Lavie Tidhar was in Dar-es-Salaam during
the American embassy bombings in 1998,
and stayed in the same hotel as the Al Qaeda
operatives in Nairobi.

Since then, he and his now-wife narrowly
avoided both the 2004 Sinai and 2005 London,
King's Cross attacks.

It was these experiences that led to
the creation of *Osama*.

Praise for *Osama*

"Bears comparison with the best of Philip K Dick's paranoid, alternate-history fantasies. It's beautifully written and undeniably powerful." – *The Financial Times*

"A strange, melancholy and moving reflection, torquing politics with the fantastic, and vice virtuosically versa."
– China Miéville

"Not a writer to mess around with half measures... brings to mind Philip K Dick's seminal science fiction novel *The Man in the High Castle*." – *The Guardian*

"The author is young, ambitious, skilled and original. *Osama* is an ingenious inversion of modern history... excellent, evocative and atmospheric." – Christopher Priest

"Intensely moving." – *Interzone*

"A novel about the power of fantasy, about the proximity of dreams and reality, about ghost people and ghost realities. Lavie Tidhar has written a fine, striking, memorable piece of fiction here, one that deserves to be widely read."
– Adam Roberts

"A provocative and fast moving tale that raises good questions not only about the heritage of Al Qaeda, but about the slippage between reality and sensational fiction that sometimes seems to define our own confused and contorted experience of the last couple of decades." – *Locus*

"Moving seamlessly between intense realism and equally intense surrealism, *Osama* is a powerful and disturbing political fantasy by a talent who deserves the attention of all serious readers." – *Strange Horizons*

"*Osama* is an unsettling, oddly poignant look at what might have been, a world that is not necessarily better – because human nature precludes that – but simply different; it shows Tidhar's originality and growing accomplishment in one of the best novels of the year so far." – Colin Harvey

First published in hardcover 2011
by PS Publishing

First published in paperback 2012 by Solaris
an imprint of Rebellion Publishing Ltd,
Riverside House, Osney Mead,
Oxford, OX2 0ES, UK

www.solarisbooks.com

ISBN: 978 1 78108 076 4

10 9 8 7 6 5 4 3 2 1

A CIP catalogue record for this book is available from the
British Library.

Designed & typeset by Rebellion Publishing

Printed in the UK by CPI Group (UK) Ltd, Croydon, CR0 4YY

OSAMA

A NOVEL BY
LAVIE TIDHAR

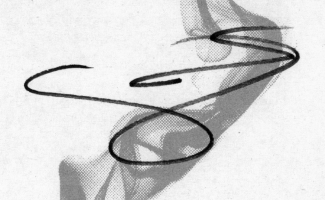

SOLARIS

For Elizabeth,
who was there

The following is a work of fiction

'Always start with a big explosion'
Mike Longshott

PROLOGUE

-- a fake Yemeni passport --

THE HILLTOP HOTEL stands on Ngiriama Road in downtown Nairobi. On the busy street outside are shoe-shiners; scratch-card stands; taxi-drivers; dusty shops selling stationary, rice, spices from Zanzibar, tinned foods and fresh tomatoes; down the road a little is an Indian restaurant. Electric fans move dust around inside the low-ceilinged buildings. The Hilltop itself is a run-down establishment catering mainly to backpackers.

The men in room 107a were not backpackers. They had checked into the hotel using fake passports, and were in the final stages of preparing to commit an act of mass murder. They did not, perhaps, see themselves as murderers, though under both the American and Kenyan penal code that is what they would be considered. The men believed they were acting on God's behalf, and perhaps they were right. God was on their side. Soon they would be successful.

MOHAMMED ODEH ARRIVED in Nairobi on the fourth of August. It was a Tuesday. He had come off a night bus from Mombassa at 7:30am, and checked into the Hilltop Hotel under a fake Yemeni passport, into room 102b. He went to sleep, getting up just before noon. He met with the others. He was dressed as a Muslim cleric, complete with a long beard. Later, he changed his clothes, putting on trousers and a shirt. He also shaved his beard.

He left on Thursday evening. He spent his last few hours in Nairobi shopping. He had his shoes shined on Moi Avenue, near the American embassy. At 10:00pm he got on a flight to Pakistan.

AUGUST SEVENTH WAS a Friday. The US ambassador was meeting with Kenyan Trade Minister Joseph Kamotho at the Ufundi Cooperative Bank near the embassy. The United States Embassy was a concrete building comprising seven floors: five above-ground, two below. Standing at Post One was Marine Corporal Samuel Gonite. The detachment commander, Gunnery Sergeant Cross, was making his rounds.

Mohamed Rashed Daoud Al-Owhali was dressed that morning in black shoes, a white short-sleeved shirt, blue jeans and a jacket. He carried a 9mm Beretta. He also carried four stun grenades. At 9:20am he made a phone call. The truck, a Toyota Dyna, had already been loaded with boxes full of eight hundred kilograms of TNT, cylinder tanks, batteries, detonators, fertilizer, and sand bags. Al-Ohwhali entered the truck on the passenger seat. Driving was a Saudi man known as Azzam. Leading the way in a white Datsun pickup truck was a third man. He was known as Harun.

They arrived at the embassy compound just

before 10:30am. Azzam drove the truck to the rear parking lot. A mail van was leaving, and he waited for it to pass before driving up to the drop-bar. Al-Owhali stepped out of the truck. He walked towards the lone guard when he realised he had left his jacket - and his Beretta - in the truck. He still had the stun grenades. He shouted at the guard, demanding that he raise the bar. The guard refused. Al-Owhali pulled the pin out of one grenade and threw it at the guard. There was an explosion. The guard ran away, shouting. Azzam drew the Beretta from Al-Owhali's jacket and began firing at the embassy windows. Al-Owhali began to run. A moment later, Azzam pressed the detonator button.

THE EXPLOSION TORE a crater in the ground. It blasted windows and tumbled concrete, and made men and women fly through the air as they died. Nearby Haile Selassie Avenue was strewn with debris. The windows of the Cooperative Bank House facing the avenue were blown by the blast. The American ambassador was knocked unconscious by the blast and cut by flying glass. The small bank building behind the embassy collapsed onto the chancery's emergency generator, spilling thousands of gallons of diesel fuel into the basement of the embassy. The diesel fuel ignited.

Two hundred and twelve people died in the attack. Four thousand were wounded. One woman, a Kenyan tea-lady from the Ufundi House offices, was trapped under the rabble. Her name was Rose Wanjiku. Rescuers, including marines and an Israeli special rescue unit, tried to reach her. She communicated with them constantly. She had been buried for five days. She died several hours before they finally reached her.

MOHAMMED ODEH LANDED in Karachi on the morning of August seven, a short time after the attack. As he went through immigration the first news of the bombing could be heard on the radio. He smiled. He passed through the airport and stepped out into the sunshine. Once outside, he located a phone box, and dialled a number.

'Emir?' he said into the silence of the mouthpiece. He took a deep breath. 'With the grace of God, we are successful.'

PART ONE
THE SECRET WAR

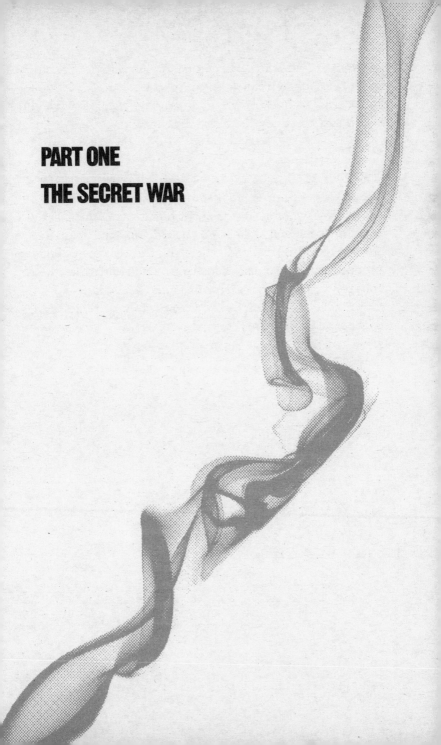

-- puddles of light --

IN THE SUMMER the sunlight falls down on Vientiane and turns walls and people translucent. Puddles of sunlight collect in street corners, and scooters pass through them and splash light onto shop fronts and down to the canals that run through the city toward the Mekong. The sunlight stains shirts with dark patches of sweat, and sends dogs to seek shelter in the shade of parked cars. Peddlers move sluggishly along the road with their wares of bamboo baskets, fruit and red-pork baguettes. The whole city seems to pause, its skin shining, and wait for the rains to come and bring with them some coolness.

Joe put down the book on the low bamboo table and sighed. The small china cup before him contained strong Lao mountain coffee, sweet with the two sugars he liked to use, which was overdoing it, he knew, but that was the way he liked it. Beside him was an ashtray containing two cigarette stubs. Also on the table was a soft packet of cigarettes and a Zippo lighter, a plain one, which sat on top of the cigarettes. He sat, as he did every morning, in the small coffee shop facing the car park of the Talat Sao in downtown Vientiane. Through the glass windows he could watch the girls walk past.

The book was a worn paperback with a garish, colourful cover. It showed a multi-story building in the final stages of collapse, a dusty African street, and people running away from a blast. The book was called *Assignment: Africa* and, in an only slightly smaller subtitle, announced it as the third title in the series *Osama Bin Laden: Vigilante*. The unlikely name of the author was Mike Longshott.

19

Joe reached for the packet on the table and extracted a cigarette, his third. He lit up with the Zippo and stared out of the window. Soft jazz played in the air. Every morning Joe came here, making the half-hour walk from his apartment on Sokpaluang Road, past the bus station and the adjacent fruit and vegetable market, past tuk-tuk drivers, dogs and squawking chickens and the large sign that extolled the virtue of Keeping Our Country Clean – All Good Citizen Must Pick Up Litter, across the traffic lights and into the Talat Sao, the Morning Market, and into the small air-conditioned coffee shop that served more as his office than his office ever did.

He sat there for a long time and was not disturbed. Staring out through the glass windows, he could see friends meet and walk away, laughing. A mother walked past with her two children, holding their hands. Three men shared a cigarette outside, gesturing with their hands as they talked, then wandered off. A girl appeared on the steps and seemed to wait for something to happen. Five minutes later a boy appeared through the doors and her smile lit up her face, and they walked away, though without acknowledging each other. A village woman came in through the car park carrying baskets. A businessman in a suit walked down the stairs accompanied by an entourage, all hurrying towards a black car and its sheltered air-conditioning. A long time ago Joe had learned that it was sometimes easiest to feel alone amongst people. He no longer let it disturb him, but as he sat there, isolated from the outside by the transparent glass windows, he felt for a moment disconnected from time, all contact between him and the rest of humanity removed, cauterized, his connection to the people outside no more than an amputee's ghost-limb, still aching though it was no longer there. He took a drag on the cigarette and exhaled, and some of the ash fell down on the book, and left a grey mark where Joe brushed it off.

Joe took a last sip from his coffee. There was nothing left

at the bottom but foam. The piped music had changed, jazz giving way to a soulful tune he recognised but didn't know from where. He put out the cigarette. A small girl went past outside holding a teddy-bear. A teenaged student in pressed black trousers and a pressed white shirt went past carrying books. Two teenage girls went past eating ice-creams, and when the boy in the white shirt saw them he smiled, and the girls smiled back, and they went off together. The wordless song playing in the air niggled at Joe, that persistent sense of knowing without quite putting a name to things, which always annoyed him. He watched the skies above the buildings and saw that they were changing.

It was a minute darkening, a momentary dimming of the light, and as he watched he saw a piece of paper on the ground outside move of its own accord, leap into the air and take off, like a dirty-white butterfly, and he knew the rains were coming.

He paid, and stepped through the doors outside, and he could smell the change in the air. The old lady selling English primers in the shop opposite looked up too, and he could see on her face the same longing that he recognised, for just a moment, in himself. Then he strode down the car park, his boots crunching on the gravel as he walked, and he whistled a tune. It was only when he was almost outside his office that he realised it was an old Dooley Wilson song, from another smoky café, in another time and place.

-- a scattering cloud of geckos --

AS HE WALKED along the wide, shady avenues of downtown Vientiane, Joe was struck again by the Japanese influence on the cityscape. Amongst the low-lying, traditional buildings along Lan Xang avenue, for instance, there emerged the half-completed shell of the new Kobayashi Bank building, a towering glass and chrome egg visible from far in the distance, an alien entity in this sedate, regal environment. Against the wall of a shop whose outdoors stalls were heaped with pineapples and watermelons and lychees, above the head of the brown-skinned proprietor (a Hmong, Joe judged) who was sitting in the shade rolling a cigarette, there was a faded poster showing the Lao king and the Japanese emperor bowing to each other respectfully, below the words *Asian Co-Prosperity Sphere*. You could see Japan in the cars, and in the blare of music that came through tinny speakers here and there, and in the notices for language schools that promised *Number One Nippon, English Tuition, For Your and Your Children's Future.*

He crossed Lan Xang and soon came within sight of That Dam, the black stupa rising against the sky like a reminder of long-gone wars. Once it had been coated in gold, and shone in the light, but the gold had been stripped, by Thai or Burmese invaders, no one was quite sure anymore, and never replaced. Grass grew through the cracks in the stone of the steps. It was a peaceful place; he had always liked it.

He reached the depilated building on the corner. There was a spirit house outside, with miniature figurines standing in its courtyard, and offerings of rice whisky and food, and a burning incense stick. He paused by it for a moment, looking at it vaguely, then stepped into the hallway, which was cool and dusty and dark. He climbed up the steps, noticing the single light-bulb had burnt again. The building was quiet. There was a noodle soup place open to the street on the ground floor, but hardly anyone ever ate there. There was also a second-hand bookshop, but it wouldn't be open for a while; not until Alfred, its proprietor, could shake off the previous night's effects and convince himself to open up for business, which was unlikely to happen before noon.

Joe opened the door to his office and stepped through, surveying the room as he did every time he entered. The windows, a little grimy, showed rooftops and wide open skies above the Mekong. His desk was plain wood, unvarnished, with a much-folded square piece of paper supporting one of its legs. On the table were scattered papers, a paperweight in the shape of an elephant, a dull metal letter opener, a desk-lamp, and an ashtray made of a polished coconut shell. Ash and two cigarette stubs from the day before were still sitting in the ashtray, and he made a mental note to have a word with the cleaning-lady, though it never seemed to make a difference. There was no phone on the desk. In the top drawer was a Thai knockoff of a Smith & Wesson .38, illegal, and a bottle of Johnny Walker Red Label, half-empty or half-full, depending.

Also in the room were: a wastepaper basket, woven from bamboo, and like the ashtray unemptied; a metal filing cabinet, empty but for a pair of scuffed black shoes two sizes too small for Joe, which were the only effects left behind by the office's previous occupant; a solitary bookshelf; on the wall, a small painting showing a burning field, the flowers crimson, the smoke coiling across the canvas in jagged lines of white and grey, the figure of a man blurred in the distance, his face hidden behind the smoke; three chairs, one behind the desk, two before it; in one corner, a potted plant that had long since passed away.

It felt like home. As he stepped fully through, half-closing the door behind him, he startled a small gecko on the wall. As the gecko shot up, other geckos appeared, and for a moment it seemed to Joe like an explosion, the geckos racing away from the epicentre – which was him. He smiled, and went to his desk, and sat down, putting the paperback on his desk. He shared his office with no one but the geckos. Every time he came in it seemed to him that there were more of them. They would hide unseen in corners, and he would startle them each time with the opening of a drawer, with the legs of a chair dragging across the floor, and they would scuttle away. Once, he came across a solitary gecko squatting by the wastepaper basket. Its left front leg had been hurt, and it was motionless for so long that Joe had thought it dead. He wondered what happened to it – did it get in a fight with another of its kind? He never found out. Later, when he looked again, the gecko had moved: the last Joe saw of it the gecko was crawling slowly through the gap under the door, until finally the tip of its tail disappeared and the wounded gecko was through, passing beyond the safety of the office into the corridor beyond.

Joe went around the desk and sat down. He thought of lighting a cigarette and decided against it. He turned the chair to the window and stared outside. The skies were clouding over, and he could smell the oncoming rain.

-- contour of a woman through the rain --

THE RAIN FELL down all at once. In the distance, thunder broke into shards of sound and exploded in the vast open skies above the Mekong, and lightning flashed blue against grey. Joe stared out of the window, watching a barefoot child run through the puddles, a green leaf as large as a serving-tray held above his head against the rain. The air was humid and smelled of vegetation and earth, and Joe knew that later, in the night, the snails would come out and glide across the road like sedate locomotives, leaving their rails behind them as they passed, and that the frogs would be luxuriating in the pools that were, to them, grand palaces of water. A burst of song came and went on the wind, bookended by static. A solitary bird flew high overhead, swooped and disappeared out of sight, little more than a black dot on the horizon.

It was when the rain had begun to ease, and sunlight streamed down through the fresh incisions in the cloud cover, that he first saw her. She was crossing the road, head bent, intent on the path she was following. There was no traffic. Light rain fell and sunlight came through behind her, but he couldn't see her face. For a moment it seemed to him the whole world was still, a frozen backdrop, the moving girl the only living thing inhabiting it. Then the clouds closed overhead and the girl was gone, and Joe sighed, and turned away from the window and reached for his cigarettes.

'Hello,' a soft voice said, close by, and Joe started, dropping the Zippo lighter he was in the process of picking up a half-inch above the table. He looked up. She looked back at him.

The window was behind her, and behind the glass the sunlight was passing through the rain, and for a moment the raindrops seemed like thousands of miniature prisms hovering in the air. 'I didn't hear you come in,' he said. He glanced at the half-open door. The girl smiled. 'You looked thoughtful,' she said. 'I didn't want to disturb you.' She had long brown hair and was quite petite, with eyes that were slightly almond-shaped, and though she was clearly European, she looked more like an Asian girl in her build. She looked like a girl who would always have a problem buying the right size clothes in Europe, and no problem at all here. There were fine lines at the corners of her eyes when she smiled, and he wondered if they were from laughing or crying, though he didn't know why. He said, 'Can I help you?'

'You are a detective?' She didn't sit down and he didn't offer her a seat. She seemed comfortable standing there, while rain and sun clashed behind her. He wondered what her accent was. He said, 'I –' and shrugged, his hands encompassing the bare office, the silence of the rain. Then he said, 'What is it you want?'

She came closer then, standing against the edge of the desk, looking at him. She seemed to study him, as if there were more behind his question than he understood. Her hand fell to the surface of the desk, resting on the paperback that lay there, and she turned. Her fingers felt the book's spine and cover, and she picked it up, taking a step back from the desk, her back still to the window. She opened the book and leafed through the yellowing pages.

'"The Hilltop Hotel stands on Ngiriama Road in downtown Nairobi,"' she said, reading. She had no problem pronouncing the road name correctly. '"On the busy street outside are shoe-shiners and scratch-card stands and taxi-drivers –"'

'No, that's wrong,' Joe said.

'No?' She looked taken aback, for some reason.

'I think there is a pause there, not an "and,"' he said. It reminded him of something, as if he had once known someone to do this, to substitute words for punctuation when reading a book out loud. Someone who liked to read out books; it made him uncomfortable. 'It's just a pulp novel,' he said, feeling defensive. 'It helps pass the time.' He didn't know why he was apologising, or trying to justify himself to her.

The girl closed the book and laid it back down on the desk, carefully, as if handling a valuable object. 'Do you think so?' she said. He didn't know what to answer her. He remained silent. She remained standing. They looked at each other and he wondered what she saw. Her fingers were quite long and thin. Her ears were a little pointy. At last, she said, 'I want you to find him,' and her fingers caressed the book; he couldn't put a name to the look she had in her eyes then; he thought she looked lost, and sad, and a little vulnerable.

'Find who?'

'Mike Longshott,' she said, and Joe's surprise became a laugh that exploded out of him without warning.

'The guy who writes this stuff?'

'Yes,' she said, patiently. Behind her the rain was petering off. Her voice seemed to be growing quieter, as if she were standing farther away than she was. Joe went to pick up the book and his fingers touched hers. He looked up, suddenly without words. She was bending down, her hair falling around her face, only a small gap of air separating them now, and she moved her hand over his, and there was something terribly intimate about it; intimate and familiar. Then she straightened up, and her hand left his, and she shook her head and gathered her hair behind her shoulders. 'Expense is not an issue,' she said, and she reached into a pocket and brought a slim, square object out and put it on the table.

'What is it?' he said.

'It's a credit card.'

He looked at it, shook his head, let it pass. Instead he said, 'How will I contact you?'

She smiled, and again he noticed the fine lines around her eyes and wondered.

'You won't,' she said. 'I'll find you.'

He picked up the card. It was matte-black, with no writing on it, merely a long string of numbers. 'But w –' he said, looking up, and saw that, just like that, she was gone. Behind the window the rain had finally stopped, and the sun shone through the breaking clouds.

-- second bomb --

THE SECOND BOMB exploded four hundred and fifteen miles away, in the compound of the former Israeli embassy to Tanzania, which had since been taken over by the American diplomatic mission. Tropical heat lay over the asphalt road and the low stone buildings. In the fish market, flies already hovered above the corpses of karambesi, yellow-fin tuna and wahoo. In the sea-shell market beyond, hundreds of exoskeletons of critters in the phylum Mollusca lay on tables, shining a multitude of colours in the sunlight.

The American embassy was located on 36 Laibon Road, Dar es Salaam. It consisted of a three-storey Chancery originally built for the Israelis, and a four-storey annex added later by the Americans. The threat of political violence in Dar es Salaam had been classified as Low. That was later revised.

Ahmed the German drove the bomb truck. He spent the night before in House 213 in the Ilala District of Dar es Salaam. He was blond and blue-eyed. The truck was a Nissan Atlas. He stopped the truck at Uhuru Street and his passenger, K.K. Mohamed, climbed out, returning to the safe house to pray, as the German drove on to the embassy compound.

Blocking the way to the compound was a water

tanker. The driver, a Tanzanian, was called Yusufu Ndange. He was the father of six children. It was 10:30am. Perhaps unable to penetrate into the compound, perhaps aware of the pressure of time, Ahmed the German pressed the detonator at that time. He was less than eleven meters from the embassy wall.

The water tanker absorbed much of the blast. It was lifted three stories in the air and came to rest against the Chancery building. Yusufu Ndange died instantly. So did the five local guards who were on duty that day. The remains of the assistant of the tanker driver, who was seen by witnesses shortly before the blast, were never found. The ceiling collapsed at the American ambassador's residence, but no one was home at the time. Five African students standing nearby also died. In total, the attack claimed eleven lives; Ahmed the German made twelve.

K.K. Mohamed abandoned the safe house and boarded a flight to Cape Town. The flight time was four hours and thirty five minutes. When he landed, he took a deep breath of the cool, winter air, and went to find a phone box.

-- an otherworldly map, like the surface of the moon --

JOE LAID THE paperback face-down on his desk, its pages open and touching the unvarnished surface of the desk like a palm print. There were many questions, but he did not feel like asking them. He opened the drawer and extracted the bottle of Red Label. He stared at it, shaking the bottle just to see the amber liquid slosh inside. There was a question: did he want a drink?

He contemplated the bottle for a moment longer, then unscrewed the cap and drank. The whisky burned his stomach. He screwed the cap back on and put the bottle back in the drawer, shutting it. He stared at the book.

He picked up the credit card and examined it, then put it back down. How did he even go about using it? None of it seemed right. He picked up the book again and turned to the copyright page. The publisher was called Medusa Press. It had a Paris address. The copyright notice was for Medusa Press. There was no mention of Mike Longshott. It was unlikely to be the man's real name in any case. No one could really be called Mike Longshott. He stood up and went to his bookshelf and scanned the spines. He had two more *Osama bin Laden: Vigilante* books, and he took them off the shelf now and returned to his desk. He checked the copyright pages, and they were identical. Medusa Press, Paris, and the address was a post office box, not a street address. He lit another cigarette and wondered why that was, and how he should go about finding out more, and then there was a loud bang from downstairs and someone cursed, volubly, in English, and Joe smiled. Alfred had evidently surfaced and was in the process of opening his bookshop.

He got up, tucking the black credit card into his pocket, and went downstairs. There was a connecting door into the bookshop and he used it. As he stepped inside, he could smell the lingering scent of opium in the air. Sometimes when he came through it smelled sweet; sometimes it smelled like burned foliage; and if Alfred was forced to comment on the persistent smell that clung to his aging body so devoutly, he would have quoted the painter Picasso, who he claimed to have once known, and call it the least stupid smell in the world. Whatever it smelled like, what words were used to describe it, it was always there, in Alfred's clothes and his black beard flecked with white, and in the books themselves that, when opened, would exude a faint trace of the scent from their pages.

'You no-good son of a bitch,' Alfred said. 'Oh, hi, Joe.'

Joe smiled and waved with the hand holding the cigarette.

Alfred turned back to May. 'Get out of my sight, May. I never want to see you again. Go!'

'Hi, Joe,' May said, and Joe smiled and waved again. There was a chair wedged in between two tall book cabinets, and he sat down. 'You smoke too much, old man. Every night you need more. Soon you will do nothing but smoke.'

May was strikingly pretty. She had long black hair and delicate features, and though she'd never, as far as Joe knew, had the operation below, she had small, firm breasts proudly displayed by her tight, red top, courtesy of her regular dose of estrogens. She was *kathoey*, and had been Alfred's girlfriend for a long time.

'Nonsense,' Alfred said. 'I have a perfectly healthy opium habit. Had it for years. Marvellous plant.'

'Makes you slow.'

'Makes me strong!' Alfred shouted. 'Strong like an ox!' he made an unmistakable, lewd gesture with his fist, and he and

May collapsed in laughter. 'I would give you many babies if you weren't half man,' Alfred said sadly when they had calmed down.

'I might be half man but I am all woman,' May said. Joe knew she could match Alfred's smoking with her own.

Alfred nodded and sighed. 'That is true,' he said.

'I love you,' May said.

'I love you, too, sweetheart. Now go and leave this old man to run his business.'

May blew him a kiss, waved to Joe, and disappeared into the sunlight outside. Alfred sighed again and turned to Joe. 'Silly girl,' he said. 'And if I didn't smoke? I might not even see you.'

Joe wasn't sure how to take that, and let it pass. You had to let things pass, with Alfred. 'You want some coffee?' Alfred said.

'Sure.'

Alfred got up and went to the small electric plate, single ring, which sat on a low table beside the open door. He spooned coffee into a long-handled pot already filled with water and turned on the dial. The electric ring began to glow.

He was a tall man, Alfred, though a little stooped now; he wore jeans and a chequered shirt and a belt with a large metal buckle. His feet were bare. He moved softly, making almost no sound: he claimed to have been with the Foreign Legion, fighting on the French side in the Vietnam War, and sometimes that he'd been an adviser to the Khmer king before a misunderstanding – whose nature he never expounded on – made him depart the country in some haste. Alfred was a man full of stories; now he filled his life with those of others, the small shop filled with worn, battle-weary books that had seen more of the world in their time, he liked to say, than he had and, like himself, had finally come to rest, for a while at least. He was a reluctant seller of books, which was, Joe thought, not a bad thing, seeing that he rarely had any customers.

'Did you see a girl walk out of the building as you came in?' Joe said. Alfred turned towards him, his eyes bright, and chuckled. 'That'd be the day,' he said.

'Did you?'

Alfred shrugged. 'I've not seen anyone. Why, you working a case?' he chuckled. 'Is she a suspect? You should have tailed her. You could do with finding yourself a piece of tail, Joe.'

Joe let that, too, pass. The water was coming to a boil, and Alfred stirred in sugar and then poured the black, muddy drink into two small glass cups. '*Salut*,' he said. He drank the hot coffee noisily.

'You know those books you gave me a while back?' Joe said. Alfred had recommended them, almost pushing them into Joe's hands. 'This Osama bin Laden series?'

Alfred sat down behind his desk and put the coffee cup directly on the table, where it would leave a ring to join the countless others that had turned the surface into an otherworldly map, like the surface of the moon. 'You got a cigarette?' he asked Joe.

'Sure.'

'Ta.'

He accepted the proffered cigarette and Joe sat back between the bookcases. 'What about them?' Alfred said.

'You know who wrote them?'

'Got a light?'

'Sure.' He got up again, flicked the Zippo, and offered the flame to Alfred, who inhaled deeply and blew out a ring of smoke. Joe sat back.

'Longshott,' Alfred said. 'Mike Longshott.' He giggled. 'I assume it's a pseudonym.'

So did Joe, but – 'What makes you think that?'

'Come here,' Alfred said. He rose and circumnavigated the desk, heading for a bookcase two down from Joe. 'Let's see, Medusa Press... the only titles I seem to sell. To be honest, the only books I don't mind selling. Very popular, in certain sections of society.' His fingers ran along the shelf, plucking out books. 'There you go.' He thrust them into Joe's hands and went back to the desk, leaving behind gaps on the shelf like the white keys of a piano. Joe looked at the books.

They were identical in size and look to the *Vigilante* books he already had. The first one was called *I was Commandant Heinrich's Bitch*. Joe stared at the cover. It depicted a blond man in uniform holding a horse-whip in one hand. Behind him were guard towers, a barbed-wire fence. At his feet was a large-breasted girl in badly-torn clothes that revealed a lot of her flesh. She was holding on to the man's leg, looking up at him with an undecipherable look in her eyes.

'Smut,' Alfred said. 'Filth. Utter junk, of course. Wonderful stuff.'

Joe put it down carefully and looked at the next one. *Confessions of a Drug-Crazed Nymphomaniac*. The cover showed a bare-chested blonde woman reclining on a sofa while the sinister shadow of a man towered above her, administering an opium pipe to her slack mouth.

The third book was simply called *Slut*.

The author of the first two books was called Sebastian Bruce. The author of the third title went by the moniker of Countess Szu Szu.

'Medusa Press,' Alfred said through the smoke of his cigarette, 'are, on the whole, purveyors of unadulterated pornography. Uncut, I should say. Dirty books, in common parlance. Sell quite well, too, when I can get them past customs. Which is most of the time, to tell you the truth.'

Pornography? And yet it seemed to fit. Sex and violence, he thought. Hand in hand through the smoke. The image startled him, seeming to awaken something inside. The smoke smelled sweet and the silence was complete – he shook his head, searched for his cigarette, realised he had left it in the dirty-glass ashtray on the second shelf and that it had burned away. He shook the pack out of his pocket, liberated another cigarette and lit it. 'Know anything else?' he said.

Alfred looked at him and the old eyes were suddenly hooded. 'No,' he said. 'If it's Mike Longshott you're looking for – if it's Osama bin Laden you're after, for that matter – then I suspect you would not find the answer here. But Joe –'

'Yes?'

The old man stood up. There was ash in his beard. He scratched a vein in the craggy, limestone visage of his face and lumbered towards Joe. Suddenly the space in the bookshop felt that much closer. 'Are you sure you want to find out?'

-- a man reading a newspaper, standing up --

WHEN HE SLEPT, he no longer dreamed, if he ever had. Sleep was a blankness, an empty space. When he woke each morning, the bed remained undisturbed as if no-one had slept there. He rolled over and went to the window, staring out at the busy road outside. A young girl was cycling past, holding a parasol above her head, the road rolling below her. A brown mongrel dog chased a goat. Already coals were being lit, meat prepared on top of miniature grills, the smoke of burning fat rising in the air. Scooters went roaring past. Students in white shirts and pressed black trousers congregated around a drinks stand. There was a man outside reading a newspaper standing up.

Joe shuffled to his small kitchen and put the kettle on to boil. Fleetingly, he thought about Alfred.

'Why wouldn't I?' he had said, and the old man had shrugged, and said, 'Are you happy here?'

Joe had said, 'What do you mean?' and Alfred had smiled, and said, 'I guess that too is an answer.'

The books were piled up on the low bamboo table. He poured hot water into a mug and spooned coffee and sugar into it, stirring, and carried the drink over to the table with him. He stared at the paperbacks. *Assignment: Africa. Sinai Bombings. World Trade Centre*. What the hell was a world trade centre?

You would not find the answer here, Alfred had told him. Joe sighed and sipped his coffee, knowing Alfred was right, had only articulated what Joe himself already knew. Paris, he thought, but the thought tasted sour.

He took out the black credit card and stared at it again.

Expense is not an issue, the girl had said. But Joe knew that wasn't right. There were always expenses, and they always mattered. Life was owed, always waiting, always afraid of the tread of the debt-collector – he shook his head and sipped from the coffee. Morbid, he thought. He carried the coffee to the window and stood there, looking out. An old man rolling a cigarette in the shade of a papaya tree across the road. Two kids racing each other on bicycles, floating past. A man reading a newspaper, standing up. He looked at him for a long moment. He couldn't see the man's face. The man's shoes were black and polished. He finished the coffee, carried it to the sink, and left it there. When he went downstairs and opened the door to the outside, the man with the newspaper was no longer there. Joe crossed the road, walking the short distance to the call box by the temple. He put a couple of coins in and dialled.

'TransContinental Airways, how may I help you?'

'I'd like a ticket to Paris.'

'When would you like to leave?'

He didn't need to think it over. 'Next available flight.'

'Just a moment, sir.'

He could hear her shuffling paper, searching through the time tables on her desk, matching the next flight with the passenger manifesto, checking seat availability –

'Sir?'

'Yes?'

He dropped another coin in the slot. It was hot in the call box, and he pushed the door open with his foot and held it.

'The next flight is at thirteen hundred hours today, going via Bangkok.'

'That sounds fine,' he said. A group of orange-robed monks walked past and disappeared through the arched gate of the temple. An old brown woman was roasting bananas outside the gate, smoking a long-stemmed pipe as she turned the blackened bananas over and over. 'You can pay through our offices on Lan Xang avenue,' the woman said, 'we accept cash, cheques or –'

'I'd like to pay with a credit card.'

There was a small silence. A fly buzzed into the call box and Joe tried to get it, but his palm connected only with air and he lost his hold on the door. The fly buzzed as if laughing at him.

'Of course, sir.'

The *sir* was a little more pronounced this time, he thought. He pulled out the black credit card. Here goes, he thought. He read out the mystical string of digits to the woman over the phone, and gave her his name. He thought they might need something else, but that seemed to satisfy her. 'Just a moment, sir.'

He waited, trying to trap the fly, but it moved too much. He pushed the door open again and wiped his face with his shirt, staining it. The sun poured in through the glass, almost blinding him, and for a moment he could not see beyond its confines, and his world was reduced to this one rectangular box – 'Sir?'

'Yes?'

'Please pick your ticket up at the airport. Check-in is one hour before the flight, and you would need to change planes in Bangkok.'

'Thank you,' Joe said, a little dazed, and the voice on the other end said, 'Pleasure, sir. Have a good flight.'

'Thank you,' he said again, and then replaced the receiver on its holding arm. He stared at the card again, seeing nothing, then put it back in his pocket and stepped outside.

-- a yellow-white coat of paint --

HE DECIDED NOT to go to the Talat Sao that morning. His carefully-constructed routine had been interrupted, subverted. As he walked back the short distance to his apartment along the Sokpaluang road, he wondered what he should be feeling. Was it freedom that caused such a pulse of sudden, inexplicable fear to pass through him? I should have told her no, he thought, but his mind slid away from the image of the girl that rose in his mind. She had put her hand over his, and her hair had fallen around her face, framing it – no.

What then?

As he approached his building, he saw something out of the corner of his eye and, turning, was just in time to see the back of a man disappearing through the door of the small convenience store. He noticed close-cropped hair, a large neck, tanned, pale-blue shirt, unremarkable black trousers, polished black shoes. 'Son of a bitch,' Joe said.

He turned and crossed the road again, almost hitting two girls on a scooter who narrowly missed him and then looked back at him, emitting embarrassed giggles. He waved to indicate he was all right and they sped away, still giggling. He went to the store, navigating his way between crates and spent cartons, and pushed the door open. There was a strong smell inside of drying fish.

'Sabaidee, mister,' said the girl behind the front table.

'Sabaidee,' he said, returning her *nop*. She had put her palms together in the customary greeting and so he answered with his own. The girl was watching a small television set showing a Japanese game-show. On the screen, a Japanese man was capering on a stage in a European clown's costume, while two contestants to either side of him were trying to hit him with long bamboo sticks. The man ducked and jumped, at once comical and strangely graceful, avoiding their aim.

'What's this?' he asked the girl, who had already returned her full attention to the screen. She looked up. '*Catch That Clown*,' she said. 'They get one hundred yen each time they manage to hit him.' She shrugged. 'They never do, but it's funny.'

Joe smiled and she returned to her screen. Catch that clown, he thought. He searched through the narrow aisles, but there was no sign of the man with the polished black shoes. 'Did anyone come through here just now?' he said. The girl seemed to contemplate the question. 'Been quiet,' she said at last, handing down her verdict, and turned up the volume on the television set.

What did that mean? There was a back way into the store, of course, but it led into the family's own residence. If so, the man must merely be an uncle or cousin or some other relative hanging around, which, when he thought about it, was the most reasonable explanation. He shrugged and picked up a tin of soup and a new packet of cigarettes, paid, and went back outside.

A man was climbing into a stretched black Mercedes parked outside Joe's building. Joe caught sight of polished black shoes disappearing inside. Then the door was softly closed shut, the tinted windows allowed no gaze inside, the powerful German engine purred to life, and the car pulled out into the road. 'Wait!' Joe shouted, and he ran towards the car, which was already speeding away. A scooter went past him, too close, and a boy in a student's uniform said, 'Watch where you're going, asshole!' as he sped away. Joe cursed. The black car was ahead of him and gaining speed. He ran after it. An elderly lady cycled past him, her bicycle loaded with egg trays. She looked at him sideways with a bemused expression. 'Stop!'

The car wasn't stopping. But a window rolled down on the right-side of the back seat, and a hand emerged, holding a gleaming object, and Joe stopped, not believing what he saw. It was a gun.

The shots echoed loudly in the street. The old lady swerved, her bicycle wavered, and then she fell, the bicycle skidding away across the hot tarmac, the trays coming loose from the strings that bound them, releasing their load of fresh eggs onto the road, where they rolled and burst, covering the tarmac in a yellow-white coat of paint. At the first sound of a shot, Joe fell facedown onto the road and rolled away towards the pavement. The hand withdrew into the Mercedes. As the window rolled back up, a piece of paper – caught, perhaps, in the updraft – came floating out of the window. The car sped away and soon disappeared behind the bend.

Joe stood up. He was shaking. He ran to the old woman, but she had not been hurt. He helped her up. She too was shaking. She did not speak to him. She watched the broken eggs on the ground and began to cry, without sound, the tears flowing down her lined face, like water through a web of ancient Roman aqueducts. Joe went to her bike and picked it up. She took it from him without a sound. She would not look at him. Other people had come out to watch. They stood outside the shop-fronts and gazed, pointing and murmuring between themselves. Joe cursed and decided it was time to be gone from there. 'Here,' he said, offering the woman some money clumsily. 'For the eggs.'

She took the money from him without comment, tucking it away in a hidden pocket. When she walked her bike to the side of the road, a group of women descended on her, escorting her to the shade and offering her tea. The woman gave them a small, sad smile. No one seemed to pay Joe any attention.

Good.

As he turned to go, a piece of torn paper hit him on the

face and he snapped at it, his anger suddenly released, and he crumpled it into a ball with one violent motion.

They had shot at him. Why the hell had they shot at him? He jogged away from there as a bus went past and left yolky tire-marks on the asphalt. When he got to his building he went right in, climbing up to his apartment and locking the door behind him. Then he stood with his back to the door, taking deep breaths. He brought his hand to his face, and realised he was still holding the ball of paper. He smoothed it open and looked at it. A dirty scrap of old newspaper, barely-legible but for the date: eleven September, two thousand and one. He shrugged, crumpled it back into a ball, and went to deposit it in the rubbish-bin. Then he packed up some clothes, threw in the three books, and left the apartment.

-- caravana de la muerte --

ON THE ELEVENTH of September, nineteen seventy three, at zero seven hundred hours, the Chilean Navy had taken over Valparaíso. By zero eight hundred, the Army held Santiago. By zero nine hundred hours, the Army had control of most of the South American country. In his final speech, President Salvador Allende said, "They have force and will be able to dominate us, but social processes can be arrested by neither crime nor force. History is ours, and people make history... These are my last words, and I am certain that my sacrifice will not be in vain, I am certain that, at the very least, it will be a moral lesson that will punish felony, cowardice, and treason." By twelve hundred hours, Hawker Hunter jet fighter planes finally arrived over the presidential palace in downtown Santiago. They dropped their load of bombs over the palace. Allende died shortly after. One story has it that he died by his own hands, with an AK-47 rifle that was a gift from Fidel Castro, and was engraved on a gold plaque: 'To my good friend Salvador from Fidel, who by different means tries to achieve the same goals.'

The Army Commander-in-Chief, Augusto Pinochet, became president of Chile.

It was an event few knew or cared about outside

of Chile. Over the next several years, thousands of people died or disappeared. The Chilean national stadium was used as an internment camp for over forty thousand people. In one instance, an army death-squad called the Caravan of Death, or Caravana de la Muerte, flew across the country by helicopters, carrying out executions. Overall, at least three thousand people had died.

Was the United States behind the coup? 'We didn't do it. I mean we helped them,' Secretary of State Henry Kissinger told President Nixon five days later over the phone. The time was 11:50 A.M. The conversation began with football.

'Nothing new of any importance, is there?' the president had asked.

'Nothing of very great consequence,' Kissinger had said.

When he heard of Allende's election to president, the U.S. Ambassador to Chile, Edward M. Korry, said, 'We shall do all within our power to condemn Chile and all Chileans to utmost deprivation and poverty.'

A communiqué to the CIA base in Chile on the sixteenth of August, less than a month before the coup, stated: 'It is firm and continuing policy that Allende be overthrown by a coup... We are to continue to generate maximum pressure toward this end, utilizing every appropriate resource. It is imperative that these actions be implemented clandestinely and securely so that the USG and American hand be well hidden.'

It was a date few remembered outside of Chile.

-- the imprisoned singing of live frogs --

'WHERE TO, MISTER?' the tuk-tuk driver said. His name was Mr. Kop and he was high on life, and amphetamines.

'The airport,' Joe said. Mr. Kop cranked up the engine and grinned. 'Bor pan yang,' he said, 'bor pan yang. No problem, no problem. Mr. Kop he take you any place you want go.' The engine made the *tuk-tuk-tuk* sound that had given the vehicle its name. Mr. Kop released the gear and sped off down the road, Joe holding on at the back, the artificial wind coming through, cooling against his scalp.

They had tried to shoot him. Why would anyone want to shoot him?

The worst moment was outside, just before he had hailed down Mr. Kop. Indecision. An irrational part of him wanted to head over the Mekong, into Siam and a train or bus to Bangkok, or disappear entirely in that great empty space of the continent that lay beyond the river: isolated villages, small fields, a scarcity of roads, a great open silence.

It only lasted a moment and then he dismissed it and Mr. Kop had stopped for him and he told him the airport. Mr. Kop drove as fast as his ancient vehicle allowed him, taking every bump on the road with relish, singing to himself as he drove, and grinning and twitching a little. Soon they were on the smooth, wide road to the airport and the Mekong was visible, still dry, the rains having not yet filled it up. The distant sand-banks had the colour of Mr. Kop's teeth. Joe leaned back and stretched out his legs. He thought fleetingly about the girl.

He paid Mr. Kop outside the terminal building and went

inside. He had seen no black cars along the road. He came to the TransAtlantic Airways desk and a girl looked up at him with a pleasant smile. His ticket was there, ready, and the girl directed him to Gate Three. The terminal was small, old but clean. The concrete floor was worn smooth. The sunlight streamed in through high windows. He bought himself an espresso at the kiosk by the entrance and sipped it standing up outside. He lit a cigarette and watched people come and go past.

They couldn't know he was going to the airport because he had only made the booking that morning, and so he felt reasonably calm. He had not spotted a tail on the road either, and that was good too. There was the other possibility, of course – that they knew he would be going to Paris because that way the trail leading to Mike Longshott lay and they knew about that, about Longshott and Osama, but it wasn't an option he was entertaining just then. He finished the espresso and bought another and searched for black shoes. An elderly Indian man went past, dressed in a suit, wearing an expensive-looking gold wristwatch. A Chinese family went past, the father ramrod-straight, the mother plump and wearing a loose dress and a worried expression, then two children, a boy and a girl, the boy holding a soldier doll, the girl a paper-bound book, a Lao nanny bringing out the rear of the campaign with the youngest member of the regiment in her arms, a boy or a girl, it was impossible to tell. Three white men casually dressed – the kind of casual it cost money to achieve – two in their twenties, one with silver hair and black shades, talking to each other in French. During the war the airport had been used as a base for a loose unit of French pilots who worked under the guise of a civilian airline company. They were called Ravens, and flew missions across the border, into Vietnam. The Secret War, they called it. Some of the old-timers stayed on, still, but the only remains of French Indochina these days were the coins that now sold to tourists in the Talat Sao. A woman carrying a bamboo basket with two chickens inside. Five Africans in flowing robes, and escorted by Lao functionaries – a diplomatic delegation from Ivory Coast or Senegal, maybe. Two young European women carrying backpacks. One smiled at Joe as she went past him. A bearded Muslim cleric wheeling a suitcase. Two Japanese, a man and a woman, power-walking, movements synchronised, not speaking. A group of Hmong villagers, carrying baskets, one imprisoning the singing of live frogs. Dark shapes peered at Joe through the woven bars of their jail. Joe ground his cigarette into the espresso cup, threw it in the bin, and went to catch his plane.

IN TRANSIT

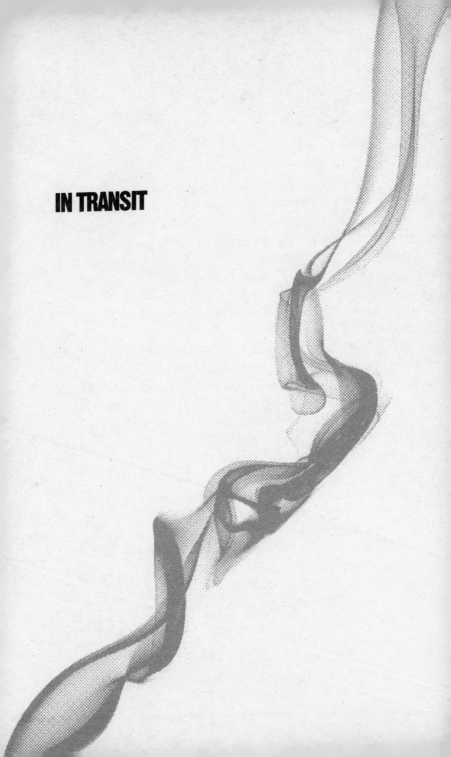

-- a cold and waterless sea --

HE ALWAYS FELT most alone when he was flying. On a plane, he felt as if he did not exist. There were the overhead lights and the bulky earphones and the canned music, dead notes and dead voices scratchily coming through a tiny socket in the armrest. Outside the world was vanished; once he was above the clouds, all he could see was a white landscape, sheer mountains, deep gorges, bottomless chasms where the clouds momentarily opened, with nothing at all beneath. The cloudscape was not real. It was insubstantial, had no concrete existence. The blue sky was a cold and waterless sea.

The flight to Bangkok took one hour. Once there, at the modern chrome and glass airport with the king's picture hanging everywhere, he waited. Airports were made for waiting, sometimes forever. He sat on a public bench and watched people come and go past him, unnoticed by them. When he went to the restroom his urine smelled of coffee. He washed his hands and toweled them dry. There was no day or night inside the terminal. It was a place where time stood still, a pause, a place where there was only a before or after, but no now.

For some reason he thought about the cat. He had tried adopting one a few months before. It was a little stray kitten, dirty-black, with big round eyes and a skinny neck and a big belly, bulging from intestinal worms. It had come up to him outside the Morning Market, just like that, and put its paw on his foot, and looked up at him.

He took it home in a blue plastic bag and fed it tuna and held it on his lap. It was a little cat, two months old and comical

51

with its loping, ungraceful gait and its enthusiasm. He called the cat Small One, because it was small, and one. There was a veterinarian clinic on Don Palang road, and the nurse came to the apartment and she said Small One needed an injection for worms and also for an ear infection, and she injected him twice. Joe had paid her and she left, and twenty minutes later Small One was dead.

Small One's body could not take the injections. He ran across the room, faster than Joe had seen him move before, and then stopped as abruptly, and crawled under the chair, feet splayed, his body wracked with spasms. His eyes stared at Joe as he peed himself, lying there in his own pool of urine, unable to move. Joe had put him in his box and mopped up, not thinking, and then held Small One close to him, and felt him go, the body becoming limp in his arms and the eyes remaining open but no longer seeing Joe, and there was no heartbeat.

He hated the nurse for doing what she did but he hated himself more for not stopping her, not telling her Small One was too small, too fragile for the injections. He let her do it because he thought it was the right thing to do, and she did what she thought was right, too.

He had buried Small One at night. The moon was one day short of being full. He dug the earth and put Small One into the ground in his box, and covered him again.

'TransContinental Airways flight to Paris now boarding at gate thirty-five,' a woman's voice said on the public announcement system. Joe stood up; he had been day-dreaming. It was the only kind of dreaming he did any more. He picked up his bag and looked up at the great departure board, where destinations and flight numbers on moving slats click-clacked into position incessantly, when he felt a hand on his arm and a voice said close by, 'Please, don't go.'

He turned, startled. A small, rotund Asian woman stood beside him. He had not heard her approach. She wore a baggy dress and soft-soled shoes, and her face looked up at him pleadingly with short-sighted eyes. Joe said, 'I'm sorry –' and the woman sighed and said, 'I am sorry too. You are lucky. You can find your way. I am still looking.' And her eyes left him and went to the departure board, and she sighed, and said, 'It should be silent and shining with words of light. Not like this. It should be... it should be like the marker to paradise, I sometimes think. But I don't know where my flight is. I don't know which gate to go to. I've tried them all.'

Joe put his hand on the woman's shoulder. He couldn't say why he did that. He felt in himself something responding to her, sensing her pain, not a knowing but feeling, and it was strange to him. 'Sit down,' he said. 'Let me get you something to eat. Everything is better after you've eaten.'

'On board meal,' the woman said. 'That's all I can taste now. And apple juice. I never drink alcohol on flights. Only apple juice. In those transparent plastic cups with the wrinkles. Now I hate the taste, but it won't go away.'

'I'm sorry,' Joe said again. He didn't know what to say. He felt powerless before her. The woman was still staring at the departure board. After a moment Joe removed his hand, gently. He thought she had forgotten he was there, but then he heard her speak. 'Go,' she said. She spoke very quietly. 'I shouldn't have come to you. But sometimes I get so lonely – where are we?'

'Bangkok,' Joe said.

'Bangkok? I've never been to Bangkok before.'

He left her there. She never once took her eyes off the departure board.

-- black hiking shoes --

THE MAN WAS part Jamaican and part English, and
close to two meters tall. He spoke with a South
London accent, having been born in Bromley and
educated at Thomas Tallis School in Kidbrooke. He
had deep set eyes and thick black hair, and there
were over one hundred grams of Pentaerythritol
tetranitrate and Acetone peroxide plastic high-
grade plastic explosives hidden in the hollowed
soles of his black hiking shoes. His name was
Richard Reid.

When Richard was born his father was in prison.
By the time he left school at sixteen, he was
already stealing cars like his old man. He did
some time for mugging. "I was not there to give
him the love and affection he should have got,"
his father would later say. When Richard ran
into the old man at a shopping mall some years
after his first arrest, Robin Reid had a word
of advice for his son. Muslims treat you like a
human being, he said. And they get better food
in prison.

Richard took the name Abdul Raheem after
his conversion at the Feltham Young Offenders
Institute. A few years after that he disappeared.
His mother thought he was in Pakistan. Records
obtained later suggest that he was trained in
Afghanistan. He resurfaced in Amsterdam, where

he worked in a restaurant. From Amsterdam he went to Brussels, and from Brussels to Paris.

December was cold and dark, and the days were short. It was on the seventeenth that Richard bought a round-trip ticket to Miami, flying with American Airlines. He spent his time in Paris around the Gare du Nord, not staying in a hotel; when he arrived at the airport on December twenty-first, he looked rough.

He had no luggage. French security personnel interviewed Reid, but they could not find a reason to hold him. Having missed his flight, he returned the next day and this time successfully boarded the Boeing 767 flight.

It was a Saturday morning. There were a hundred and eighty five passengers on board. There were, as mentioned, explosives, as well as a detonator, in the soles of Richard Reid's shoes. Once the flight was airborne, and after the in-flight meal (which Richard did not share), the smell of smoke began to waft through the cabin. A stewardess, Hermis Moutardier, discovered him trying to light a match and warned him that smoking was not allowed on board. Reid promised to stop. He picked his teeth with the blackened match instead. He had a window seat, and no-one beside him. Moments later, Moutardier returned, finding Richard bent over in his chair. She thought he was smoking. 'Excuse me,' she said, 'what are you doing?' He did not reply. When she demanded an answer Reid turned in his seat, exposing the shoe now between his legs, a fuse, and a lit match. Moutardier grabbed him. He pushed her away. She tried to take hold of him again and he pushed her, hard, until she fell across an armrest in the next row of seats. Moutardier ran back down the plane, shouting, 'Get him! Go!'

When Cristina Jones heard Moutardier, she ran towards the commotion. Reid's back was turned away. Jones shouted, 'Stop it!' and tried to grab him. Reid turned and bit her left hand, his teeth fastening to the flesh below the thumb, not letting go. Jones screamed.

When he released her, Jones put up the tray table in the seat beside him. Passengers passed over bottles of Evian water to pour over Reid. They then used belts, headphone wires and plastic cuffs to tie him up. When, later, the FBI tried to take hold of him, they had to cut Richard out of layers of bonds.

'I think I ought not apologize for my actions,' Richard Reid said at his trial. 'I am at war with your country. I'm at war with them not for personal reasons... So you can judge and I leave you to judge. And I don't mind. This is all I have to say.'

'You are not an enemy combatant,' Judge William Young said. 'You are a terrorist. You are not a soldier in any war. You are a terrorist... We do not treat with terrorists. We do not sign documents with terrorists. We hunt them down one by one and bring them to justice.

'You are a terrorist. A species of criminal guilty of multiple attempted murders.

'Custody, Mr. Officer. Stand him down.'

'On the Day of Judgment,' Reid said as he was carried away, 'you will see in front of your Lord and my Lord and then we will know.'

-- an emptiness of sound --

JOE PUT DOWN the book and drank his whisky. A single ice-cube tinkled against the glass. The window shutters had gone down, and the plane was in darkness. Like the guy in the book, he had a window seat and no one beside him. Before and behind him, all throughout the plane, people were sleeping, like silkworm larvae in their soft cocoons. He could hear the sounds of their lives, the gentle snores and their bodies turning this way and that, and he wished he too could sleep. The books did not seem particularly conductive for airplane flights. They were full of exploding planes, exploding buildings, exploding trains, exploding people. They read like the lab reports of a morgue, full of facts and figures all concerned with death. He did not understand them. He thought about the words of the judge in the book. The judge said there was no war, or rather he said that the bomber, Reid, wasn't a soldier: he was a criminal. But it seemed to Joe that, though he didn't understand it, there *was* a war being fought in the book. He didn't know why or what it was about, it was an ideological battle of which he had no conception, but not understanding it did not mean that it did not exist. Perhaps the judge, like himself, did not understand it, could not understand it, and therefore would not accept it for what it was. And yet, it only took one side to declare war.

He sighed and lit a cigarette, having booked a seat at the back of the plane, and when the ash grew long he tapped it into the arm-rest's small, metallic ashtray. He wished he could look out of the window. It was dark on the plane, and quiet. He had headphones, but they carried only canned music through.

Tomorrow he would be in Paris. He was travelling back through time on this flight, the hours falling away as he went; it was like shedding old skin, emerging new again at the same point one started from. Today he would be in Paris. Yesterday, now.

On board the plane there was no time. Here, he existed in a bubble of stalled time, time halted, preserved, the hour of boarding contained within the self-enclosing metal all the while it was in the air. He shook his head. He was being fanciful. It was only the crossing of time zones that did this. Tomorrow he would readjust his watch, and it wouldn't matter what the time was on the other side of the world. It seldom mattered what happened on the other side of the world.

He finished his cigarette, and his mouth tasted of ash. He finished the whisky, swirling it around his mouth with his tongue, running his tongue against his teeth, and swallowed, and his stomach felt hollow. He pressed the button that turned off the light and sat back, his head resting against the seat. The plane hummed all around him, and he let the sound close on him until he was completely alone, and the rest of on-board humanity had dwindled into a nothingness: an emptiness of sound.

PART TWO:
DEAD LETTER BOX

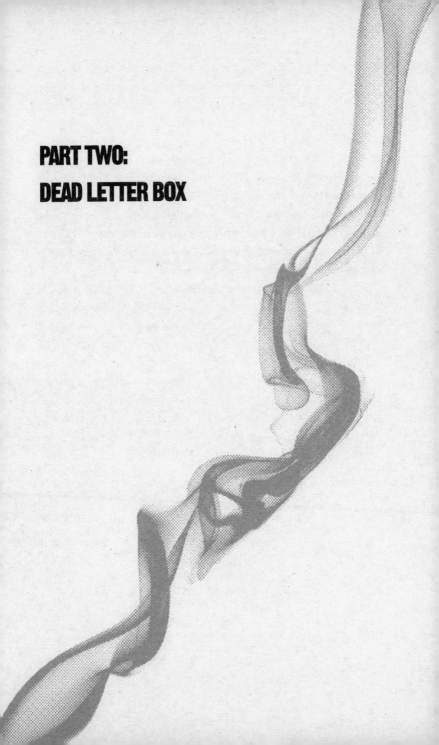

-- everywhere's a good place for a drink --

FINDING THE FAT man had not been easy.

He had landed at Orly; taken the train into Paris; checked himself into a small run-down hotel in the foothills of Montmartre. Orly was a concrete busyness. On the jetty as they disembarked a man slipped and fell, hitting his head on the ground. Outside the terminal building there was a statue of a French general: the small brass plaque read: *Charles de Gaulle, leader of the Free French Forces, Lille 1890-Algiers 1944. "Fighting France calls upon you."*

Sprayed against the concrete base was a faded inscription, partially covered in dried bird droppings. It read, *France has no friends, only interests. CDG.*

The trains were busy and the seats worn. There were sprayed messages against the sides of the carriages, and burn-holes in the upholstery. Joe's hotel room was on the third floor, overlooking a narrow, climbing street. Just outside the hotel entrance a man with an upturned cardboard box offered passers-by a chance to find the lady, his hands moving incessantly as the three playing cards, face down, changed and shifted places. Joe stared out of the window and smoked. He felt restless, tired, but not able to sleep. The air was hot and muggy, a dirty Parisian summer beginning to angrily emerge from a winter's sleep.

The first stage of the investigation had been easy enough. The address of Medusa Press was a post office box, followed by a numerical code. Consulting the local branch of La Poste, he found out that the code identified the location as set in the 8th *arrondissement*. 'It is the old post office on Boulevard

Haussmann,' the clerk told him. The building number was 102. He was going to go there, but now it was most likely too late. He would set up surveillance tomorrow, early. He stood up. The room was almost bare, a narrow single bed, a grey blanket, off-white sheets, a dresser that was either antique or old rubbish, depending on one's point of view, dirty maroon curtains, a picture on the wall of former French president Saint Exupéry against a blue background, a sink. There was a shower and bathroom at the end of the corridor. There was an ashtray on the dresser. There was a smell of disinfectant. Joe left the room and closed the door behind him.

He negotiated the stairs down to the ground floor, nodded to the Algerian man behind the counter, and strolled outside. Hats were back in fashion, he noticed. He passed the card tout and his small crowd of hopefuls, and in a street stall further down the road bought a black, wide-brimmed hat and put it on at an angle.

'Ooh, very nice, monsieur,' the large African woman standing behind her crude makeshift table of colourful cloth said. 'Very good for the ladies.' Joe smiled and paid her. He needed a drink. He needed to eat, too, but mostly he needed a drink. He walked down the Boulevard de Rochechouart, towards Place Pigalle.

'Hey, you want company?' a voice said. She was leaning against the wall, one leg lightly crossing the other, flashing him a smile. She had bleached blonde hair and long brown legs and her skirt was very short. She had a nice smile, but it didn't seem real, somehow. She looked strangely insubstantial standing there, like a mirage on a city street, shimmering in the hazy air. There was a faint but lingering smell of booze.

Joe shook his head.

'You don't like girls?'

He shrugged and walked past. Behind him the girl called, 'You like boys? I can find you a boy. Or we can party all together, what do you say? What colour you like?'

There was something her voice, a way in which it caught as she spoke the last words, a falling intonation that caught him off-guard; there was something lonely in there, and hurting, and raw, and he turned around. 'I like the colour of whisky when the ice-cube is just beginning to melt in the glass,' he said. 'When you hold up the glass to the light and watch the drink through the underside, and it's like the sky after it's stopped raining.'

The girl laughed. 'I like the colour of it neat, myself.'

'Where's a good place to get a drink around here?'

'From where I'm standing,' the girl said, '*everywhere's* a good place for a drink.'

-- a warm, safe place --

THEY SAT IN companionable peace on two stools beside the wide wooden bar. They were somewhere in Pigalle. The girl drank her scotch neat. Joe had his with a single ice-cube. He felt that separated him from the drunks. Putting that ice-cube there meant you were merely enjoying a drink. The girl had downed two shot glasses as soon as they came in. Strangely, she looked more substantial now, the hazy aura dissipating: she looked solid and very real and very close. She caught him looking and smirked. 'I have to keep drinking so I don't fade away,' she said and raised her glass in a silent toast. They drank. Joe signalled for two more drinks.

'I've not seen you around before,' the girl said. 'Are you new?'

It was a strange question, but he merely said, 'I only just got here.'

The girl nodded and seemed satisfied. 'Hard at first, isn't it?' she said. 'What a strange place.'

He looked at her again. Brown skin, long hair black at the roots. Large almond eyes looking at him soulfully. The girl hiccupped and burst into giggles. Joe smiled. He wondered where she was from. Her French was flawless. Algeria? Somewhere in North Africa, he decided.

The girl pulled a soft packet of Gauloises out of a hidden pocket and extracted a cigarette. 'You want one?'

'Sure.'

He lit both of their cigarettes with his Zippo. The girl arched her eyebrows and blew a smoke ring that hovered above the countertop. It was dark in the bar, and smoky. A fan turned lethargically over one end of the counter. There was no music.

'It's like a private space, isn't it?' the girl said. He wasn't sure if she was speaking to him or to herself. 'Sitting in here, it's like – I once had a mouse. When I was a little girl. I used to carry it in my pocket. Sometimes it would stick its nose out and sniff the air, but mostly it liked to stay inside, and I used to imagine what it was like in there, warm and dark and safe. Sometimes I feel like that here. When I can afford to.'

'A pocket universe,' Joe said, and the girl laughed. 'A pocket universe,' she said. 'That's funny.'

They sat, and smoked, and drank, and the world was reduced to a warm, safe place, and Joe held up his glass and watched the colour change as the ice melted and the girl laughed again. It could have been noon outside, or midnight, or all the hours in between, but inside, time was a contained thing, captive and still.

Joe didn't know what made him mention the books. There was method behind it: a feeling first, that the girl would know, but also logic: that a publisher who specialised in a certain type of book may be known, here, in the area around Place Pigalle, which made something of a specialization itself with that kind of fantasy. So he said, 'You ever read the *Vigilante* books?'

The girl's eyes were very alive. She nodded, slowly, and sighed out a lungful of blue smoke. 'Yes...' she said.

He signalled for two more drinks. The girl smiled and stroked his arm. He was feeling light-headed, a cloud of smoke suspended in heavy air. He waited. The fan wheezed lethargically in the corner of the bar, and Joe watched the smoke wafting above the counter-top.

'They're published here, aren't they?' he said into the girl's silence. 'In Paris.' Her eyes were studying him, he realised. They were deep and dark, like empty wells. 'Yes...' the girl said again. She looked away from him. The bartender arrived with their drinks, but the girl pushed hers away. 'I think I'm solid enough,' she said, to no one in particular. Joe looked at her figure and had to agree. Still he waited.

Perhaps it was his silence that made her pause and at last turn to him again. She was already in the process of getting off the bar-stool. 'Are you one of them?' she said. He didn't know what she meant, but he said, 'No.' The girl stubbed out her cigarette in the ashtray, hard. 'They want to find him too,' she said. 'They should leave Papa D alone.'

'Who's Papa D?'

The girl shook her head. 'I better go,' she said. She gave him a smile. She was turned in profile to him, had already dismissed him. 'Wait,' Joe said. 'Please. I need to know.'

'Why?' the girl said. And turned fully to him then. 'Why?' she said again, looking into his eyes as if searching for something there, but not finding it. She shrugged, and it was a tired, weary gesture, and shook her head, and then she was gone, and the door to the bar closed softly behind her.

-- hollow cells in a honey bee hive --

ALGIERS, THE WHITE city, Alger-la-Blanche, rises
from the Mediterranean sea like a mirage. Its
white buildings lie bleached in the sun like
whalebones. Walking along the sea front, one can
encounter both the Grand Mosque and the Casino.
Albert Camus attended the *lycée* and later the
university here. On the eleventh of December
two bombs exploded, ten minutes apart, one
in the Aknoun district and one in the Hydra
neighbourhood.

Both were car bombs. Both contained eight
hundred kilograms of explosives. The second bomb
exploded on Émile Payen Street at 09:52, between
the United Nations headquarters and that of the
UNHCR - the UN High Commission for Refugees.

The UNHCR sat in a modest building, white
with blue awnings over the windows facing the
road. There was a flag above the door, a small
courtyard, a notice-board outside. The building
had a capacity for a staff of twelve. The UN as
a whole had a total of one hundred and sixteen
Algerian employees and eighteen internationals.
The explosion levelled the building and tore
through the UN headquarters opposite, stripping
the walls and burying people under the rubble.
The death toll included seventeen UN personnel,
amongst them Algerians, a Dane, a Filipino and

a Senegalese. A policeman guarding the office was also killed, as well as a DHL agent inside the UN building. Five other people, living close to the office, also died in the blast. Forty UN personnel were injured, some severely. The man driving the bomb truck was the first to die.

Many of the survivors remained behind, helping to clear the rubble, searching for people buried inside. They included the United Nations' office cleaner, who was several months pregnant.

Twenty-two minutes earlier at 09:30, across town, the first car bomb exploded near the Supreme Constitutional Court. The building, done in a Moorish style, had been built by a Chinese construction company. As the walls disappeared, offices were revealed inside like the hollow cells in a honey bee hive. A bus passing by, packed with students on their way to lessons at the Ben Aknoun University, bore the full force of the explosion: it reduced its passengers into a thing resembling crushed pupae.

-- one of us --

THAT EVENING JOE sat alone in a darkened cinema hall and watched the light playing on the screen, dust motes dancing in the path of the projected beam. It was an old film from the 'thirties, in black and white, and there were few people in the cinema. Joe sat in the back and had a whole row to himself, and an uninterrupted view. Above his head the beam of light from the projector travelled in a steady stream, resolving itself into old images as it hit the distant screen. The story seemed to be about a group of sideshow freaks. His mind felt dirty and soggy, like a cigarette butt stubbed into water. He still couldn't sleep. He had stayed at the bar until the sunlight faded outside and street lamps began to come alive. He'd ordered the meal of the day, which was a stew with beans and fatty meat and carrots, served with bread. When the bartender brought over his plate he said, 'You're looking for the Greek?'

The food smelled good and it made Joe's stomach rumble. Briefly he thought about the woman he had met at the airport. *On-board meal, that's all I can taste now,* she had said. He grimaced. He lifted up his spoon, thought of the bartender's question. The man was watching him patiently. He had a bald head and a pug nose and hair on the back on his hands. His eyes were a clear, calm blue. 'I don't know,' Joe said. 'Am I?'

The man shrugged. 'No business of mine,' he said affably. 'Enjoy your meal.'

Joe ate. The bartender went back to polishing glasses. When Joe was finished, the bartender returned and removed his plate. 'Wait,' Joe said.

'Yes?'

'Do you know who I'm looking for?'

The man shrugged. 'Who are we all looking for?' he said, with just the hint of a smile on his face. Joe said, 'I need to know.'

'We serve drinks and stew,' the bartender said. 'Everything else's extra.' He wandered off, carrying Joe's plate.

Joe smiled; then he carefully inserted a twenty franc note under his by-now empty glass. When the bartender returned his eyes didn't miss the note; and with a slight nod he went to refill Joe's glass, putting a measure of whisky in and a new ice cube. The note had disappeared. 'One for yourself?' Joe said. The bartender shook his head. 'I never drink,' he said.

'More for the rest of us,' Joe said. The bartender smiled. 'Sure,' he said. He pulled up a chair and sat on the other side of the counter. Joe said, 'Talk,' and it made the bartender smile wider. 'You didn't sleep with her?' the bartender said. 'The girl that brought you here?'

'Why would I – ? No,' Joe said. The bartender nodded. 'Interesting,' he said. 'She's not all there, you know,' he said, as if imparting a great secret. 'Which can make it *interesting*, if you follow my meaning. At least, I think it would. Fuzzy around the edges, that girl. Especially if she's not drinking.' He shrugged again. 'Not that there's much chance of that.'

'The Greek,' Joe said, ignoring him with some effort. 'Papa D. Who is he?'

'Ah, so you *are* looking for him,' the bartender said. 'I thought as much. Didn't mean to pry, mind, but I can't help overhearing things.'

'Sure,' Joe said. 'You can't.'

The bartender gave him a long look, then seemed to decide to let it drop. 'Not sure what I can tell you,' he said at last. 'The girls call him Papa D. His name's Papadopoulos. Not sure what his first name is, if he even has one. Strange little man. Tubby.

Book publisher, if you can call the things he publishes books. Half-Greek, half-Armenian, half-fuck-knows-what. Papa D.'

Joe lit a cigarette. The bartender fell silent, seemingly exhausted with the effort of producing such a concise biography. His math, Joe thought, was a bit off. He blew out smoke and said, in carefully-bored tones, the voice of a man checking items against an inventory on a clipboard, 'What is the name of his publishing company?'

'Medusa,' the bartender said. They locked eyes. The bartender's said, *Don't fuck me around, boy.* Joe smiled and shrugged in a good imitation of the man. 'You ever see him around?'

'I see a lot of things,' the bartender said. Joe said, 'See this?' and extracted a second note. He had used the black credit card again at the airport upon landing, taking it into the branch of the Crédit Lyonnais and asking to withdraw money. To his surprise, they gave him some.

The bartender took the note and looked at it critically. Joe pulled on the cigarette and when he looked back the money had disappeared. There was something terribly familiar about the situation for him: his job required him to pay people for information, but he wondered how often the bartender went through the same routine, and what sort of questions he was asked. He also wondered if anyone had been asking the same questions he had.

'Fat and small, like I said,' the bartender said. 'Looks a bit like a mushroom – just as white, too. Don't think he sees the sun much.' He and Joe exchanged a glance. Neither of them was seeing much sun either, just then.

'Know where he lives?'

The bartender shook his head. 'No,' he said.

'Know where to find him?'

The bartender thought about it. 'No,' he said.

Joe waited. 'He comes here some times,' the bartender said at last, reluctantly. 'If not here, the shops around, you know.

The sex shops. They sell his books. Also, he likes to pick up the girls. Like your drinking friend there. But Papa D, he doesn't usually have the money.'

'Seen him recently?'

The bartender shook his head.

That was then. He pulled himself back to the present, the even soothing sound of the projector in the booth above falling over him like a blanket. It didn't help. He thought there was something wrong with the film, black and white figures going through an alien ritual while he was frozen, on the wrong side of the screen. The other watchers seemed frozen in their seats, bent statues made of weathered stone.

On the screen, the sideshow people were having a party. A tall woman was marrying a midget. Around the table were a pair of conjoined twins; two girls with no arms; a legless man and an entirely limbless one; a dwarf with a head resembling that of a bird; a skeletal man; a figure who was a man on one side of the body, a woman on the other; the midgets; and others. They were shouting. The words echoed around the dark cinema hall. *One of us*, the sideshow people were crying. *One of us. One of us.* Joe tried to light a cigarette and found that his hand was shaking. He rose from his seat and walked hurriedly through the door at the back, through the narrow corridor, the silent, empty foyer, and into the night outside. The air felt humid, feverish, but not of the tropics: a city's smell hung on it like limp laundry, a smell of pavement slabs and concrete blocks and cars and fumes and smoke and food and urine and spilled alcohol and spilled tears, it was a smell of many lives. He walked back through empty streets to his hotel and climbed up the silent flights of stairs and to his room; and sleep at last claimed him.

-- being a detective --

FINDING THE FAT man had not been easy. In the morning Joe woke early, and took his coffee standing up beside an outdoors kiosk, with Sacré Coeur towering overhead. He took the Métro to Boulevard Haussmann and was stationed outside the post office at number 102 when it opened.

Joe was the first customer.

He located the post box easily enough. The post office was an old, run-down establishment on the ground floor of 102. There were apartments above. Inside, the sound of traffic was strangely diminished, and the lighting, too, was dim, and the floor was stained concrete, and the spots on the floor and walls could have been old blood stains from the German war or they could have been spilled coffee – either way, they weren't telling. The woman guarding the boxes did not ask him for identification, but he still made a show of jingling keys in his pocket and going confidently, as if merely to collect his morning post. There were rows upon rows of small wooden doors set in the walls, thousands of boxes: already the first customers of the day were coming in, each wrapped in their own private universe, each going to their own small address, and for a moment the feeling came to Joe of the weight of expectations there, the pressing body of letters waiting just behind the little locked doors, beyond the thin makeshift wooden walls and the metal grilles that separated the inside and outside of this outpost. He thought of wild mail, living freely behind those doors; of lost mail, like buried treasure, waiting to be unearthed in dark booby-trapped tombs; and of the mail that wasn't there but was hoped for, the unreal mail that would never be written or delivered, but still hoped for every day, still expected against all hope: *We made a mistake, your daughter is alive. Please accept our apology, your son has been found well and is on his way back home.* And then he shook his head, because he was being fanciful, and he had located the box, and now all he had to do was wait for the man to come and collect his post, because one thing a publisher had to do every day, if nothing else that day, was check his mail. He was tempted to break the lock and look inside, but decided against it. There would be time later, but for now he needed only to watch, and wait: which was ninety-five percent of being a detective.

By noon he had seen no sign of a man fitting the description of Papadopoulos. At one o'clock he bought half a baguette with ham and cheese and a thin mayonnaise, and washed it down with two small black coffees. At half past one he had to go in search of a bathroom, which he at last found in a local brasserie, where they grudgingly let him use it. At two o'clock he thought he saw someone fitting the description and followed him for forty-five minutes through twists and turns and stops that seemed very promising, until the man at last went into a butcher's shop on Rue de Londres with pig heads staring mournfully through the glass: the man turned the sign on the door from *Closed* to *Open*, put on a white apron, and went behind the counter.

Joe decided to call it a day. As he walked back, the great grey structure of the Gare St. Lazare rose above him, and he watched the dark railway lines spread out from the station like a spider bite, their paths crisscrossing and hatching, and the great metal beasts of burden trudged along them, fleeing across the earth. His footsteps led him to the back of the station. It seemed a wild wasteland that took him by surprise. Beyond the gate, at the back of the station, pools of standing water littered the ground, and amidst them, like a still landscape, were strewn abandoned objects, broken and unwanted, like sacrificial offerings to St. Lazare. Joe paused as his shoes squelched in the water, and watched a man leap from a floating wooden ladder, his reflection caught in the smooth surface of the water. He saw bicycle tires, and disused pipes, a wet newspaper, an army helmet, clothes pegs, a broken torch, an upturned beer crate, a pair of spectacles with the glass missing, a toy monkey with its eyes missing, something that looked like the inside of an electronic device of some sort, all wires and copper, lines in complicated patterns, a milk bottle, an empty packet of cigarettes, a floating ticket stub for a train or a cinema, a broken pencil, white toilet paper strewn this way and that like bandages that had been torn away from a rising corpse. All that and, as his eyes wandered over the sea of debris, that geography of abandoned human lives, further away and to the left, disappearing behind a corner: polished black shoes.

'Hey!' Joe shouted. 'Wait!' And he ran, following the shoes, but as he turned the corner there was nobody there. Joe swore. Then he said, 'Enough,' and turned, and went to the St. Lazare Métro station. The clouds were amassing overhead, and as he descended the steps into the underworld of the train network, a fine rain began steadily to fall.

-- everybody comes from somewhere --

HE THOUGHT ABOUT a post office box that wasn't being collected, and he thought about a man in black shoes, and he wondered who was watching whom, and why, and then he thought about the train station, the grey edifice rising out of the Parisian soil like a ghostly castle, and he thought about trains: he liked trains. They made him feel safe. He thought about rain, because just as he was descending down to the platform, he glanced up, and a ray of sunlight had come through the clouds behind the rain, and for a moment he thought he saw her, the girl who came to him for his help, and she was looking at him, and her eyes were clouded. He had blinked, and the world was grey again, the clouds joining overhead, and the girl had gone, and he had most likely imagined it. He pictured her face, but it was like rain falling down on his memory, obscuring her face behind the drops, and he wondered why the thought of her made him feel the way he did, and then he drank what remained in his glass and ordered another one, *s'il vous plait*, *merci*, and lit a cigarette and thought of nothing at all.

This was the third or fourth bar he'd tried, each one dingier than the other, in each subsequent one the music quieter, the lights dimmer, the drinking more intense. There were women there, from Asia and Africa and Europe, a cosmopolitan blend who all wore the same exaggerated makeup, the same too-short skirts, the same look in their eyes that was at once an evaluation and a wariness and an invitation, and deeper than that, a great restless tiredness resembling fear, and the men who came to the bars returned that look with one of their own, a corresponding mix of hunger and reticence and unvarnished need and a little bit of shame: they were a dance, Joe thought, an intricate wavering pattern criss-crossing and hatching like the web of train lines outside St. Lazare, criss-crossing and hatching, but never quite meeting, and if they ever did it would be fatal. It was the third or fourth bar, he couldn't now recall, and the only illumination was provided by fat candle-stubs scattered across the room, and couples were dancing to the tune of some slow, mournful African jazz. There were hairy hands on naked thighs, lips touching ears, whispered words, a groping in the half-light, fabric rubbing against fabric in the close-dance, and beyond that, sitting against the bar, the solitary figures waiting or still deciding or, like himself: the lonely ones who wanted only drink.

It was there that she found him, the girl of the day before, and she sat herself on a stool beside him and her skirt rode high up her thighs and she smoothed it with a practiced hand and shook her hair back and looked at him, not smiling, not speaking either, but companionable.

'You shouldn't be drinking alone,' she said. He didn't reply.

'None of us should,' she said. He looked at her sideways. Her wide almond eyes looked back at him steadily. She made a gesture with her fingers, signalling the bartender. The man ambled over, replaced Joe's glass without comment, and put a shot glass in front of the girl. Not looking at him, she put a note on the counter. The bartender took it and ambled off.

The girl held Joe in her sight. Her eyes were like screens; he wondered what he was projecting onto them. The girl said, 'Where are you from?'

Joe broke eye-contact. The sight of his glass was welcome. He took a sip, and then another. He had had several drinks already, going from one bar to another, searching for a fat, pale man – like a mushroom, the bartender a day and several bars ago had told him – and with an eye for working girls. There were several men he had seen who might have fit the description, but none of them had turned out to be Papadopoulos. He felt the weight of the girl's expectation beside him and turned, unwillingly, and said, 'Here and there.'

'Here and there,' she said flatly, repeating him, and he shrugged. '

All about,' he said.

'All about,' she said, imitating him. Her hand grasped his on the counter; her fingers were long and brown and strong where they held him. He faced her. He wondered if the bleached blonde hair was a wig. She had very full lips. They seemed soft, but her eyes were hard. 'Everybody comes from somewhere,' she said.

He turned from her and looked away, at the swaying drunken couples and the solitary drinkers slouched on the bar. Candlelight flickered in an unseen, unfelt breeze. There was nothing beyond the windows. He spoke very quietly then, his lips barely moving, speaking to no one but the emptiness of this compressed world, and it was as if he didn't even know that he was speaking. 'Then where do we come from?' he said. He turned to her, but she was not looking at him any more. She too was looking away. 'And where do we go?'

She was crying. Her face was turned away from him; her glass was empty. Her hands were withdrawn, closing her off from him; they were a screen to shelter her.

They didn't speak. When she took away her hands, her makeup had run, but she seemed not to notice, or care. She said, 'Is that why you are looking for him? You think he could lead you? Where? Forward, or... or back?'

He didn't know what she meant and he didn't reply, but he offered her a cigarette and she accepted, and he lit it for her, and one for himself, and signalled for a drink, the actions reduced to ritual between them, something established, a pattern worked out. There was comfort in ritual. 'I need to find Papadopoulos,' he said, and then, looking at her face as he spoke – 'Papa D.'

The girl, flatly: 'I haven't seen him.'

'No,' Joe agreed. 'I haven't seen him either. But you must know where he stays? Did you ever go back with him to his place?'

He had some hope as he was saying the words, but the girl merely shook her head and looked tired. She said, 'I don't know where he lives. If he can afford a girl he never goes far. There are cheap rooms. I don't know where he lives.'

'Would you tell me if you knew?'

The girl shook her head again. When she looked at him, he felt trapped: he could not move away. The large brown eyes examined him, stripping him down without emotion, looking inside, a doctor checking for tell-tale signs of a terminal disease. 'No,' she said. 'Why should I? He never did us any harm. And he cares, Joe. He cares. Life isn't a pulp novel, Joe, and death isn't either.' And she got up and threw her head back and downed the drink, the last drink, and put down the glass on the counter and walked away, and he watched her, and it was another ritual established, another pattern followed, agreed upon, comforting. They both needed comfort, not of sex or even drink but of a reason, any reason, and in the absence of that there were only empty rituals. And the door closed behind her and the couples danced, seeking warmth in each other's bodies, and the slow recorded jazz played on, and the smoke from Joe's cigarette formed Lazarus castles in the air, grey and insubstantial, and he thought, I never told her my name.

-- into Monceau --

THE NEXT MORNING he was stationed at the post office again but this time he wasn't watching for the man. He was only watching the post box. Joe was a tourist. He was buying stamps. He engaged a teller in a long conversation on first day covers; he chose and replaced postcards; he spoke terrible French, but was determined to make use of it for conversation; when he couldn't make himself understood, he resorted to speaking loudly and slowly in English; he wrote out long messages to absent friends, scribbling them on postcards, leaning on the counter, saying to everyone how beautiful he thought the city was; in short, he made himself a nuisance of the kind that was happy, it was clear to everyone in sight, to remain at the place all day.

It was lucky for all concerned that the boy came a mere one hour and fifteen minutes after the post office opened.

Joe had almost missed him. The boy had brown hair and dark skin and he was small and he went unremarked through the adults who came to check their mail. He carried a small brown bag on a strap on his shoulder. Joe had hardly paid him attention, the small, shy figure passing through the cavernous hall of waiting boxes, going to one end of a row of boxes –

There.

For just a moment, there was post in the boy's hands. Envelopes. A small package. A couple of single-sheet flyers. And then they were gone into the small brown bag and the boy turned to leave. No one could have seen him.

And, to the relief of the employees of the Avenue Hausmann branch of La Poste, the annoying tourist with the bad French and Parisian manners had suddenly lost interest in the display of pre-Independence Algerian stamps he had been giving so much noisy attention to in the past quarter of an hour, and with only a brief *merci* had finally and rather unexpectedly left the premises.

Joe was relieved, too. Focusing attention on himself came hard to him, almost as a physical exertion, an actual sense of discomfort, as if to draw these people's attention was to bodily grab them, and do so while moving through a viscous, gelatinous liquid that was resisting and restricting his movements. It was a strange feeling, and it left him, as he in turn finally left, light-headed and a little disoriented. As he walked down the wide avenue it seemed unreal to him, the cars moving along seeming like translucent crawling beetles, and the trees were hands, raised into the sky with fists that opened and closed, and as he looked at them he could see their veins, a map of blood vessels traversing the stump of a hand. He tried to shake the feeling away. He needed sugar, he thought. He felt like a man who had given blood: he needed coffee, a slice of cake, and he would be fine. Instead he lit a cigarette and coughed, and kept his eyes on the boy and his distance from him, and worried about who else might be following.

For it occurred to him that he was not alone. There had been someone – perhaps several someones – watching him in Vientiane, and in Paris too he got echoes of them, nothing concrete, nothing established, but little echoes coming back a little off, a tone of voice, the way an answer had been phrased – too smoothly, too quickly, as if the person being questioned had had occasion to formulate the answer before. There could have been someone else on the same trail, they could even be using Joe – it was a possibility he didn't like to contemplate, but there it was, and so he worried, and smoked, and followed the boy at a distance, and at the same time watched for a tail, but he could see no one following, and it occurred to him how ridiculous he was being, and yet –

They had shot at him. And perhaps it was merely a warning shot, but they were watching him, he had to go on the assumption that they were, whoever they were, whatever they wanted – and it occurred to him that, sooner or later, he would have to find out. The boy, meanwhile, was walking along with no care in the world, an anonymous, small brown boy, turning away from Avenue Hausmann, going north, Joe following, the road becoming narrower and quieter, and when he looked in the reflection of shop windows he could still see nothing and no one behind. It was a hot day. The cigarette had scorched his fingers and he had dropped it and now he was sweating, and still the boy was going ahead with the mail meant for someone else, until at last he had crossed a road and disappeared into a green grassy space, and Joe paused: it was the back of the Parc Monceau.

He hesitated before going in, and he didn't know why. He had never been there before, and yet it felt as if he had. The knowledge of a memory, rather than the memory itself, nagged at him. He knew the park, without quite knowing how or why he knew it.

He walked down the tree-lined Avenue Ruysdaël, and into Monceau.

-- fabriques --

IT WAS A small green place, a little self-contained bubble of a world inside, and yet away from, the city proper. On a bench in the grass an elderly man sat, slowly eating a sandwich. The man seemed entirely occupied with the laborious process of eating. He brought the baguette to his mouth and took a bite from it, nibbling the sides so that they were equal, then brought the baguette down again to the off-white napkin spread on his knees, and chewed. He chewed with great concentration, all teeth involved in the process, while his hands held the partially-eaten baguette over his knees and his eyes stared into space, grey bushy eyebrows moving up and down with the rhythm of his eating. At last the man swallowed, waited, allowed the food to travel before lifting the sandwich again and repeating the process.

Joe continued to follow the boy, but more with his eyes. The boy had been there before. He knew his way through the quiet. Joe wished it were the same for him. There were curious structures dotted around the park. There was a Chinese fort. There was a Dutch windmill. There were Corinthian pillars. And the word came to Joe as he followed the boy's progress towards – yes – the miniature, brick-made Egyptian pyramid that sat nestled under the trees.

The word was *fabriques*. Those things, those structures erected in Moceau in miniature, were things made to resemble the real, but not real in themselves. They were architectural fabrications, an invented scenographic landscape: they were lies, constructed for the purpose of art – but they were not real, Joe thought. They were not real. The park was a fictional space in the midst of the city.

Outside it, buildings were erected by the forces of commerce, by the human need for habitation – by the dual forces of greed and need. And the buildings were there for a reason, and people lived inside them, worked inside them, slept and ate and fucked and died inside them, and made the city, the space where people lived, real and substantial, just as the park was not. He stopped and stared out across the grass at the mottled grey and white pyramid, and he saw that as the boy went around it and came out the other side, his brown shoulder bag was gone, and he almost smiled. He followed the boy's progress, standing still on the grass, and listened to the quiet. A couple was walking, hand in hand, and the girl wore a summer dress, though it was not yet summer, and when she turned her head, for a just a moment, he thought about his client, the woman who had hired him, and he felt something he couldn't put into words, but which hurt, and he turned away from the couple.

Statues littered the small park. The figures of still and silent men, frozen in pose, staring out to the distance, men who once moved and loved and laughed: Chopin, his fingers still, his music dead, and Maupassant, whose frozen fingers could no longer write but, of course, they were not real either: they were the replica of the men who composed music and words, but not real: they too were *fabriques*.

The English word for *fabrique* was folly, and Joe wondered what it meant, that difference in languages. Was it really folly, to exist in a world that was a fabrication, that was not real, but only made to seem it? Or did existence itself count for something, the statues, though not real, nevertheless existing as a reminder of what had been before, markers of memory in the terrain of shadows and half-truths that was the past? As he circled the park he was checking the lanes, the people passing, watching for watchers, for anyone who may have followed him, for shadows that shouldn't have been there – and then he didn't have far to look because they came directly at him, three of them, and they were smiling, which was never, Joe reflected, a good sign.

There were three of them and they wore black suits that must have been new once, and black ties that made them look like undertakers or – to take a word from the pulps – the mob, but they were neither, and another word from the pulp novels came into Joe's head, and it was G-men.

They smelled like government. They came up to him and stood around him in a loose semi-circle and they were grinning as at a long-lost friend. The one in the middle had greying hair and was the oldest of the three. The ones on either side of him were younger, black hair slicked back: the one on the left had a small discreet scar running down his right eye like a tear. 'Joe, Joe, Joe,' the one in the middle said. 'What are you getting up to?'

'Do I know you?' He was less tense than perhaps they thought he should be. But he had expected them, expected *someone* to be there, sooner or later, and their coming had almost been a relief. They could have been the ones from Vientiane, but somehow he didn't think so. They were watchers, yes, but he thought they didn't *like* to watch: they liked to control.

'Does he know us?' Grey Hair said, turning to the other two, who Joe had decided were merely the muscle. It was the one in the middle he had to listen to – and the others to watch out for. 'I don't think he does,' the one on the left said.

'Maybe we should talk louder,' the one on the right said.

'Or maybe he should listen harder,' the man with the grey hair said.

'Should I?' Joe said, ignoring them.

'Should you what?' the man with the grey hair said, as if oblivious.

'*Should* I know you?'

Grey Hair shook his head. 'No reason why you should,' he said. Then: 'It will go better for you if you merely listen.'

'I'm listening,' Joe said. He wondered if he could take all three of them – or if he could outrun them. He glanced at the muscle on the right and saw the bulge of a gun under the once-new jacket.

'He's listening,' Grey Hair said, and nodded, and said, 'Did you hear that, boys? He's being very gracious to us.'

'Fuck you,' Joe said. Grey Hair nodded.

The punch came from his left and sank into his kidneys and the pain was unbearable and then he was hit in the small of the back and his legs were kicked out from under him and he fell, the two muscle boys holding him, lowering him almost gently to the ground. Grey Hair kneeled beside him. 'We'll be dealing with all of you, sooner or later,' he said. Joe moaned. Grey Hair slapped him. 'Pay attention!' he said. Joe tried to focus. The man was a grey blur above him. 'Go back, Joe, go back to your little hidey-hole and your make-believe play-pen and stay out of trouble. Only kids want to play detective. And kids should know when to do what they're told.'

'Who are you?' Joe said. The words bubbled out of his mouth. His lips felt covered in saliva, thick and stringy, and he couldn't wipe it off.

'The name would mean nothing to you,' the man said. Joe realised that he had an American accent, as did his two assistants. 'You stink of government,' he said. Grey Hair nodded again, and the pain that shot through Joe's right side made him arch his back and moan again. 'It's nothing personal, Joe,' Grey Hair said. His voice was soft, surprisingly gentle. He reached down and touched Joe's hair, smoothing it. His touch made Joe flinch. 'We are only concerned with the greater good. I won't tell you again, after this. Stay away.'

Grey Hair stood up. The two men either side of him rose too. From Joe's perspective on the ground they looked like shadows, hovering above him, the black of their clothes contrasting with the whiteness of their skin until they seemed to him, for just a moment, like ghosts.

He wasn't fast enough. He saw the shadow on the left move, but it moved too fast, and its foot connected with the side of Joe's body and he thought he heard a bone crack through the pain. Then they left him.

-- cheap suits and American voices --

HE WAS INTERESTED not in the mail but in who came to collect it, but more than that, he resented being worked over before lunch. When the men left, Joe remained on the ground for a long time, staring up at a blue-grey sky where clouds wrapped themselves into the shapes of pyramids and windmills, a backdrop as false as the one below. His ribs hurt, and his mouth had the warm salt taste of seawater or blood.

No one approached him. There were few people in the park and none had come over. At last he rolled over, groaning, and rose to his knees, and then he was sick all over the grass.

When he felt well enough to stand, he did so, and the world spun. It was a curious sensation. He would fix his eyes on a point in space and they would move of their own accord, swinging away from it. Again, he would focus, anchor his vision in a concrete spot, only for his eyes to betray him and swim away again. He steadied himself against the trunk of a tree and took deep breaths, and at last the world began to settle again. Cheap suits and American voices, he thought, and something else too – what were they afraid of?

He went with unsteady steps and sat down in view of the pyramid. It felt good to sit down. The pyramid had a small opening at the bottom, an empty doorway jutting out from the main structure. The bricks were mottled browns and greens descending to a grey-white closer to the ground. There were two decorated stone urns outside it. He thought the boy had deposited his bag inside the opening of the pyramid, but he was in no hurry to go and check. He fished out his packet of cigarettes and was dismayed to see it was crumpled. Nevertheless he shook one out and straightened it as best he could and lit it, and drew the smoke into his lungs with a shuddering breath, and held it still for a long moment before exhaling. The pyramid was a dead letter box. He watched it and listened to the sounds of traffic in the distance, and breathed in smoke and the smell of the trees. There were more clouds overhead now and he could feel the rain coming, and when it did the drops were soothing on his skin and he raised his head and opened his mouth to trap the drops; his tongue felt swollen. He turned his head as a ray of light shone down through the clouds, touching the ground on the far side of the pyramid, and for just a moment he thought he saw her again, the girl who had come to him, wavering there between the sun and the raindrops, looking at him, and then she was gone and took the sun with her. His head hurt and he knew he should leave and go back to his hotel but he persisted and then he saw Papa D's other courier and felt little surprise, more like a suspicion confirmed: it was the girl from the bar, and she was wavering a little unsteadily across the bare-ground path to the pyramid, and when she arrived she reached inside and her hand came back with the small brown bag. She slung it over her shoulder and then paused and pulled out a small flask from a coat pocket and unscrewed the top and took a deep pull before screwing the top back shut and secreting it away in her coat. She wore a long black coat that reached almost to her feet and a wool hat over her hair and she didn't look around her as she began to walk away.

Joe longed for that drink. Instead, he rose from his seat, carefully, feeling the pain travelling through him but trying to ignore it, and began to follow the girl.

She walked the short distance to the end of the park and out of it again and down below, into the Métro station of Monceau. Joe felt the pain through his body and his clothes were damp from the rain and clung to his skin and made him itch. He followed the girl down below, purchased a ticket, and followed her at a distance on and off trains until they had crossed the Seine and surfaced again at St. Michel.

The sunlight hurt his eyes. In the square the pigeons seemed suspended in mid-flight. Above the fountain, the saint was frozen in the act of slaying a dragon. The water seemed to hover like mist. An accordion player teased out sad, despondent notes from his instrument. A girl was painting the Notre Dame cathedral in the distance, sitting on a folding-chair beside a small easel, brush and palate in hand. The wind picked up out of nowhere, snatched a hat from a man passing by and threw it in the air. Joe followed the girl, who made for the narrow twisting alleyways of the Quartier Latin. He lit a cigarette and blue smoke followed him as he passed, like the steam being snatched from a moving locomotive. The streets were paved and old and thronged with people, but no one paid him attention. He caught his own reflection in the window of a flower-seller: he looked like a wash-cloth that had been squeezed dry.

The thought made him smile. He followed, safely anonymous in the crowd. The girl marched on, finally passing through the courtyard of a church and entering the narrow Rue de la Parcheminerie. Joe could smell roasting coffee and smoke and cooking meat and the pervasive smell of frying garlic, and his stomach growled; and at the same time he felt nauseous. At number twenty-nine there was a bookshop, untidy heaps of books scattered outside, more books pressing against the windows inside the shops, looking out as if trying to escape. There was a side door. The girl disappeared through it. Joe leaned against the wall and watched. It was comfortable to rest against the stones. The Rue de la Parchminerie smelled of cooking foods and old paper and dust. There were few people walking past. There was a light up on the second floor, but the curtains were drawn shut. Five minutes later the girl emerged through the door and began to walk down the road. Joe went to the door. There was no occupant's name. He tried the door, but it was locked. There was a small intercom and a buzzer, and he pressed the button and heard a man's voice say, 'What is it now, Marlene?' in an exasperated tone, and then there was a buzzing sound, and when Joe pushed the door again it opened.

He climbed up the stairs. The stairwell was dark and musty, and wet-looking moss grew on the walls. At the top of the landing was a door and it was being opened as Joe climbed, and he reached it and found himself face to face, at last, with his quarry.

-- the fat man --

THE BARTENDER'S DESCRIPTION, Joe thought, had been accurate enough. A pale, fat man, shaped a little like a closed-cup mushroom. He wore a flowing white robe and a dandyish hat and his feet were bare, the toes bulging and puffy. 'Who the hell are you?' he said and made to push the door closed, but Joe was already there and holding it from shutting, and he said, 'I just want to talk.'

'Sure,' the fat man said, and blinked. 'They all just want to talk.'

'Please,' Joe said. The fat man looked at him and said, 'What happened to *you*?'

'I think some people didn't want me to find you.'

The fat man suddenly grinned. 'And they didn't persuade you?' he said.

'No.'

'Pity.'

But his hand left the door and he moved aside, and gestured for Joe to come inside. 'You look like you could use a drink.'

'That,' Joe said, 'is truly perceptive. My name's Joe. I'm a private detective.'

The fat man laughed. 'I've always wanted to be a private detective,' he said. 'Sit down. Scotch?'

Without waiting for an answer he made for a small drinks cabinet in one corner. Joe looked around him.

The apartment was full of books. An old wireless box sat precariously on top of a wooden cabinet. There were prints on the walls showing women in various stages of undress. The majority of the books were paperbacks. They lay everywhere, like fallen comrades, on the two brown armchairs and the round coffee-table before them, on shelves, in piles on the floor, in cardboard boxes. The light was dim, and the blinds were thick red velvet and let in little natural daylight. There was a double bed in one corner, the bed-sheets pulled back, more books lying exhausted on top. Above the bed on the wall was a large poster showing a man with clear, penetrating eyes and a long beard, and beneath it the caption read: *Wanted: Dead or Alive. Osama bin Laden, Vigilante.* A sweet, cloying smell hung heavy about the room.

The fat man came back with a glass for Joe, and one for himself. Joe took it gratefully and drank. The liquor tunnelled through him and he felt distant explosions erupt deep inside him, their warmth spreading out through his body. He was still looking at the poster and the fat man, following his gaze, said, 'More trouble than it's worth, this Vigilante business. They want me to stop, you see. But the money's good. Are you a fan?'

He made 'fan' sound like a dirty word. Joe slowly shook his head. At last he was here, had located Longshott's publisher. The man seemed to take an inordinate amount of precaution regarding his location. And yet he had let him in with little argument... interesting. He said, 'Who wants you to stop?'

'Besides the critics, you mean?' He laughed and put out his hand. 'I'm Papadopoulos, by the way. Daniel Papadopoulos, purveyor of fine literature to the masses.'

'Papa D...' Joe said.

The fat man looked up. 'Yes,' he said. 'The girls like to call me that. I think I bring out the maternal in them. Or is it the Oedipal?'

'Maybe it's a bit of both,' Joe said. He examined Daniel Papadopoulos. There were fine cobweb lines at the corners of his eyes, and – now that he looked closely – what looked like a fading bruise on the man's face, below his left eye, masked unsubtly with white make-up. 'I'm looking for Mike Longshott,' he said, and Daniel Papadopoulos sighed. 'Are you one of them?' he said, and he in turn was also examining Joe. 'Refugee?'

He wasn't making sense, but Joe merely shook his head and said, 'I don't think so.'

'You mean you don't know.' The look in the fat man's eyes made Joe uncomfortable. 'That's all right. Live and let, well, live, is what I say. If you get my meaning.'

Joe didn't. He said, 'Who did this to you?' and pointed at the bruise. Papadopoulos shrank back. 'The same people who worked you over, maybe?' he suggested.

'What did they look like?'

'Like gangsters,' Papadopoulos said, and Joe thought – I'm not the only one who reads too much pulp. 'Gangsters with the law on their side. They smelled like bacon.' He smiled, though there wasn't much amusement in his eyes. 'They were pigs. The worst kind of gangster of all is a gangster with a badge. '

'You mean they were policemen?'

'Full marks, boy.' Joe stared into the fat man's eyes. Papadopoulos didn't meet his gaze. Joe thought – he talks big, but he's frightened.

'Did they say who they worked for?'

'No.' Papadopoulos paused and chewed on his lower lip. It was not, Joe thought, a pleasant sight. He lit a cigarette. His mouth tasted raw and full of smoke, like the inside of a collapsed building. He washed it away with the scotch. 'Maybe. When they were leaving I heard one of them – the leader, big guy, grey hair –'

'I think I ran into him, yes,' Joe said.

'He said – I think they thought I was out by then – he said something about reporting back to the...' The fat man fell quiet.

'To the – ?' Joe said.

'I think they loosed a tooth,' Papadopoulos complained. His hand was on his cheek, massaging it. 'Let me think.'

Joe waited. Daniel Papadopoulos was being very forthcoming – but then, men who had been beaten up were sometimes eager not to repeat the experience. Though he sensed there was strength in the man, a conviction behind the pale watery eyes that would not be easy to scrub off. He drew on the cigarette. There was an ashtray on the low coffee-table, a brass plate with a brass girl reclining on it with her legs wide open. The stub of a cigar was resting between her thighs. Joe ashed on the carpet instead.

'CPD,' the man said. 'I think. I think that's what he said. They had to report back to the CPD.'

'What's the CPD?' Joe said, and the fat man shrugged and said, 'How the hell should I know?'

'Where is Longshott?' Joe said.

'Longshott, Longshott,' Daniel Papadopoulos said and grimaced. 'I wish I'd never heard the name. Nothing but trouble.'

'And the books?'

The fat man brightened. 'Sell like, how you say? Like hot cakes. Better than *Slut*, even.'

'I see.'

'Though Countess Szu Szu does sell better overall.'

'I'm sure she does.'

'Still, very profitable, those ridiculous stories. Always start with a big explosion! Boom! Poof!' he brought his hands together in a loud clap. 'Mike Longshott. What a ridiculous name.'

'So who is he?'

Daniel Papadopoulos shrugged. 'How the hell should I know?' he said.

'You don't know who he is?'

The fat man shook his head. 'Never met him. Don't imagine Mike Longshott's his real name, either.'

Joe said, 'Mr. Papadopoulos –'

'Call me Daniel. Please.'

'Daniel. I'm confused.'

'The world does that to you,' Daniel Papadopoulos said, sympathetically. Joe sighed. 'I don't understand,' he said. 'You are Mr. Longshott's publisher. Surely you've met the man?'

The fat man looked amused. 'What on earth for?' he said. 'I never have any contact with writers. If I do, they just keep pestering me about getting paid.' He shrugged, said, 'Look. Couple of years back I get an envelope in the mail. A manuscript submission. I get several a week. It was called *Assignment: Africa*. Good title. I read it, I thought I could sell a few copies, I wrote back to him, sent him a cheque... that's it. Never met the man. Every six months or so, I get a new manuscript in the post. More explosions, collapsing buildings, crashed planes, dead people. He has a busy imagination.'

'So,' Joe said, 'you have an *address* for Mr. Longshott.'

'Well, yes,' Daniel Papadopoulos said. 'And he's very prompt at cashing the cheques, too.'

'Can you tell me what the address *is*, Mr. Papadopoulos?' Joe said.

The fat man regarded him for a long moment. 'Why?' he said at last.

'Because I need to find him,' Joe said.

'Other people want to find him too,' Daniel Papadopoulos said.

'And did you give them the address?'

'They've been after me,' the fat man said, ignoring the question. 'Not just the government people. Others, too. Like you. I have to be careful with Medusa Press anyhow – a lot of people don't like some of the titles –'

'Like *Slut*?'

'Well...' Daniel Papadopoulos shrugged. 'Small-minded,' he said. 'So I only use that post box on Hausmann, and this little system of mine, but it doesn't seem to make that much of a difference, in the end. Everyone can be found if you try hard enough.'

'Even Mike Longshott?'

The fat man suddenly smiled. 'That I don't know,' he said.

'Did you give them the address?'

'No.'

Joe looked at the fat man. 'Will you give it to me?' he said. 'Please?'

'Why?' the fat man said again. His eyes were on Joe's face, looking at him, not quite seeing him. 'Ghosts,' he said. His voice war faraway. 'I have nothing against ghosts. But I don't like being haunted.'

'Mr. Papadopoulos,' Joe said patiently, 'I don't wish Mr. Longshott any harm. I am merely trying to locate him. Please.'

The fat man's eyes focused again, and he smiled. 'No threats, ha?' he said. 'It makes a change.' He went over to the drinks cabinet and replenished his glass. He didn't offer the bottle to Joe. 'To be honest with you, I'm a bit curious myself. And you're a private detective...'

'I can only take on one client at a time,' Joe said. The fat man shrugged. He looked suddenly tired, the animation gone out of him. His face was blotchy, his eyes bruised. 'If you find him, will you let me know?'

He had nothing to lose. He needed the publisher's help. He said, 'If I can, yes.'

The fat man laid down his glass on the small coffee-table. 'Let me write it down. I want you to get out.' He was visibly shaking now, and the glass when he put it down had bumped against the table with some force. The fat man located a piece of paper and a pen on one of the bookcases and scribbled a couple of lines. 'Take it,' he said. 'Now get out. Close the door behind you.'

'Thank you,' Joe said, but the fat man was no longer listening to him. As Joe was leaving, he could not resist a final look: peering through the doorway, he saw the fat man reaching for a high shelf and bringing down a large, leather-bound volume. When he opened the book, Joe had seen enough. He left and closed the door behind him.

The book had been hollow, and he had recognised the paraphernalia inside.

-- dead-end --

BACK IN THE Montmartre hotel, Joe washed, the water warm and rust-coloured, spluttering out of the ancient shower-head. A lone cockroach scuttled as far away from the water as possible. Joe's body hurt. After he had dried himself and pattered back across the dark hallway to his room, he lay on the bed and stared up at the ceiling. Stains that had no definite shape stared back at him, and his tired mind tried to impose order on them, the non-shapes forming through the filter of his mind into definite ones: planes, and trains, and collapsing buildings. He had recognised the smell in the publisher's rooms, at last; should have recognised it sooner; the same smell that clung to his friend Alfred, the smell of processed poppies, but he didn't know what it meant, if the fact had significance. He stared at the scribbled note from Papadopoulos. Paris had been – not a dead-end, no, not quite – it had been merely a dead-letter box. Longshott wasn't there: only his books were.

There were questions he had to ask, but again he did not feel the urge to ask them. Yet he would follow the trail. There was nothing left for him in Paris now, but for the disquieting, niggling sense as of a fading dream, that he had once been to Monceau, that there was a girl with him then. It was a spring day and they had eaten at a nearby brasserie and, bursting, had taken the walk and gone to the park and sat together on a bench: nothing more. He shook his head on the hard pillow and got up and decided it was time for a drink after all. Somewhere it was always time for a drink. Outside he could hear children shouting and the slap-slap-slap sound of running sandaled feet against the hard surface of the road and as he stared out of the window the three-card man was still there, still enticing passersby to find the lady. He realised that the hat he had bought on his first day was still in the room, had been hanging on the dresser, and he put it on, fitting it at an angle, and left the room. As he walked towards Pigalle he checked his reflection in the shops' windows and for a moment thought he'd seen a man with black shoes following behind him, but when he turned could see nothing beyond the milling crowds; and anyway, he didn't care. Paris was a maze of streets that led nowhere, a map whose directions led elsewhere, a confusion of chalked arrows all pointing to a dead-end. The bar he went to could have been one he had been to before or it may have been a different one, he really couldn't say and didn't care. It was quiet and he ordered scotch and didn't bother about the ice. Later, he went back to the hotel and got his things and checked out. The sun was setting over the city as he walked down crowded streets towards the Gare du Nord. It was as he approached the great building of the station, its arches and turrets framed against the darkening sky, that he saw the girl from the bar again.

She was lying against the wall, curled up. He almost hadn't noticed her. It was only the sound she made, a faint mewling sound, that stopped him. He crouched beside her. There was something strange about her. Her brown skin seemed faded, and when he gently raised her head with his hand and looked in her eyes he seemed to see the wall through them, as if the eyes had lost all substance, had become windows into an empty house. There was a bottle held in the girl's hand, but it was empty. The girl blinked when he touched her. 'Oh, it's you,' she said.

'It's me,' he said. And, 'Are you all right?'

The girl tried to laugh. The sound came out of her like gurgling water. It seemed to him, later, when he tried to remember it, as if all the sounds she made were merely the sounds of the street, as if she spoke in traffic noise, and in the words of the public announcement system, and in the sound of the wind. No one disturbed them. People went past without looking. It almost seemed to him, as he held her, that there was no one and nothing there, that what he was holding was merely a heap of old, cheap clothes left by the side of the station. 'I can't any more,' the girl said. 'I was on a bus. The bus was full of people. I was on a bus, and...' her eyes closed. For a moment it was as if she wasn't there. 'I was on a bus...'

'Wait!' He didn't know what made him·shout.

'No more drink. No more sex... I don't feel it when I do it. It's like I'm not really there. Not really here. I was on a bus...' She looked up at him, but there was nothing in her eyes. 'Can you take me home?'

He didn't answer, and she sighed, and the sound was like the wind stirring leaves along the pavement. 'Maybe there is somewhere else...' she said, and then she said one strange word: she said, 'Nangilima.'

Then, somehow, she was gone. He wasn't sure, afterwards, what had happened. All he knew was that she was not there any more. He got up from his crouch and looked around, but he couldn't see her and the people who walked past never shifted and, like a drunk, he walked away, into the great hall of the station, the clockwork inside him still, somehow, ticking, and at the counter he said, 'Londres,' and paid for the ticket, and less than an hour later he was on the train.

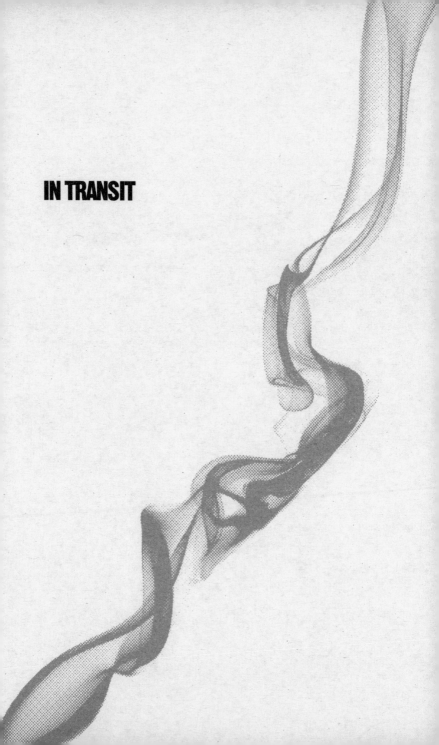

IN TRANSIT

-- missed connections --

THE TRAIN CHUG-CHUG-CHUGGED out of the Gare du Nord, passing through industrial landscapes like spray-painted grey fields where nothing grew. The street lights cast ghostly glows over the bare walls of this unfashionable part of town. He was leaving the city behind gradually, and he thought he had missed something there. There had been – clues, he thought, scattered over pavements, dropped in ashtrayed bars, garish neon signs saying: You are following the wrong trail.

But what was the trail? These were the facts: his name was Joe. He was a private investigator. He had been hired to find a man, and given more-than-adequate funds to do so. Everything else...

These were the facts. Facts were important. They separated fiction from reality, the tawdry world of Mike Longshott from the concrete spaces of Joe's world. Everything else...

He sat in the dining car and smoked and watched the lights of Paris, like a cloud of scattered moths, disappear in the distance. He had always liked trains. There was a sense of timelessness in the way they moved across a landscape, a comfort in their rhythm and their constant pattern, an order of sound and movement. The train's whistle sounded and it made Joe smile. The dining compartment was half-empty, and beside the heavy weight of smoke he could smell brewing tea and floor polish, and as the train gathered speed the windows rattled, just a little, and the wheels turned with a soothing constancy and the windows steamed up and the car was like a cocoon, and he felt no desire to leave it.

And yet there was a little part of him that did. It was a part that, while he was staring out of the window and pulling on his cigarette and letting the lights in the dark world outside all run together as the train sped past them, asked *questions*. That part made him restless and irritable. It was a part that suggested he got lost underground. That he had taken the wrong line, had missed his connection, but rather than admit it to himself he continued to ride the train to somewhere else.

No. There were facts. Everything else – the Monceau *Parc* with its fabricated landscape, the men in black, the way Papadopulous had asked him, *Are you one of them? Refugees?* – none of that had significance beyond, perhaps, its connection to the immediate case. It was important, and he felt the need, somehow, to reiterate it to himself, not to confuse reality with fiction.

That seemingly resolved, he ordered tea, which made him suspect he wasn't feeling all that well, since he only ever drank tea when he was sick, and he lit another cigarette before realising the previous one was still burning in the ashtray. He watched a white round man with a bulbous nose and a floppy hat and a grimy blue backpack enter the car through the connecting door, followed by an incredibly lovely Chinese girl at least fifteen years younger than him; she wore a long-lens Japanese camera around her neck and her hair was long and untied. They found an empty table and sat down and spoke to each other in low voices, fingers touching across the table, the man breaking off the touch to gesticulate, the girl smiling at him in obvious affection. There was something very real and solid about the two of them, and he wondered what she saw in the guy; they had wrapped the world around themselves and recreated it for themselves and yet they were fully a part of it, strange and bemusing and inexplicable with their relationship he would never know the true nature or origin of, their shared history that was private between the two of them, their lives that were separate and had now joined and later may split and rejoin, remain, or part. At another table sat a man with a

Slavic face, a thick dark moustache braided with silver, hairy brown hands hugging a coffee mug. Three young women with pale skin sat together, also, talking rapidly in French, bags of shopping by their feet. He felt a curious dislocation from these people, a distance he could not – did not want to – articulate. They possessed the car – the space inside it – the space around themselves – in a way he could not quite comprehend, only knowing – again, with that small, rebellious part of him that he was trying to shut down – that he could not, did not, share it.

There was the girl, back in Paris. He didn't even know her name. But he knew *her*. The connection between them worried him. And then she had gone – like leaves blowing down the street, like clouds converging over the setting sun – and he could not rationally explain it. His mind turned away from it, from her memory, and from the memory, also, of the Parc Monceau where for a moment he had a curious sensation of having already been there, having walked hand in hand with a girl... He drank from the cooling tea, and the taste in his mouth was of leaves soaked for too long, and he swallowed and got up and went to his compartment, and into a black and dreamless sleep.

-- red flowers, blossoming --

WHEN HE AWOKE it was to get on the boat and then there was the voyage across the sea and the spray of cold seawater as he stood on the deck and looked out. Then there was a moon and the cliffs of Dover, chalk-white, shone in its light, not ghostly, but like the face of a mute corpse, turning its face away, in death, from the ferry approaching across the black waters of the channel. The ferry docked and snatches of music came across from the land and were snatched by turn in the wind: a jazz orchestra band coming through on BBC radio. It was a cold, clean night.

He bought milky coffee in a Styrofoam cup from a lone vendor and smoked a cigarette and stamped his feet as the other passengers disembarked, the men puffy-eyed and hostile, the women with their hair in disarray, holding their hands up against the wind, looking defensive and unhappy. For Joe, though, there was a kind of peace in the moment. The point of transit was like the epicentre of two opposing forces, like the equilibrium found when an equal pull is exerted on a body from all directions, creating the moment of stillness that is free-fall. For Joe those were the moments of exquisite calm, a perfect present with no future and no past. He loved the waiting times, the empty times, the endless moments that came in-between the going and the gone.

A light rain, driven by the wind, came across the water, and Joe's cigarette stub, extinguished, floated at his feet, hovering above the ground, and for a moment he stared at it, transfixed, as if observing an alien artefact, or a strange, unknown remnant of an ancient civilization. Then he laughed and the sound made the great open space around him seem warmer somehow, and he joined the rest of the passengers on the way to the waiting train. The cliffs of Dover, chalky and pale, were being left behind, their faces, many now, staring out across the sea. Joe stared back through the window; inside it was warm and the humidity fogged up the windows and he had to wipe the pane with his sleeve. He pressed his face to the glass, which was cool against his skin, and peered out. He wondered what the faces of Dover saw when they gazed out to sea. Across the channel the poppies grew, somewhere there beyond the water, in the French landscape he had so recently passed through; he pictured a field of poppies growing where, beneath, a field of humans had been sowed and reaped. The train gathered momentum, but for a long time Joe's face remained glued to the glass, staring out, beyond the gentle English moonlit landscape sprayed with silver rain, seeing, as if through a fine haze, endless red flowers blossoming across the silent world.

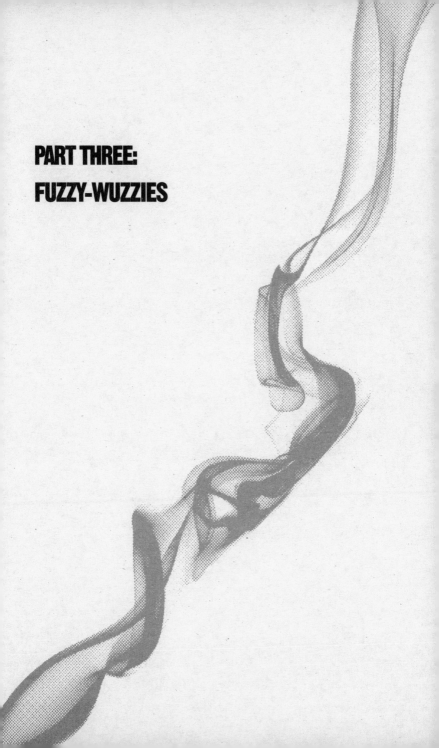

PART THREE:
FUZZY-WUZZIES

-- the angel of Christian charity --

THERE WERE TOURISTS milling all around the statue of Anteros in
Piccadilly Circus and the sun was seeping through dirty grey
clouds, putting a sheen of sweat on girls' upper lips and on
the men's foreheads. Cars went round the circus like herds of
primitive herbivores, and in the high façade above the Café
Monico opposite Anteros, large wrought-iron signs were
advertising Lipton, Wrigley's and Delicious Coca Cola. A large
clock gave out Guinness Time. Joe stood underneath the statue.
The god of requited love and the avenger of love scorned was
a boy with wings resembling those of the pigeons milling all
around the circus. It stood, one leg raised in the air, on its plinth
above the fountain, its bow held aloft, its eyes glazed. It was
made of aluminium. It had been modelled on a sixteen-year-old
Italian boy, Angelo Colarossi. The boy had since then grown old
and died, while Anteros remained youthful. A tour group went
past Joe and stopped beside the fountain, and their guide, bald
and sweating in the lightless humidity, said, as if continuing an
earlier monologue, 'And this is the famous Angel of Christian
Charity, erected on this site in eighteen ninety two, moved again
to this exact spot following the Second World War –'

'I thought this was Eros,' a man in the tour party said. He
had a thick Dutch accent and corn-yellow hair.

The guide smiled and wiped sweat off his brow. 'A common
inaccuracy, sir,' he said. 'Though indeed, originally, it was
meant to be the *brother* of the God of Sensual Love –'

A double-decker bus went past, the people inside looking
down through their windows on the milling crowds. Joe saw

111

a young couple kissing on the steps of the fountain, quite unconcerned with the touring party or anyone else. The girl had long black hair and the boy's was shorn, and neither were much older than the angelic Angelo Colarossi at the time he had posed for the statue.

'Ah, the Criterion!' the guide said, with something like relief, turning away from the fountain. 'Wonderful theatre. Built by Spiers and Pond on the site of the White Bear Inn – come, follow me, all together now! – and opened with W.S. Gilbert's little-known *Topsyturveydom* – moving on, we have –'

Joe smiled as he lit his cigarette. The site of Piccadilly Circus, at least, did not appear to be a stranger to topsyturveydom. Amongst the tourists, the school kids who had mysteriously failed to make an appearance at school, the buskers, the pickpockets, the drug pushers, the gypsy women selling paper flowers, the young musicians with their second-hand guitars, the commuters coming and going from the tube station directly below – amongst all these, the world did indeed seem to be in a permanent state of topsy-turvy. He stood below the Angel of Christian Charity and waited, smelling sweat, car fumes, marijuana smoke, passing perfumes, frying onions, burning sausages, spilled beer, and finally the smoke of a cheap cigar as he saw the man waiting in the entrance of the theatre (the tour group having moved on). He went up to the man.

'You Joe?' the man said. Joe nodded. They shook hands. The man was bald and round. His eyes were deep-set and small. He wore a dirty-brown raincoat, and puffed on a thin brown cigar as he spoke. He noticed Joe's look and said, 'Hamlet.'

'Hamlet?'

'The cigar. Like *to be or not to be*, you know?'

'Sure. Shakespeare.'

'Right.'

'So which is it?' Joe said.

'Which is what?'

'To be, or not to be?'

'Ah,' the man said, and smiled, revealing nicotine-stained teeth. 'That *is* the question, isn't it.'

The man's name was Mo and Joe had found him in the telephone guide resting by the phone in his hotel. He was looking under *Private Inquiry Agents*. He had to admit Mo looked the part. He had a grubby, well-used look, like a paperback that had been carried in a backpack for a long length of time. And he looked unremarkable. None of the people passing them by gave them more than a cursory glance. They could have been two disembodied shadows, standing there outside the theatre, while humanity surged on all around them.

Joe stayed at the Regent Palace Hotel across the road. The building suited him. His room on the fifth floor was small and had no windows. The showers were at the end of a wide and empty corridor. An army could have gotten lost in the Regent Palace. As Joe walked down endless corridors he encountered no-one else, and the only sound as he passed was of his shoes against the floor, a rhythm resembling that of a beating heart, counting seconds and minutes and the passing of time. When he checked in, the concierge had told him, reminiscing, 'You know, in the old days, if you wanted a girl for the night, you used to ring the desk and ask for an extra pillow.'

'And today?' Joe asked. He paid in cash. The concierge shrugged and looked into his eyes and said, 'You just ask for a girl. My name's Simon. You need anything, you call me.'

'Thank you,' Joe said. Then he had gone up in the elevator; he had not seen another hotel guest since.

Joe liked London. He liked its crowds, its constant movement, its hurried busyness. There was a different kind of being alone, of not being noticed, in London. It was a city where it was easy to disappear, to become a face in the crowd that no one would ever glance twice at.

'You want we should go someplace we could talk that's more comfortable?' Mo said. Joe followed the man's eyes to the large Guinness clock above the signs opposite. It was just past twelve o'clock. 'Say, a pub?'

'You got the information for me?'

The man tapped his temple. 'Right here,' he said.

Joe looked at the clock again. Everyone knew that after twelve was already the afternoon...

'Sure,' Joe said.

-- Romeo and Juliets --

...AND SOMEWHERE IT was always just past twelve. Mo had a
bitter. Joe had a French lager. They both had a shot of whisky
just to help the beer go down. They had walked a short distance
up Shaftesbury Avenue, turned left, and were now seated in the
Red Lion pub, hemmed in by the Windmill Theatre on one side
and the Pink Pussycat club on the other. A black girl with a
blonde wig was standing outside the door of the Pink Pussycat
smoking a cigarette. A beggar walked past pushing a shopping
trolley. The Red Lion had large windows and cheap beer and
Joe was paying. They finished the first round and ordered
another. Neither, it seemed, could find a reason not to. 'I'll have
a Gin and Tonic,' Mo said. 'Malawi-style.'

The bartender said, 'What's Malawi-style?'

'You put a pickled chilli instead of a slice of lime in the glass,'
Mo said. 'Gives it a kick.'

The bartender shrugged.

'Just a beer for me,' Joe said.

Two Chinese men in suits walked past. A large poster on
the side wall of the Windmill Theatre promised Fully Nude
Shows. The girl outside the Pink Pussycat finished her cigarette,
dropping the stub to the ground, and remained standing,
holding her arms across her chest. Joe lit a fresh cigarette. Mo
lit a new cigar. The smell of the Hamlet had a life all of its
own. Mo must have seen something in Joe's face, because he
shrugged, and said, 'When business is good, I prefer Romeo
and Juliets.'

Joe let it pass without comment.

'I'm a bit of a Shakespearean,' Mo said. Then he smiled and said, 'At least when it comes to cigars.'

There was something about the man, Joe thought, that wasn't quite right. Sitting in the pub with only the dim sunlight coming in through the windows, Mo's skin had the colour of tobacco leaves, his thin eyebrows the colour of smoke. 'First thing I can tell you is, getting access to members' records isn't going to be easy,' Mo said. 'The Castle is your typical private members' club. There are at least ten in the Soho area alone and they all take privacy very, very seriously. It's part of the appeal. The Castle's clientele seems to be varied: about half are actors, some writers, directors, that sort of people, and the rest is government – councillors, MPs, a couple of ministers. So they don't want anyone snooping around. There was a case a few years ago, one of the waiters at another club opened his mouth to a journalist, all kinds of stories – drugs, orgies, underhand deals conducted in the dining room, you know, the usual – and I only found out about it accidentally. The story never got published, the journalist involved lost his job, and I never heard shit about the waiter again. No one else ever did, either.'

'What does that mean?' Joe said. Mo was beginning to irritate him.

'It means that people respect privacy around here,' Mo said. 'And if they don't, they can be made to respect it. Savvy?'

'Yes,' Joe said, a little testily. 'Do go on.'

'The Castle has three floors; a basement, and the first and second floors. The ground floor' – he was counting the way the British do – 'as far as members are concerned, is only a reception area. That's where the kitchens, et cetera, are located, out of sight. The members' entrance is through an unmarked door at number twenty-two Frith Street. There is a discreet exit through the back, and also a staff entrance two doors down on Frith Street again. To become a member you have to be first recommended by an existing member, then approved by a committee. The membership numbers are restricted. On the first floor is a dining room where guests can be entertained. The second floor holds bedrooms for members wishing to stay the night. In the basement are a private dining room, a library, the smoking lounge and a postal room for use of members wishing to route their post via the club – and that's really what you wanted to know, wasn't it?'

'Yes.'

The address Papadopoulos had given Joe in Paris was for the Castle Club, in London's Soho area. Royalty payments for the Osama books went to Mike Longshott, care of the Castle Club. Mike Longshott, therefore, must have been a member of the club. And membership numbers, as Mo pointed out, were restricted. It was Joe's first solid lead. Somewhere inside the Castle there would be information leading him to Longshott – there had to be.

He took a last swig from his beer and laid down some notes for Mo. The bald man stuffed them inside his raincoat, but seemed in no hurry to leave the premises. 'Everybody's looking for something,' he said suddenly. 'Only some of us get paid to find it.'

Joe was taken aback. Mo smiled and signalled the bartender for another drink. 'I hope you find it, whatever it is,' he told Joe.

Joe nodded. 'And you?' he said. 'Anything you're looking for?'

Mo shrugged. 'I mainly do divorces,' he said. Joe smiled and walked to the doors. As he was about to leave, a small brass plaque on the wall caught his eyes. 'In a room above this pub, in 1847, the second Congress of the Communist League was held. In the same room, Karl Marx wrote *Das Kapital*.' Below that, in smaller letters, was the legend: '"Our age, the age of democracy, is breaking." Frederick Engels.' Joe stepped outside and lit a cigarette.

-- voices at a funeral --

THERE WERE TWO shots. The air was a foggy haze. The girl in the doorway opposite had disappeared. There were no pedestrians. The sunlight had a murky quality. It was very silent but for the gunshots. He hadn't taken more than two puffs on the cigarette – it stayed between his fingers, the smoke curling up so slowly to the sky, but you couldn't see the sky in London. A moth fluttered past. Brick walls. Great Windmill, a pedestrian street. The sound of traffic coming through from Shaftesbury Avenue, but muted, like voices at a funeral. A torn piece of newspaper blowing past his feet. Someone had spray-painted 7/7 on the wall further up, the direction from which the three men were approaching. He saw black shoes, no faces. The door opened behind him, Mo emerging into the street, oblivious, saying – 'I'll give it to you for free – if you get stuck try looking out for Madam Se –'

Gunshots, three this time. One took the bald man in the head. Joe spun, slow-motion-like, his hands trailing bands of light. The sound of the shots was very loud in the street. A glass window exploded. There were screams from inside. Glass fragmented, rippling out of the blast core, flying through the air, the shards catching the light as they blew. There were momentary rainbows. Mo, falling, like a body in water. The cigarette was still glued to Joe's fingers.

Take stock. Turn. Mo still falling, falling, the ground a long way away, his body trailing light like coloured smoke. Three men coming, three men with guns, Joe trapped in a triangle between the Pink Pussycat, the Windmill Theatre and Marx's pub. Up the road a sign said Bookshop. Mo hitting the ground and Joe thought – Strange. There was no blood. Time speeded up and he staggered, the three men still coming, two of them circling him, the third stopped where he was. Joe ducked a blow, kicked out, heard a man grunt in pain. Someone swore. A pistol butt connected with Joe's head and he fell back, hit an obstruction, fell. The ground came at him hard. Mo's body a rise above the plane of the street. Mo's face, turned to Joe, pale thin lips, moving. A whisper. Joe strained to hear.

'One of us...'

The eyes closed. The lips settled into a line. A face like the surface of an asteroid, passing in the darkness of space. Fading out. Hands reached for Joe. He fought them. From somewhere, a shout: 'Don't knock him out!'

Pain flared in the back of his head. He thought, *Too late*.

Fade to black.

-- forget the detective --

DEATH DEFYING ACTS. He was awake, he knew that, but not quite. He was hovering in that space between full wakefulness and sleep. Random acts of senseless violence. One of us. One of us. All I can taste is airline food. Now I hate the taste. Through his half-closed eyes, Great Windmill Street. Outside the Pink Pussycat, a white girl standing with her arms crossed, her hair the same blonde as the black girl who was there before. Angels of Christian mercy watching over him. He groaned.

Fade out.

Awake again. Suspended in a bright white world. The ground beneath him soft, the air perfumed: disinfectant, sweat, patchouli. The sweat his own. The world soft, like a bed. Half-closed eyes: his client, leaning towards him, her face filling his vision. Lips tight, eyes wide. Voices in the background, softly, softly. Something in his arm. A machine pinging. 'I think he said something. Did he say something?' – and fade.

When he awoke, the street was dark and a group of Japanese businessmen in dark suits were piling into the Pink Pussycat. He groaned again and felt the back of his head – there was a large, painful bump there. He blinked, once, twice, tried to sit.

'Sorry, didn't see you there –' A man pushing a shopping trolley, looking startled, hurried away. Joe looked at the junk poking out of the cart and thought of a life. He turned his head, slowly, this way and that. No sign of Mo. Behind him the pub was shut, the window boarded up. No sign of the men who assaulted him. He groaned again and thought of a drink, fished in his pockets, withdrew a crumpled packed of

120

cigarettes, put one in his mouth. His hands shook and it took him several tries before he managed to light it. He took a deep drag and felt the smoke burning his throat, slipping into his lungs. He sat back, against the wall, and smoked. Bright lights flashing. People walking past, night people, no one glancing in his direction. He blew smoke and knew he was in over his head.

How long had he been out?

It was night time. And no one had come for him, and the men didn't get him, and the window got repaired and Mo removed while he was out cold, it was as if the world was cleaned around him while he slept. He said, 'No,' and tasted smoke. He pushed himself up. He was shaking. He stood bracing himself against the wall. Bright flashing lights, a windmill of neon spinning. 7/7 sprayed against the wall up the road, and a *Bookshop* sign. Fuck it. He pushed himself away and went downstream, towards Shaftesbury Avenue.

They might be waiting for him at the hotel, but he didn't care. When he pushed his way in through the doors of the Regent Palace, the first thing he heard was loud Irish music coming from the hotel's pub. Noise, a blast of warm air, the smell of booze and cigarettes. The doorman took one look at his face, shook his head, said nothing. Joe walked in.

Ashes to ashes, dust to dust. Perfume, smoke, laughter. My-name's-Simon on reception, sitting behind a large brass adding machine, the buttons gleaming. Extra pillow. A flash of something hovering at the very back of his mind – white sheets, the ground soft as a bed, 'I think he said something –' No. He staggered into the pub, ordered a whisky, straight, no ice, drank the first one at the counter, ordered another: he felt better after the third, paid for a beer and a fourth, took it to a dark corner, sat down. Irish music and loud voices, faces walking on the pavement outside, lives blowing in the gutter-wind – no. He drank from the beer: it cooled him down. The whisky had burned through him, warmed him up – he hadn't realised how cold he'd felt. Oscillating temperatures.

In too deep – that's what it amounted to. He should relinquish the case. Forget the Castle, forget the Mike Longshott trail – it probably led nowhere in any case. Let go of Papa D, of the girl outside the Gare du Nord. Let go of Mo, drink a toast and forget the detective. Do what the men from the CPD said, and stay away. Forget his employer, the fine lines in the corners of those big, slightly almond-shaped eyes, forget the way she put her hand on his and it was too familiar... Let it go. Let go of Osama bin Laden, let go of books where bombs go off and people die, let go of this war you have no scale for, that you don't understand. Let go of the crumb trail, the talk of refugees, the sideshow freaks in the old black and white movie he'd watched in Paris, chanting *One of us, one of us.*

It was getting late. The three-piece band had wound down, softer music came on, some sort of jazz, no, he knew that song; he touched his eyes and they were wet, and when he blinked he saw the world through a film of moisture, like rain, and she said, 'We have all the time in the world.'

Then she was there, sitting opposite him, blurry, he could only see her blurred through the film over his eyes, an intersection of light and water: he thought she smiled.

He said, 'I saw a man die today.'

She said, 'Maybe he was already dead.'

The silence lingered between them. Joe shook his head, said, 'No.' The girl reached across the table, touched his hand. Her hand was warm. 'No,' she said, agreeing. He blinked, the tears still there. The pub quiet now, the voices hushed. She said, 'Do you remember – ?' and Joe said, 'No' – his vocabulary shrinking to that one word, one single perception.

'Find him, Joe,' the girl said, and he noticed her ears again, a little pointy, and lovely for that. 'Find Mike Longshott. Find Osama bin Laden.'

He wanted to say, *No one ever catches him in the books. Now you see him, now you don't.* And then he thought how the writer resembled his hero, a jack in the box, a disappearing act. He said, 'Why?' Her hand on top of his trembled. He had the urge to take her hand in his, lace his fingers with hers and not let go.

She shook her head. 'For...' She was fading, he couldn't see her clearly any more. He rubbed his eyes and they were dry. When he looked up she was gone. Left on the table was a calling card. He picked it up. It said *The Blue Note*. Nothing else. He finished the dregs of his beer and stood up, and walked out, through the wide corridor of the reception area, up a wide and empty elevator, down an empty echoing corridor, and to his room. Later he had a shower and shaved and watched the dried blood from the back of his head swirl down through the plughole, turning and turning in a diminishing spire of loss.

-- bruisers and cruisers --

THE NEXT DAY he decided to watch the Castle. He walked through Soho, passing signs for Adult Bookshops, Adult Cinemas, Adult Shows – an entire wonderland of adulthood, sculpted into the red-grey bricks of the narrow streets. Italian restaurants; Chinese restaurants; Indian restaurants. Newsagents selling cigarettes and soft drinks and newspapers. Pubs. Bars. Clothes shops. Ticket agents selling tickets to shows on Shaftesbury Avenue at half-price. Mini-cab stands. A man sidled up to him as he walked, said, 'Hashish? Marijuana?' He pronounced it like a name, Mari-Joanna. 'You want girls? Boys? Opium?'

Joe shook his head, no, no, no again; the man sidled away, shaking his head. Joe walked along Old Compton Street and wondered who Old Compton was, and smiled.

Frith Street: old stone houses spilling down to the pavement. Outside number twenty-two, a coffee-bar, tables outside, on the left: a small, unmarked door. He went up the stone steps, pressed a buzzer.

'Yes?'

'I'm here to meet a member.' Said as a question.

'Who are you looking for, sir?'

'Mike Longshott? I believe he's expecting me.'

Silence the other end. The sound of papers being moved. 'We have no member by that name.'

'My apologies,' Joe said. 'Is this not the Century Club?'

'No, this is the Castle.'

'I must have the wrong address.'

Silence on the other end. Conversation terminated.

Joe smiled.

He sat at the coffee bar outside and ordered a cappuccino. A wide-screen television inside showing BBC coverage of a European sports league. He sat with his back to it, watched the approach to the Castle. Not long to wait: a man came out, dark suit, a large frame, a once-broken nose – making sure he was gone.

Well, he wasn't. The bruiser went back inside, seemingly satisfied. Joe lit a cigarette, added sugar to his coffee. The bruise at the back of his head still hurt.

He sipped his coffee. He watched the club.

09:30 – a black cab pulled up to the curb, a man in a brown suit came out, holding a briefcase and a cane. Climbed up the stairs, the door swallowed him, the cab drove off.

09:42 – a man and a woman, casual clothes, the woman smoking, the man gesturing with his hands as he talked – up the stairs, into the club.

09:48 – an elderly man with a wild mane of white hair, stepping out of the club, blinking in the light, walked off towards Soho Square, zigzagging a little.

Nothing for another fifteen minutes, and he ordered another coffee, went to the bathroom. Through the counter, through a too-low door, down stairs, a cubicle underground. Emerging back into the light to find his coffee waiting for him, and a horse-drawn carriage, no less, outside the Castle, men in livery holding open the doors: two Japanese officials emerging in full regalia, a white man with square glasses, receding hairline and a suit, the three of them went into the club. He could be waiting all day.

10:16 – three men in casual clothes, talking loudly, coming from the direction of Chinatown.

10:22 – a cab pulled to the curb, waited. Four minutes later two women came out of the club, climbed inside. Strong features, prominent noses, mute and expensive clothes – the cab drove away.

Another trip underground for Joe. Standing under London all sounds were muted, the small dark space closing in on him. He hurried back up the narrow stairs.

Third coffee, and he was beginning to lose the thread of what he was looking for. Only a sense, a feeling that he would find something, an end to follow, if only he waited long enough. But he'd had enough of the coffee. He felt wound up, kept fidgeting with the cigarette.

10:43 – black car, diplomatic registration plates, no flag flying, three men in black suits, the older man gesturing, telling a joke – they were too far away for him to hear the particulars – the other two laughing. Grey Hair and his two muscle-boys, last seen Moceau. The car drove away, the three went up the stairs, disappeared inside the club.

Cosy. Did they know about Longshott, then? Too many unanswered questions. He left money on the table and stood up, stretched. Went back to number twenty-two and stared at the door. A small blue plaque on the wall: "The first television broadcast was made on this location in 1926." He waited. He didn't have to wait long.

The door opened. The bruiser from earlier. The suit an excellent cut, the face cut also, from long ago. 'Can I help you, sir?'

Joe liked the 'sir.' The man's massive frame blocked the door. 'I was just leaving,' Joe said.

The man waited, face impassive. Joe thought of the people coming and going from the club, of the man in front of him. Bruisers and cruisers, he thought, and smiled.

'Sir?' The man detached himself from the doorway. A bulge under his jacket. Concealed gun. 'If you don't mind.'

Joe left.

-- convict's last --

HE WALKED BACK to the Red Lion. It was still early. The Pink Pussycat was closed. The broken window of the Red Lion was still boarded up. Two African men walking past; a woman in a sari; a red-headed girl with pale Irish skin; a group of builders, heading for the Red Lion – Joe left them to it.

Spray-painted on the wall, there was that number again. 7/7, lucky number doubled. He wondered what it meant. There was that Bookshop sign again. He went up Great Windmill, stepped through the door to the shop. A bell tinkled faintly.

The interior dark, a little musty. Dusty books in piles on the floor, movie reels stacked on shelves behind a counter, a black cat sleeping on a rocking chair. Leather outfits like something out of World War Two hanging loosely on hooks. Behind the counter, straightening up: an old man, white candy-floss hair sticking out, glasses perched on the edge of his nose. 'Can I help you?'

'What sort of books do you have?'

'Dirty books,' the man said, flatly.

Joe trailed a finger on a spine, left a line in the covering of dust, said, 'I can see that.'

'Very funny. You want to buy something?' the implication being – if not, get out.

'Do you have any Medusa Press titles?'

The old man grimaced. 'Sure. We got the latest titles just come in from Paris.'

'Could I see them?'

The man gestured at a pile of books by the door, a little less dusty than the rest. 'Help yourself.'

Why was he looking at the books again? He didn't know. He had a feeling he had missed something, in his talk with Papa D. He squatted down and began sifting through the titles, forming a new pile as he shifted books starting at the top.

Confessions of a Dungeon Slave.

Alien Sexperiments – this one a science fiction title.

The New Translation of the Kama Sutra.

Countess Szu Szu's Guide to Erotic Love.

Papa D had been busy.

He went through some more of the same. 'Do you stock any of the Osama bin Laden books?'

'*Vigilante*?' the owner made a face. 'I might have the new one somewhere. Hold on.'

The man came from behind the counter. Liver-spotted hands. A thick moustache salt-and-peppered. A turkey neck. There was something about him that suggested a convict's last, unnourishing meal. A pile of unopened mail by the door. 'There it is. Came in last week.' He tore open the bag. Five slim paperback volumes slid out. He passed one to Joe, left the rest on a random pile and shuffled back to his stool. There was a distinct smell, very familiar by now, permeating the shop. Joe tried to ignore it.

'You get a lot of business here?' he said. The old man shrugged. 'Some.'

Chatty. He looked at the book in his hands. *The European Campaign*. In big bold letters below: *An Osama bin Laden: Vigilante Novel*. Smaller letters above: *By Mike Longshott, author of "Assignment: Africa," "Sinai Bombings," etc.* The cover depicting an exploding double-decker bus on a crowded street.

'Ever read them?' he asked the old man.

A shrug. 'Sure.'

'What do you think?'

'Load of rubbish, innit.'

'How much for this one?'

The old man shrugged again. 'You want film?' he said. 'I have original reels.'

Joe wondered: original reels of what?

'Film posters? Memorabilia?'

'Just the book would be fine.'

'I don't make money on books,' the old man said.

'It does say *bookshop* above the door,' Joe pointed out.

The old man shrugged. 'That's just for respectability, like.'

'Right.'

The man named a price. Joe paid. 'You got anything else?' he said, not sure why he did so. The old man squinted at him. 'Like what?'

'Stuff,' Joe said.

'Stuff,' the old man said. 'What the fuck does that mean?'

Joe shrugged. 'Forget it,' he said. The old man suddenly chuckled. 'You mean opium?'

'Sure,' Joe said. 'Opium.'

'Fought two wars over opium,' the old man said. 'No shame in saying the name. I get mine in Chinatown, funnily enough. On account of tradition.'

'Any place good?'

The old man looked him up and down. 'Wouldn't have figured you for an opium eater,' he said. Joe shrugged. The old man said, 'Try Madam Seng's on Gerrard Street. Good ambience, and I supply them with the movies. Old black-and-white stuff.'

'Thanks,' Joe said.

'Don't mention it.' The old man was still looking at him curiously. 'Have I seen you before?' he said.

'No.'

The man shrugged. 'Maybe someone like you,' he said.

'Like what?' Joe said.

The man shrugged again. 'You know. A fuzzy-wuzzy.'

A *fuzzy-wuzzy*? What the – ?

Joe took the book with him. As he left, the doorbell rang again and the cat on the rocking chair opened one eye, only to close it again a moment later.

Joe walked up, leaned against the wall, and looked at the book in his hands. *Fuzzy-wuzzies?*

He leafed through the pages.

-- we are at war and I am a soldier --

AT 07:21, FOUR men entered the train station at Luton. Hassib Hussain wore dark shoes and trousers, and was bare-headed. Germaine Lindsay wore bright white trainers and carried a shopping bag. Mohammad Sidique Khan wore a white baseball cap. Shehzad Tanweer brought up the rear as they entered the station. All four carried backpacks.

Mohammad Sidique Khan was born at St. James's University Hospital in Leeds. His father, Tika, was a foundry worker. Mohammad went to South Leeds High School and later to Leeds Metropolitan University. Later still, he worked at Hillside Primary School in Leeds, a mentor for the children of recently-emigrated families. He was described by colleagues as a 'quiet man.' He was married, with one girl. At the time of his entering the Luton train station, his wife was pregnant with their second child. She later had a miscarriage.

In a filmed segment found after the event, Khan said, 'Our words have no impact upon you, therefore I'm going to talk to you in a language that you understand.' He was thirty years old. 'Our words,' he said, 'are dead until we give them life with our blood.'

Hassib Hussain was eighteen. He had also gone to South Leeds School, where his teachers described him as 'a slow, gentle giant.' He liked cricket, and was a member of the Holbeck Hornets football team. He lived with his brother at 7 Colenso Mount, Holbeck, Leeds. Shehzad Tanweer was twenty-two; Germaine Lindsay was nineteen.

The four men met up at Luton Station. They drove there in a red Nissan Micra, which Tanweer had rented several days before. They left the car parked by the station. They waited for nearly half an hour at Luton before boarding the 07:48 Thameslink train to King's Cross. They arrived at King's Cross at twenty past eight. Half an hour later three of them would be dead.

-- hobbies for the dead men --

JOE LOOKED UP from the book and drew a deep breath. This was insane. Longshott's obsessively neat facts and figures seemed designed to snare him, entrap him: names, times, street addresses, hobbies for the dead men. London. He thought: fuzzy-wuzzies, and giggled. Was he searching for Longshott, or was Longshott searching for him? The pulp writer was leaving him a trail of crumbs to follow, and he was following, and the world was slowly unravelling around him, a threadbare tapestry that could no longer quite comfort him against the chill. I could throw it away, he thought. There was a bin nearby. I could drop it and walk away, go back, and if she follows me I will say –

But he had no idea what he'd said. He remembered those pointy ears, pinned back, the soft brown hair; something in her eyes that he could put no words to. She always looked, he thought, like she had more to say to him.

Is that what it came to, he wondered – is it simply that I am afraid to say no to her? All this, the bloodied trail he followed, the shades that fell in his path, fell and were stilled, the questions he didn't want answered: was it all for her sake, or for his?

His head ached, and he leaned it against the old bricks and closed his eyes. The book felt heavy, unwanted in his hands. He stood up, walked, turned left, and found a pub with unbroken windows, loud music, and few clientele. He purchased a pint and carried it to a table scarred by extinguished cigarettes. He leaned back in his seat, took a swallow of beer, and opened the book again.

-- the reality of this situation --

THE FOUR MEN separated at King's Cross station.
Crowds milled through the halls and corridors,
up and down escalators, to and from platforms,
into and out of trains. Their backpacks were
full of homemade explosives.

Mohammad Sidique Khan took the Circle Line. So
did Shehzad Tanweer. One went west; the other
east. Germaine Lindsay went on the Piccadilly
Line. All three activated their charges at
8:50am, within fifty seconds of each other.

Hassib Hussain was meant to travel on the
Northern Line. Instead, he had discovered, in
the last hour of his life, what every Londoner
knew off by heart: you can never rely on public
transport.

The Northern Line was closed.

Not sure what to do, the slow, gentle giant
went above ground. He stopped at a Boots store
in King's Cross Station. At 09:35 he boarded the
number 30 bus to Hackney Wick. The bus was a
Dennis Trident 2 double-decker. Its registration
number was LX03BUF. At 09:47, as the bus passed
through Tavistock Square, Hussain detonated the
bomb in his backpack. He was later identified
by the remnants of his skull, credit cards and
driving license.

Below ground, subterranean London was a world

of smoke and fear, twisted metal and bone
fragments, a world of darkness, despair, death –
and an overwhelming desire to live, as survivors
fought to escape out of the tunnels. Passengers
not killed in the attack were left in packed,
dark carriages. Air filtered in through the
smashed glass windows. Passengers talked, trying
to reassure each other. From time to time there
were screams. They could not leave the train
because the live tracks would have electrocuted
them. When they did disembark, they journeyed
single-file through the tunnels, ghostly in the
half-light of the emergency lights. The air was
full of dirt that worked its way into people's
lungs and made them choke. When they reached the
stations they were lifted up onto the platforms,
where they joined others like them, dirty,
blackened, bleeding hollow-eyed people who were
as yet not sure they really were alive.

'I and thousands like me are forsaking everything
for what we believe,' Mohammad Sidique Khan said
in his recorded statement. 'Now you too will
taste the reality of this situation.'

-- a trail of graffiti --

HIS HEAD HURT – a blackness behind his eyes, shooting stars. He looked down and saw that his drink remained almost untouched on the table. He felt no desire to drink. He raised his hand and looked at his palm, the lines etched into the skin like tracts that led nowhere, that terminated at dead-ends. The skin around his nails was nicotine-stained yellow. There was a small scar at the base of his thumb and he couldn't recall where he got it, or how. He left the pub, went outside, and drew in a breath of muggy London air. What did they believe, he thought. What did he believe? He could not taste a reality in his situation. He began to walk, staring at the walls as he passed, not knowing which way he was going, not caring, the darkness behind his eyes expanding and constricting like a heart.

He followed a trail of graffiti. Near an off-license someone had spray-painted the message, *Vera Lynn was right*.

7/7 again. 9/11. 7/8. 11/12. It was as if a mad mathematician was let loose in the city with unlimited cans of paint.

We are Edwin Drood made no sense.

Mum I miss you.

On the side of a red phone box: *Refugees go home*.

Behind his eyes, expanding and constricting, the darkness blocking out thought. An adult cinema, an usher staring at him curiously, white-blond eyebrows raised; on the wall, that term again. *Fuzzy-wuzzies, I can see you.*

Somehow he found himself on Charing Cross Road and the mute fronts of myriad books stared out at him from beyond a prison of glass. Turning, and there was that poster again he had last seen at Papa D's place, in Paris, the man with the long beard and the clear, penetrating eyes that seemed to look inside him, to sift through the dust and debris that made up his life, and to know him. *Wanted: Dead or Alive. Osama bin Laden, Vigilante*. A display of garish paperbacks. Some sort of crime fiction bookshop. Walking, walking, down Shaftesbury Avenue where it was quieter and cooler, on a building of chrome and glass someone had spray-painted the message *Madam Seng is a Snake Head* and he paused, because there it was again, and suddenly he had too many leads to follow and he guessed they would all be dead-ends and he didn't want to start. The darkness behind his eyes was alive, rattling doors in his mind that he wanted tightly closed. He walked, not conscious of any particular direction, folding away from Shaftesbury Avenue until music stopped him. An organ played, pouring out a sea of notes that washed over him, halted him, lifted him, and he saw a church and beside it, right where he had halted, the doors of yet another pub.

-- the angel of St. Giles --

THE INTERIOR OF the pub was dark and there were people inside
and the sounds of conflicting talk. A fire was burning despite
the heat outside, but Joe did not find it suffocating; he found
it comforting. There was a bar area and the barman was tall
and dark and unspeaking, like an extra in a silent movie, and
Joe ordered a shot of whisky and drank it and still felt cold. He
ordered another one and lit a cigarette and went to stand by the
fire. He was shaking, and he didn't know why.

Conversations came wafting like smoke:

'So I said to him, is that really a way to run a business? We've
got ten tonnes a month coming in from India, we need two
people just to do the customs clearance, and he wants to –'

'It's the shipping costs. Good thing for us the Saudis know
what's expected of –'

'If we could break open the Japanese market it wouldn't be
so bad, but –'

'The Asian market has always been too-good a promise –'

'And he says, do you have a passport? Well, do you?'

'I liked him in that film, the one with –'

'And he says, well, how much if we buy this amount a *month*,
and you won't believe it –'

'It was a ghost movie. I'm sure that –'

'Ten tonnes a month!'

'I'm sure that's not right.'

'With that actor who plays a detective, and he has to –'

'You have to follow the paper trail, that's what it comes
down to. Always keep your eye on the paper trail –'

'Co-Prosperity Sphere, sure, but how does it benefit *us*?'

'Hong Kong –'

'Don't say Hong Kong to me, you know perfectly well that –'

'A passport for what? I mean, it's not like we're back in World War Two, is it? So I said to him –'

'It's the Saudis, it's a good thing we've got our hand firmly on the rudder, if you know what I'm saying –'

'With that actress who plays the love interest, what's her name –'

'Opium. You can use it to finance wars or heal the sick. That's what he says to me. The cheek of it! As if we're not already paying enough –'

'You know that joke, the one with the elephant –'

'Ten tonnes!'

'Does he die in the end?'

Joe shuddered. In the fireplace, the flames danced to the beat of an unseen drum. He saw a small blue plaque fixed to the wall: *The Angel Inn. Here, in the middle ages, the condemned would stop for a final drink before proceeding to the gallows in St. Giles' Circus.*

Below, in black marker pen, someone had scribbled: *So have a drink!*

'The Americans would have you believe *they* won the war single-handedly –'

'The Russian Deal –'

'And there's a pink elephant in the room! A pink elephant! And no one wants to admit to seeing it. You know that expression –'

'I need another drink. You want one?'

'What's the time?'

'Time for another drink.'

'Oil isn't the problem, it's the –'

'But I can't remember who the bad guys were. Was it ever even explained?'

'Ten tonnes! And what does he want to go for instead? What? *Tea*. How much bloody tea can you *drink*?'

'Built the empire on –'

The talk swirled round and round in Joe's head, snatched sentences meaningless, the volume too high, the voices of the condemned, dead men talking, the flames dancing in the fire and he smashed his glass against the wall, the fragments cutting into his skin, blood running between his fingers, and he left a bloodied handprint on the wall as the conversations died around him and the bartender came from behind the bar and said in a quiet, almost voiceless voice: 'Perhaps you should leave now, sir.'

Joe stared at his hand, made a fist and released it, watched the tiny glass shards moving like silent boats across a bloodied sea. He could no longer find shelter in those places of the world where peace could be bought for the price of a drink. The realisation physically hurt him. He closed his eyes and when he opened them again saw only the impassive face of the bartender, heard that empty, featureless voice again say, from inside hollow eyes and bleached-white skin: 'I think you should leave. Now, sir.'

The conversations returned, the voices louder, drowning out thought. Joe nodded. 'I think you're right,' he said. The bartender nodded. 'This way, sir,' he said; and, gently taking hold of Joe's elbow, he led him to the door.

-- the one clear thread --

LONDON WAS FULL of angels, it seemed to Joe. He didn't know
what was happening to him. The darkness behind his eyes was
pounding at him; he could not find solace in drink; his mind
refused to quiet down, was dancing like the flames he had been
watching, was forcing him down dark pathways he did not
want to take. London was a road-map, its directions less than
helpful. People went past him. His hand was throbbing. He
flexed his fingers and found satisfaction in the pain. A waking
up. He walked, turned the corner, and was at St. Giles' Circus,
but there were no gallows there.

Traffic crawled past him. The Circus was a four-way traffic
jam. He waited for the lights to change, crossed over to the
butt-end of Charing Cross Road where it meets Oxford Street,
and found himself before the open entrance to the London
underground.

He stared inside. People came and went, shoving past him.
Stairs led down into the ground. Light bulbs cast a yellow glow
over the entranceway. He could hear rumbling far down below,
and voices seemed to call out to him, to whisper through the
throng of people, a wedding feast for the circus performers,
chanting through a silver screen. He shook his head and
suddenly it cleared, and he knew that he was scared.

He turned away. There were leads for him to follow, a goal
that was clear in its simplicity. Do the job he was hired to do.
Find the man he was hired to find. Be a detective. He felt relief,
and the blackness was gone, and he felt light-headed. He lit
a cigarette and it tasted good, and he turned away from the

entrance and walked down Charing Cross Road, ignoring the books in the windows, and realised he was hungry and still hadn't eaten that day. There was a maze around him, but he didn't need to follow every turn: all he had to do was follow the one clear thread that would lead him out. At a stall in Leicester Square he bought himself a sandwich and ate it as he walked back to the hotel. At the Regent Palace he found comfort in the quiet abandoned corridors with their faint smell of disuse, had a long hot shower in a cubicle and, back in his room, bandaged his hand and then lay in the bed. Someone had come in while he was gone and changed the sheets, and they felt cool and soft against his skin, and he sighed and, turning over, clutched the pillow against his chest and fell asleep.

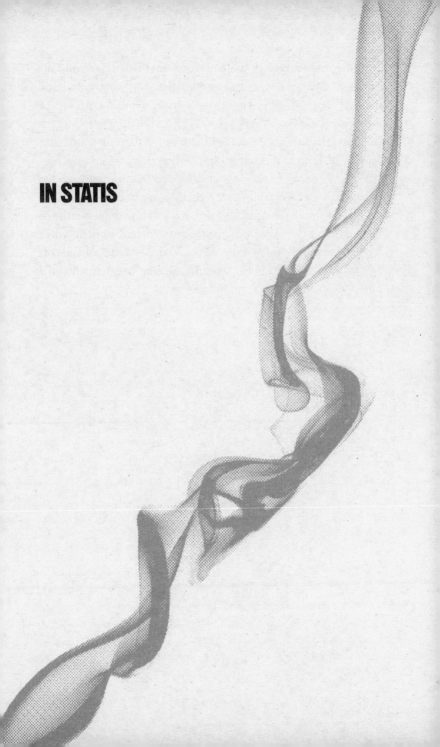

IN STATIS

-- men like clouds --

EARLY MORNING. THE room in darkness. A scratch at the door. The bed cold underneath him, feeling disused. Joe in the space between sleep and waking – aware, but disinclined to move. Someone outside trying the door, quietly. He never dreamed any more. Something clicked the other side of the door. Joe's hand throbbed, the pain reassuringly real. The door opened, softly, letting in a band of light. A dark shape in the doorway, face obscured by shadows, but he could see the black shoes, a short-sleeved chequered shirt, thought back to Vientiane – which seemed a life-time ago.

Electric light: the sudden brightness made him blink back tears. A shape moving with big easy steps, a hand on his face, holding him down, something put over his eyes. He didn't resist, didn't see the point. A voice murmuring in his ear, the hint of an accent: 'You are blind, like worm.' Joe let it pass.

'Why you keep going?' the voice said. 'Even with your eyes open you are blind. Why grope in the dark, tap-tap-tap, like a blind person with a walking stick? I am sorry about your friend.'

His friend? He thought about Mo, the lingering scent of cheap cigars, 'I mainly do divorces,' a name in a phone book made momentarily real, then cancelled with the sound of gunshots. 'Why you not give up?' the voice said, and it sounded perplexed. 'You have good life, before. Drink coffee, sit in office, is peaceful, no?'

Somehow he wasn't scared. It was like a dream, he thought: the closest to dreaming he could come. The words, 'Are you going to kill me?' came floating into his mind and stayed there, movie dialogue unspoken.

'I am not wishing to kill you,' the man said. 'Death is merely a gateway to another place. I used to think it was paradise, but it isn't.' A short laugh like a cough, bitter like coffee. 'I spit on it.'

Ambiguity. Spit on what? The bed was like hard clouds, and he was floating. The man above him had no face, he was convinced of it now. A man with no face. It made him laugh, but inside. Only inside. 'You are brave,' the man said. 'But stupid, too. Yes, I think you are very stupid.' One hand was still on his face. Cloth on his eyes, worms' cocoons woven into silk and dyed black. 'You stay here,' the man said. 'For you, paradise, now. All good, no? What you miss? Why you make trouble?'

No answer expected. The man speaking to himself, not to Joe. 'When I was kid,' the man said unexpectedly, 'I look out window, I see clouds. All time, clouds are different. I see faces in clouds. Ears, eyes, mouths' – he pronounced it *mouthes* – 'eyes, I see eyes, many eyes. I see smiling faces. I see sad faces. In clouds. Outside bedroom window. You understand?'

But Joe didn't.

The man's other hand on Joe's hair, stroking it. Sadness in the moving fingers. 'Then wind comes. Clouds move, change. Sometimes make new faces. Sometimes gone. Men like clouds. You ever think of God?'

The hand stroking his hair. No answer expected. The man said, 'Old man with long beard, yes? High up in clouds. God, for children it is God. Sometimes for grownups, too. You understand?'

Joe moved his head, an almost imperceptible shift. No. The man said, 'You stay out of trouble. Go back to coffee, sunshine, walk to office and back. Is more good.'

More good than what?

'Or you go other paradise,' the man said. His hand was no longer on Joe's head. 'Stay, go, all the same. You make trouble, I send you. Okay?'

Joe felt like laughing. But the voice above him, fragile, was still dangerous. Joe moved his head, minutely, perhaps yes, perhaps no, and heard the man sigh. 'All the same,' he heard the man say, but quietly, and then the dark material was pulled gently from his eyes and he saw the back of the man as he moved towards the door, and the door shut behind him with a soft click and then the room was dark again.

WHEN HE WOKE up again it was morning proper, a part of it already gone. Of his early morning visitor there was no sign. His hand had stopped hurting. He flexed it and the fingers responded as if they had never been cut. He felt better than he had in some time. He showered, and dressed, and went down to the lobby, and nodded hello to my-name-is-Simon who seemed never to leave reception. Just outside the hotel he found a café and sat down to order breakfast. It was a hot, humid morning, but that didn't disturb him. He had fried eggs and sausages and fresh bread and coffee, and as he ate he thought about the day ahead.

There were leads to follow. There was detecting to be done. There was work. He didn't think until his food was finished – it was a relief.

When he was done he found himself staring at the remains of his breakfast on the plate: the ruins of an ancient civilization etched in egg yolk and sausage grease. Where should he go first? He felt restless now; eager for movement. He made to leave when a shadow fell over him, and he looked up and said, 'Not you again.' He noticed the waiter glancing their way, then looking away.

A voice with a distinct North American accent, continental United States, said, 'Why are you here?' and didn't mean it in any sort of existential questioning.

'Having breakfast,' Joe said. 'It's the most important meal of the dead.'

'Of the *day*,' the man with grey hair said, sounding disgusted, and added, 'And it's a luxury you may not be entitled to for very long.'

148

'Even more important to have it while I can, then,' Joe said. Grey Hair sat down opposite. His two companions were nowhere to be seen. 'Left your muscle at home today?' Joe said. Grey Hair smiled, and Joe thought that, really, the man had a pleasant enough face when he made the effort. But the face felt as if it could slip off the smile as easily as it had put it on, and what would be left would not be nearly as pleasant. 'I thought I told you to stay away.'

'Refresh my memory.'

'You wouldn't like it if I did.'

Joe took out his packet of cigarettes and shook it, sliding a couple half-way out, offering them towards the man. To his surprise, the man took one. Joe took the other for himself, brought out his lighter, and Grey Hair leaned forward to accept the light. For a moment they were caught like that, two heads leaning towards each other, in stillness and secrecy, as if one was about to impart a great knowledge to the other. Then the tip of the man's cigarette flamed red, he pulled back, and Joe lit his own cigarette and put the lighter away. Something had changed, subtly, between them. 'You won't,' the man said, 'find what you are looking for.'

'What am I looking for?'

The man nodded, as if the question merited greater consideration than it perhaps seemed to suggest. He said, 'What do you know about opium?'

It was not a question Joe was expecting. He said, echoing something half-heard the night before, 'You can use it to finance wars or heal the sick.'

'And which one would you choose?'

'You didn't come here to talk to me about opium.'

The man said, ignoring him, 'It can't be used to heal the sick.'

'Oh?'

'It can only relieve their pain.'

'Better than re-living the pain.'

'Don't,' the man said, 'be a smartass.'

'Sorry.'

The man nodded, acknowledging the apology. He signalled to the waiter. 'Two coffees,' he said. Joe shook his head. Why did he apologise?

'Sertürner isolated morphine in eighteen-oh-five,' the man said. 'Named after Morpheus, the god of dreams. Robiquet isolated codeine in eighteen thirty-two. Heroin was first synthesised right here in London, by Wright, in eighteen seventy-four. With me so far?'

'Sure...'

'But only became popular when Bayer re-synthesised it in eighteen ninety-seven. Heroin, from the German *heroisch*. Do *you* feel heroic, Joe?'

'Only when I'm paid to.'

The man smiled and blew out smoke. Their coffee arrived, and he added one sugar and stirred it. 'Bayer lost a part of their trademark rights on Heroin after the first world war,' he said. 'Incidentally.'

'I see.'

'Joe,' the grey haired man said. 'I want you to understand something. Opium and its derivatives are still, even after more than *three thousand years* in constant use, the best known pain relief medication known to science. Period. The opium poppy is the single most beneficial plant *in the world*.'

'What do you want?' Joe said. 'I didn't realise you came here to give me a lecture in botany.'

The grey haired man shook his head. 'There are a lot of things you don't realise,' he said. Joe let it pass.

'In our own civil war,' the grey haired man said, 'opium was known as God's own drug. Our combat medics still carry morphine packs to inject severely-wounded soldiers with. The United States of America is still the world's largest consumer of opium-based prescription drugs.'

'I guess you lot care a great deal about opium, then,' Joe said. The man ignored him again.

'The world, our world, is safe,' he said. 'Safe and healthy. Opium comes from Asia, is made into medicine by German and American and British firms, and eases suffering. The money earned is taxed, which aids governance. No one, Joe, is sponsoring wars with opium.'

'I'm not sure I follow you,' Joe said.

The man said, 'Yet it still, somewhat surprisingly, poses a problem for us.'

'That's too bad,' Joe said.

The man smiled, but there was nothing friendly anymore in that expression. He said, 'Do you dream, Joe?'

The man kept surprising Joe. He thought about his black-filled nights; took a sip from his coffee; did not reply. 'A theatre seemed suddenly opened and lighted up within my brain,' the man said. 'Which presented nightly spectacles of more than earthly splendour. The sense of space, and in the end the sense of time, were both powerfully affected. De Quincey.'

'Friend of yours?'

'Joe,' the man said, 'listen to me carefully, because I won't say it again. What you want – what you would do – is open a door that we would, very much, like to keep closed. Keep tightly shut, in fact. You have to understand I am not unsympathetic. It is not easy, for refugees. But refugees must nevertheless respect the sanctity of their hosts. Do you understand?'

Joe didn't. But he nodded. The man sighed. 'Good,' he said. And, 'There is no such thing as forgetting possible to the mind,' he said. It had the same intonation of reading out aloud a memorised quote. 'A thousand accidents may and will interpose a veil between our present consciousness and the secret inscriptions on the mind, but –'

'Yes?'

'The inscription remains for ever,' the grey haired man said.

PART FOUR:
IN CASABLANCA

-- the secret inscriptions on the mind --

THERE WAS A Hamlet in full costume walking down Frith Street, declaiming a soliloquy as he passed. He was not, Joe thought, a very good Hamlet. As he passed Joe, he was shouting, 'To die, to sleep! To sleep, perchance to dream! Ay, there's the rub!' and Joe thought he had never heard Hamlet done with so many exclamation marks before. Hamlet spoiled it even further by sticking a question mark over the next line – 'For in that sleep of death what dreams may come?'

Joe tossed him a coin. Hamlet turned, gave him a short bow, and continued on his way, changing his patter inexplicably to a rant about Ophelia.

Joe was back at the Castle. This time, he was watching the tradesmen entrance. He'd reached his quota of quotations for the day. He should have started earlier, but had been derailed by breakfast and the man from the CPD, and talk about opium that left him more confused than before. Was Longshott involved in pharmaceuticals in some way? He shook the thought from his mind. He knew the next visit from the grey-haired man could prove fatal; and he didn't intend, if he could possibly help it, for the fatality to be himself. He settled down to watch and wait instead.

At 09:45 there was a late employee arriving from the direction of Leicester Square, running and out of breath, and she disappeared inside the tradesmen door but Joe didn't quite spot what opened the door – was it a key? Was she buzzed in?

At 10:03 there was a delivery truck, parking on the curb, burly men offloading crates of frozen foodstuff. A woman appeared at the door, vacated her place for more Castle employees who ferried the cargo inside. A camera, then? And employees only inside the building – no tradesmen let through. Interesting.

He could actually keep an eye on the main entrance too, but it seemed to be a quiet morning. At 10:22, at last, something more interesting than frozen lobsters – a solitary figure strolling over, brown paper bag in hand – a boy who, unconcernedly, turned right at the Castle's tradesmen entrance and paused briefly before the door. The door opened. The same woman stood in the entrance. A brief conference. When the boy left, he was no longer holding the brown paper bag. The boy had the black hair and pale skin of a Han Chinese. The boy turned the way he had come. Joe followed him, at a distance.

He was still trying to fathom the grey haired-man's words to him. De Quincey's words, really. There is no such thing as forgetting. Was memory, then, the secret inscription? And, what was the point in a secret inscription? He wondered if he was forgetting something, then wondered how he would know. What he did know was that he should be keeping an eye out for the CPD men. The others too, the ones who shot at him. Recently, it seemed, both parties had decided to talk to him instead. He couldn't decide if that was an improvement. They didn't strike him as people who liked to talk a great deal. Neither would probably bother again. Still, he had to give them full marks for effort.

He followed the boy a short distance, across Shaftesbury Avenue and onto Gerrard Street. Here was the heart of London's Chinatown. The typeface advertising businesses was English made to look a little like Chinese characters. There were deep-red, roasted ducks hanging from hooks in the restaurant windows. Cleaver-wielding chefs stood behind the glass, hacking away at the carcasses of chickens and pigs. There was frying garlic smell everywhere, and that most exotic of ingredients for the British, the ginger. There were greengrocers selling tamarind and lychees and bok choi. There were travel agents advertising the wonders that could be had on a package tour to Kuomintang China. Pictures of Chiang Kai-shek hung everywhere. Even the red phone boxes were transformed into miniature Buddhist temples, but without so many stairs.

The boy turned left on Gerrard Street, and Joe followed. Into Newport Place, where several columns rose out of the ground, culminated in a decorated roof, and formed an open pagoda which took him by surprise. For a moment it was as if he were back in Vientiane, at his office overlooking the black stupa. Then it was gone, and it was merely a gaudy pagoda that looked like a bus shelter from the rain.

The shops in Newport Place were different. Joe knew that a small alleyway, Little Newport, joined it to Charing Cross Road, but here there were no books. The atmosphere was laden with a different kind of smoke than that of Gerrard Street: cooking, but not of ducks or noodles. The boy went past the pagoda and disappeared through an unmarked door. There was little advertising in Newport Place. There was one pub and its windows were grimy and the interior was dark and he could see no one inside. It was called the Edwin Drood and he thought of graffiti and felt suddenly cold.

He'd seen places like this before.

He approached the door the boy had gone through. He knocked and the door opened, just a crack, showing nothing beyond but a face, not Chinese but darker, Hmong perhaps, or one of the Tai groupings, and it said, 'What you want?'

'To come in.'

He couldn't see anything beyond the door but he could smell it. The man in the doorway said, 'Forget it, mister. No place for you.'

Joe worked on a hunch. 'I want to see Madam Seng.'

The face, disembodied, as if let loose from any mortal anchoring of flesh, sucked its teeth. 'No Madam Seng here. You go.'

Joe fished in his pocket, came up with a note. 'This refreshes your memory?'

The face smiled and, for just a moment, dropped the accent. 'My memory is just fine as it is,' the man said.

'Too bad your manners aren't,' Joe said. He lunged for the face, but the man who owned it was faster, and the door slammed on Joe, almost catching his fingers. There was the loud sound of a key being turned in the lock.

'Son of a *bitch*!' Joe said, not without feeling.

-- the body in the library --

HE KNOCKED HARD on the door, but there was no reply, and he didn't expect one. Passers-by stared at him. He stepped away from the door, glared at it, but it still wouldn't open. 'I'll be back,' he said, which made him feel better, somehow. He glanced across the road at The Edwin Drood, thinking of a drink, but the dilapidated building glared back at him from its dark, stained windows, repelling the notion. Instead he walked down Little Newport, passing stalls selling incense, Buddha statues, posters of Sun Yat Sen, compasses, animal figures shaped in copper wire, cheap makeup, even cheaper perfume, past a door opening onto a stairwell where a hand-written sign said Miss Josette was available for French lessons upstairs, another for a Miss Bianca and Greek, past a dumpling restaurant, a stall where he could have had his name engraved on a grain of rice, and onto Charing Cross Road.

This time he turned right. As he passed the entrance to the underground, he avoided looking at it. He ran into the mass of people passing to and from Leicester Square, kept a hand on his pocket, waited patiently for the lights to change, crossed the road, passed Wyndham's Theatre, passed Cecil Court with its row of rare book dealers, and went into the Charing Cross public lending library.

Joe had always liked libraries, though he could not remember having gone into one recently. There was something comforting about the intimate space, rows of books marking orderly borders, the only sound that of turning pages, whispered conversations and the dimmed noise of the traffic outside. He went to the reading corner and found the week's newspapers draped neatly on wooden sticks, looking like an exhausted flock of albatrosses. He liberated a few and retreated to an empty desk by the wall.

Three days ago.

He found nothing on page one for any of the days.

Three days ago and it seemed like a lifetime.

Nothing on page two.

Somebody's lifetime.

The late edition, three days ago. Page three. *A Shoot-out in Soho.*

He read through it. *Unknown assailants fired shots outside the Red Lion pub in Soho earlier today, breaking glass and frightening customers. One woman was treated for minor cuts. There were no other casualties. 'We are taking this very seriously,' a spokesman for the police said, 'and are following all available leads.'*

No Mo. No mention of Joe lying there unconscious. Somehow, he hadn't expected there to be.

Fuzzy-wuzzies, he thought. The word left a bad taste in his mouth. He thought – refugees. He wondered what leads the police had. Perhaps they were analysing samples of cigarette ash. He imagined them armed with round magnifying glasses, scattered around the city, backs hunched, searching for clues. He reached for his cigarettes, remembered you weren't allowed to smoke in libraries. No clue for the police, then.

A different newspaper, this one a tabloid. The same story magnified, an opinion piece, an outraged tone, immigrants are to blame, government must increase control of remaining colonies, stronger powers of arrest demanded in the House of Commons. Lords against. *How long can we let our children grow up in fear?*

Joe looked around him. No one seemed afraid in the busy children's section. They were drawing in crayons, leafing through bright-coloured books. He wondered what they were reading. He thought about Mike Longshott: the Osama bin Laden Colouring Book. You could leave the beard page-white. Make the eyes sky-blue and empty.

Back to the broadsheet, the same news item reduced to page four in the next day's morning issue. Look for it the next day too and it was gone, as if it had never happened. Goodbye Mo.

Even though he didn't expect it in the paper, it riled him. Invisible people, he thought. Did someone, somewhere, mourn Mo's passing? Did someone remember him, grieve for him, wish him back? Did he still exist, some parts of him, some fragments, his smell, his smile, the touch of his hand, his voice when he spoke, the way he cleaned his ears, did they still exist somewhere, secret inscriptions on somebody else's mind?

He put down the paper. The desk before him was a mobile geography of off-blue ink and smudged paper. He had come to the library to find a body, and it wasn't there. Nevertheless. He felt stubborn, like he had something to prove. A part of him was fighting it, telling him to leave. He didn't. There was one place at least he knew he could still find Mo in.

The phone book.

-- an explorer in a silent film --

WHEN HE APPROACHED again the Leicester Square tube station the crowds seemed to pull at him, and he had the irrational thought of fighting them. He pushed through the massed congregation instead and found himself at the entrance. Stairs led underground. A beggar was sitting in the entranceway, slumped over a backpack, reading a paperback, a dog-food bowl by his feet with coins floating inside it. He raised his head when he felt Joe watching, and Joe got a glimpse of the book, and of course it was an *Osama bin Laden: Vigilante*, the reading of choice for the homeless, and the beggar, a little more than a boy, Joe thought, said, 'This is some heavy shit, bro.'

He had not felt the same way in Paris. Yet here, the thought of going underground was suffocating him. He tossed a coin into the beggar's bowl. 'Get some new reading material,' he said. Then he went down the stairs.

He studied a map of the tube network, different coloured lines twisting and intersecting, and realised he had to take the line to King's Cross and change. The picture on the map looked like spilled intestines. He bought a ticket and went through the barrier and descended again, deeper into the ground, and suddenly it was silent, and strangely peaceful. He waited for the train to arrive, watching the rats scuttling under the platform, in the tunnel. There were adverts on the walls for products he would never buy, or use. The train came and he boarded it. The doors closed with a soft whooshing sound, quite reassuring. He found a seat, occupied it. The walls of the tunnels as they passed were ghostly, the stations unexpected bursts of white light. At King's Cross he got off and wandered through the station, a little lost, underground caverns opening above him: he had the sense of being an explorer in a silent film, wearing a pith helmet, breaking into a mummy's tomb. Instead he got directions from a uniformed black woman who pointed him in the direction of the circle line, and he got on the train and counted stations.

At Edgware Road he got off. There were no escalators, and he climbed up the wide stairs and into sunlight, and he wondered if there was a curse on the pharaoh's tomb, and if so, when it might manifest itself. He walked down the station road a short while and then turned right on Edgware Road itself. He went under an overpass and the shops all seemed to change, and as he passed a couple of young people the man said, gesturing for the benefit of his blonde-haired girlfriend, 'And this is what we call Little Cairo.'

Little Cairo. There were coffee shops where men sat and smoked sheesha pipes and food stalls where great columns of meat rotated slowly under flames, fat drizzling down their sides. There were veiled women walking kids down the road or pushing babies in their baby-chairs, and he could smell cinnamon and cumin and the men were playing backgammon, he could hear the constant sound of rolling dice, like thunder.

The blonde-haired girl said, 'That is *so* romantic.' The boy grinned and pulled her to him.

There were Mercedes cars in the street, black and polished, and men in kafeyehs, beards and moustaches, and there were shops selling toys, and clothes, and food, and many signs advertising many bargains. He was looking for Mo's office, and as he turned for the road he found a street market in progress and smelled fish. He walked down the side of the road, avoiding the main thoroughfare of the market, and passed a bakery and a flower-shop, and then stopped and retraced his steps and bought a rose, not quite sure why. The woman who sold it to him smiled as she handed it to him. 'I hope she likes it,' she said. Joe smiled, awkwardly. He continued on his way, the purple rose in his hand, passed a sign for *Sachs & Levine, Solicitors*, passed the straggling fish-tail of the market, crossed the road, and found the building.

There were some cars parked by the curb, none of them new. When he scanned the business names on the side of the door he found Mo's, in chipped white paint, the words *Private Inquiry Agent* peeling. When he stepped through the door into the hallway it was dark and quiet and there was grime on the windows, dust on the floor, and it made him think again of entering a sort of sacred tomb, and he wished he had a pith helmet after all. Instead he climbed up the narrow stairs to the third floor and found the door, tried the handle.

It was unlocked. He pushed the door open and stepped inside.

-- loss hovering between the dust motes --

THERE WAS NO one in Mo's office. There was a window overlooking the road Joe had just crossed, red-grey brick buildings with washing hanging from the windows. Few cars. There was a desk and a lamp and a box of cigars – he slid open the wooden lid and saw that only three remained inside, and their smell spread out from the box and into the room. Not Hamlets, at least. Romeo and Juliets, perhaps: the Cuban version of Shakespeare.

There was a large chair behind the desk and two smaller ones in front of it. A wastepaper basket, a metal filing cabinet, a shelf on the wall with some books on it. He didn't have to look too close to know they were Osama paperbacks. It reminded Joe of his own office back in Vientiane. Bare and minimal, a cell more than an office. He began to search it.

He found no scotch, which was disappointing, because he suddenly craved a drink. There should have been a camera somewhere, and probably negatives, but he could find nothing; it was as if the place had been professionally cleaned, or else had never been occupied in the first place. He broke the lock of the filing cabinet, but it was empty. In the bottom drawer of the desk, however, he struck lucky. The drawer was shorter, he discovered, than the ones above it. He took it out and inserted his hand in the gap and rooted there. There *was* something there. He managed to grab it, pulled it out. It was another cigar box, but heavy. He laid it on the desk and opened it.

Close, but no cigars.

There was a small but fat gun in there, a four-shot COP 357

165

Derringer, and Joe took it and slipped it in his pocket. There was an envelope with five one-hundred pound notes, which he put back. There was a drawing of a woman's face, badly made. He wondered if it was Mo who drew it. Lines had been erased and retraced until the paper wore out. Joe wondered who she was, why Mo had no picture of her that he had to attempt drawing her, over and over. He left the money and the woman's picture and put them back in the box and closed it, and returned it to its hiding place.

He took one last look around the office. The books. He went to the shelf and removed the paperbacks one by one. He scanned fly-leafs and endpapers and found nothing but hints of foxing. Next he leafed through them, shook them page-edges down, searching for anything hidden between the pages. He struck lucky, of sorts, on the fourth book he tried. A square piece of light-blue paper fluttered to the floor from within the pages of *Sinai Bombings*. He picked it up. It was a cloakroom receipt. He pocketed it and returned the book to its place on the shelf.

He took a last look at the room. It had a disused, abandoned air. He went back to the desk and closed the lid of the cigar box, gently. He was glad there was no mirror in the room. He did not want to look at it and see himself. He scanned the room again, but Mo still wasn't there. He saw loss hovering between the dust motes.

There were no sarcophagi in the room; no ancient jars, no decorations of jade and gold. There was not even a calendar.

He left the purple rose he bought in Little Cairo on the desk. Then he left the room.

-- a hill of beans --

SOMETHING WAS WRONG. He knew it, felt it, but he couldn't place the feeling with any accuracy. Something to do with the books. He retraced his steps, without conscious thought. Back again through the bustling market, past bakeries and fishmongers and greengrocers' carts, past cheap plastic toys spilling onto a blanket on the pavement, past loud music in a language he did not speak, past the smells of roasting coffees and roasting lamb kebabs, past men in jalabiyehs, a telephone booth with the handset off the hook, and he thought about cause and effects, and a kind of war that he didn't understand.

The question that had been niggling away at him was too small and too big at once. It was why.

It had nothing to do with the real world and everything to do with the fictional one, Mike Longshott's world, the world of *The European Campaign* and *Sinai Bombings* and *Assignment: Africa*. The world of *World Trade Center*, whatever that was. They were war books. But he did not understand the war, and the feeling that was pressing down on him from the inside, that made the bones of his fingers ache and not stand still, was that he should.

On Edgware Road he found a coffee shop and went inside and sat by the window. There were Middle Eastern men sitting around tables, drinking, talking to each other. Two were sharing a sheesha pipe. The proprietor came over and said, 'What can I get you?' and Joe said, 'Coffee.'

The proprietor was portly and moustachioed, with eyes like dark-green olives. He brought over a long-handled pot and a small china cup and then returned with a glass of water and a small plate holding two pieces of baklavah, fine layers of pastry overflowing with syrup.

'Business is good?' Joe said. The man shrugged. 'Inshalla,' he said. 'One can't complain.'

The coffee was bitter and Joe bit into a piece of baklavah and then drank again, the pastry sweetening the black-tar coffee. War, he thought. And then – was mass murder a *crime*, or was it a political act? And who decided?

There must be more in the Longshott books, he thought. He kept skimming through them, but there must have been something he was missing. For the first time, the books struck him as strangely unreal. He thought of all the attacks described. If you added all the wounded and the dead, he thought, they still wouldn't amount to how many people died in a single month in car accidents in just one city. It was a war about fear, he thought, not figures on the ground. It was a war of narrative, a story of a war, and it grew in the telling. For some reason he thought of a hill of beans, which was a strange thing to think about. Lives in a hill of beans. He laughed. The sheesha in the next table was putting out thick clouds of cherry-flavoured smoke. And then he thought – if this was a war, how many dead were on the *other* side?

-- cuckoo-bird mother --

'MORE COFFEE?' THE proprietor asked. Joe shook his head, stood up. He paid and left, and stood for a while in the weak sunshine of Edgware Road, thinking. The receipt from Mo's office was in his pocket. It was too late to follow his other leads. Or too early. What do people do in London? He wondered. And then he thought – of course.

He took a bus back into town. He sat on the top, in the front seat before the big windows, and looked out at the city streets as they passed by, slowly. They were grey and solid, like an accountant. There was something comforting about London, its small distinct neighbourhoods, its narrow lanes, congested roads. He watched another red double-decker bus go past from the opposite direction, looking like an Asian elephant driven by its mahout. Ahead of it were two black cabs, like beetles. He half expected them to open wings and buzz up into the sky. Something inside him felt lost. This was not the future he had expected. There were no flying cars, no silver suits, and the only aliens walking in the streets outside were human. There were Arabs and Indians and Chinese and Malay, Jews and Africans, a whole planet of refugees seeking shelter in the mothership that was London. From here wars had been launched, colonies conquered. From here, this great big sprawling administrative centre, an empire had been managed in triplicate. No wonder we come here, he thought. The city was a cuckoo-bird mother, taking children that did not belong to it, annexing them, bringing them up in a strange mix of missionary activity, trade exploitation and good intentions. When the time came and the children wanted their independence, the mother was hurt, and they fought. And now some of the annexed children, who were not children at all, came back, because they had nowhere else to go.

He got out on Oxford Street and walked down the crowded avenue, past large bright stores selling cargo. The city was a hungry, insatiable being, demanding its tea and its medication, its food and its clothes and all the things that came from elsewhere. It was a city of cargo, its giant warehouses filled to the brim with the produce of a hundred different places. He knew where to go, and it was a short walk: down Oxford Street, across St. Giles' Circus where corpses no longer sighed in the breeze, down New Oxford Street and into Bloomsbury.

There were vineyards there once, and wood for one hundred pigs. Now there were pubs and bookshops, but it was quite likely some of the books, at least, had been bound in pigskin – which said something about progress.

He turned right on Great Russell Street. It was quiet – no. It was peaceful. It was a feeling he had almost forgotten he knew. There were more bookshops here, and they specialised in what the British called the Far East, and the Middle East: there were old books in the windows with pictures of the pyramids on them, and the Forbidden City, once-grand possessions of the British Empire now reduced into the memoirs of soldiers and administrators. There were old looted coins in the windows, and the busts of long-gone emperors, and the smell of dry leather and dust, and under his feet the grilles of a sewage tunnel echoed as he passed.

What do you do in London, he thought: and the answer came easy, channelled into his mind in Mo's voice: you go to a museum.

-- knives, corpses, vases and gods --

THERE WAS A man selling hot dogs outside the gates of the British Museum and the smell of frying onions made Joe hungry. He stopped and bought one.

'Enjoying London?' the short man behind the cart said.

'Having the time of my life,' Joe said.

He chewed on the sausage in its soggy bun as he entered the courtyard. Eating it did not take long. He cleaned his hands as best he could with the thin napkin and felt grimy. His mouth tasted of onions and cheap mustard. He balled the napkin and dumped it in a rubbish bin and climbed the stairs of the museum. It was then that he thought he saw a pair of familiar black shoes in the crowd, but when he turned they were gone. He had the receipt for the cloakroom but now he decided to be careful before checking it, and so he entered the building and found grand staircases rising on either side of him and another door that led into a large, dim-lighted space.

Up and down stairs he went, checking reflections in reflecting surfaces, examining less the exhibits than the people who came to see them. In the Egyptian collection he saw three-thousand-year-old giant statues of long-gone Pharaohs. Cat-headed deities seemed to watch him from above. He saw the black façade of the Rosetta Stone, and a fragment of the Sphinx's beard, and he thought – if there had been enough room, they would have dragged the entire Sphinx in, all the way from its sandy residence in Egypt. In one display case he found the mummified corpse of Cleopatra of Thebes. He stared at it for a long moment, then turned away. In another part he saw half of the Parthenon, transported from Greece by the Earl of Elgin. Marble figures, lightly clothed, that looked confused in the cold dimness of the British Museum.

There were statues, sculptures, bas-reliefs, manuscript tablets, paintings, coins, jewellery, knives, corpses, vases, Greek gods, Egyptian gods, Buddhas, books, the loot of an entire world hoarded, stored, collected and guarded. It came from China, from Iraq, from Tasmania and Benin and Egypt and Sudan, from India and Iran and Ethiopia. It was as if the British had gone out into the world, stripped it of its heritage, and returned, laden with their cargo, to decorate their city with it.

It was a terribly arrogant building, it seemed to him. Joe thought again about the books he'd read, about their secret war. Why did they fight? He thought, there at the peaceful museum, that he could see just a hint of that, the fingers of antiquity crawling into the present day and shaking it.

At least the Sphinx was too large to be moved, he thought, and laughed, and he walked up and down stairs, circling the great building until his feet ached, and saw no one following him, until he arrived at last back where he had started and went to get a coat that wasn't his.

-- litter in the desert --

IT HAD BEEN the site of wars for millennia. Human migration travelled back and forth across its expanse of fine yellow sand, from Africa into Asia and the rest of the world, then back in a succession of colonizers. The Ten Commandments shared, in historical order, by the Jews, the Christians and the Muslims, were given to Moses in that desert, as he fled the Egyptian Pharaoh's army. In 1518 the Sinai was taken over by the Ottomans; in 1906, by the British. In 1942 Erwin Rommel and his Afrika Korps stormed their way through Egypt, on their way to taking Palestine for the German Reich; in the event, they were stopped at El Alamein. In 1948 Egyptian forces travelled through the Sinai in the direction of a Palestine hastily abandoned by the British, and in 1967 Israeli forces made the same journey in the opposite direction. The desert was littered with unexploded bombs, mines, rockets, grenades, the remnants of untold wars, all waiting patiently in the desert sun for someone who had read the Ten Commandments, but had stopped at Thou Shalt Not Kill.

That October saw the usual migration of sun-seeking tourists to the beaches of the Red Sea. They stayed in small sea-side camps, in modest, airy bamboo huts. They came there to sunbathe, to snorkel, to flirt, to relax. The smell of burning hashish was not unknown there. Further down the coast, and more upmarket, stood the Hilton Taba Hotel, a multi-storey building offering the more discerning tourist a place to stay.

The first bomb hit the front of the Hilton Hotel at 21:45. It destroyed the entrance hall, blew the hotel windows inwards into the rooms, and caused the upper floors to collapse. Corpses landed by the swimming pool, and thick smoke prevented families from escaping down the hotel stairs. Others were buried in the rubble. Fifty kilometres away in Ras-al-Shitan, the Devil's Head, two further explosions erupted, the first one taking out a restaurant and several nearby huts in the Moon Island resort. It seemed, for a while, an appropriate name.

The bombs were made with washing machine timers, phone parts and modified gas cylinders. They were packed with TNT and explosives found in the Sinai, proving once again the truth that nothing is ever wasted in a desert economy. The bombs were carried by cars. The bombers died in their respective explosions. Amongst the wounded in the three attacks were the British Consul's wife and daughter. Amongst the dead were Egyptians, Jewish and Arab Israelis, Italians and Russians.

The next year, on Revolution Day, a second attack killed eighty-eight people, mostly Egyptians, a little up the coast in Sharm-el-Sheikh.

-- Mo's last case --

THERE WAS A little bit of fine yellow sand in the left pocket of Mo's coat. The coat was made of wool and was too hot for this time of year. Cigar smoke had woven itself into the fabric, giving off an aroma that conjured for Joe images of private clubs and men in smoking jackets sipping sherry by a roaring fire. He'd put his hands in the pockets and was exploring them. He found a packet of cigars, one left inside, and as he stepped out of the British Museum he unwrapped the cigar and lit it. He stood outside in the sunshine, the coat itching against his body. He thought: maybe Mo just forgot it here. There might not be anything more complicated than that.

But he could feel the small, hard object inside the coat, against his chest. A sewn-in pocket, he thought. He walked down the wide steps and sat down in the courtyard, far enough that he could easily watch both the gate and the museum's entrance. He could see nothing suspicious, and yet had the feeling of being watched. He smoked the cigar, watching people. Also in Mo's pockets were sweet wrappers, a handful of penny coins, two pen caps with no pens, a black round stone, two creased and bent business cards, one for Madam Seng's, the other even more interesting.

He could feel the weight of the unseen object against his chest.

He realised then that his reasoning had been wrong. He had thought the shots outside the Red Lion were fired at *him*. But what if they weren't? What if, despite appearances, it was *Mo* who was the real target?

What had Mo been working on? He said he mainly did divorces. Perhaps, Joe thought, the man hadn't been entirely honest with him.

He could feel the object against his chest. He smoked the cigar down to a stub, a pile of grey-black ash collecting at his feet. He threw down what was left of the cigar and crushed it with his foot. He was waiting for something, he realised. The sense of being watched increased. He felt suddenly angry. He was tired of waiting. He stood up. 'Come on, then!' he shouted. People turned their heads to look. A couple of Japanese girls hurried away from him, towards the steps. 'Come on! You want to take a pop at me? What are you waiting for!'

There was a silence all around him. The courtyard seemed frozen, the sunlight caught in glass, dust motes and little tiny particles of sand that had travelled all the way across Europe from the Sahara desert hovering motionless in the air. He felt he was the only person alive, and all around him the living-dead were halted like statues in the frozen movements that went nowhere. 'Come on,' he said, with less force. His voice was brittle in the open air. There was no reply.

'Fuck it,' Joe said. Then he walked away.

-- lost again --

HE WALKED AIMLESSLY through the London streets. He had the sense of being followed but could see no one. The early morning's energy had left him and he felt heavy and dull. At an alleyway off Oxford Street he went through Mo's coat. He found a small notebook in the sewn-in pocket, hard-bound, with neat, blue-inked notes handwritten inside. He put the notebook in his own pocket and dumped the coat. Somewhere in the maze of streets he found a tiny pub and sat away from the window and drank beer. The pub specialised in sausages. The menu listed around twenty different kinds. The English, he thought, had once conquered most of the known world, but their cooking hadn't improved as a result. It was quiet inside The Dog & Duck. It seemed to him he was spending his entire life in bars and pubs, and wondered if it had ever been different. He couldn't remember. He knew that what he should do is dump Mo's journal, forget Chinatown, leave behind him the unwanted mysteries that were unravelling like the ball of twine in the Minotaur's maze. He had a simple task to perform, only it was becoming a lot less simple. The ball of twine was entangled, knotted, but it was still a single twine, he knew that, in a deeper part of him where his night's absolute darkness was. He didn't know how long he sat in the pub, but it was getting darker outside. It wasn't yet night-time darkness, just a grey shapeless absence of light, a London summer day. It began to rain. He lit a cigarette and his mouth tasted bitter. He finished his pint and ordered another. After the second one he felt better, like streaks of light appearing against a grimy window-frame. He thought about the smell of opium, which was sweet, but hard to describe in words. He thought about the girl who hired him and his mind conjured up her image, the serious face and the pinned-back, delicate ears, and the soft brown hair, her hand on his, her voice as she said, 'I want you to find him.'

He couldn't find anyone, and least of all himself. He thought about her and it was strangely comforting. He was feeling dissociated from the world around him, as if he were a man in a silent film walking through empty, pre-War streets in a dream, an invisible man: but thoughts of the girl eased his isolation. Or perhaps it was the beer.

Fuzzy-wuzzies, he thought. Was it the world that had become fuzzy while I remain in focus still? Or was it the other way around, the world still there, but I go in and out of focus, like that girl in Paris whose name I never learned but who knew my own, like Mo who was both there and not there, a shadow moving in a world of shadows, doing –

Doing what? Upsetting the shadows, Joe decided. That was what Mo had been doing. He pulled out Mo's journal and squinted at it, but the blue letters ran blurred. Joe took a sip from the beer and ran the liquid around his mouth, rinsing.

He swallowed and opened the journal again.

If we are here, so must they be.

There were no dates, no detailed drawings. Just a series of scribbled notes, scattered haphazardly. He leafed through the notebook and realised only the first seven pages had been used. The rest were blank. On the first page, in bold letters, as if Mo had traced the lines of the letters again and again, almost cutting through the page; surrounded in a jagged frame, the blue inked so deep it was almost black; one question.

But where?

On page three, towards the bottom. *Followed but lost them at Heathrow.*

Page four, half-way down. *Saw them again today. Tracked them down to Holborn. Lost again.*

On page two, at the very bottom, in small letters, still neat, right towards the corner: *Met R. At BN. Disagree re: inv. Tld him to F hmslf.*

Joe approved of the sentiment. He looked at the note again. *Met R. at BN...* He pulled out again the second card he had found in Mo's coat. It was almost identical to the one Joe himself carried, the one his client gave him in the pub of the Regent's Palace. Almost. He turned the card over. *Rick*, handwritten on the back. It matched – and assume BN for the Blue Note. Threads of twine all knotted together... Who was Mo following? Not Longshott, Mike, paperback writer, address unknown. *Them*. Lost them at Heathrow. Where did they go?

He thought of black shoes and a chequered shirt. Thought – Vientiane nice this time of year...

Final note, page seven, near the top. *Found them.* Boxed neatly underneath: *British Museum Underground Station.*

Joe got up. The bartender was washing glasses. Joe asked for a map of the London underground. Took it back to his seat. Studied it.

Wasn't entirely surprised to discover there was no such station.

-- another better world --

HALF AN HOUR later he was sitting at the Edwin Drood looking across the street at the unmarked door of Madam Seng's. He had to overcome a physical sensation of revulsion as he pushed open the grimy doors of the pub. The Edwin Drood was badly-lit, with oil lamps that spluttered and fumed in low dark alcoves. Where the Dog & Duck had been all Victorian splendour in mirrors and gilt, The Edwin Drood was Victorian in the sense of open sewers and resurrection men. The bartender was old, bald, with age spots the size and colour of two-pence coins on his head and small, narrow eyes and white bushy eyebrows, and the same stringy hair grew out of his ears like magic beanstalks. He glared at Joe, but served him a drink in silence, and as Joe carried the pint of warm beer to a table by the dirty windows he felt the bartender's gaze fall on him, unwavering. The smell of opium was strong in The Edwin Drood, but it was an after-smell, a clinging, lingering odour that rose from the silent drinkers. Joe half-watched them as they sat there, rigidly holding on to their drinks, not looking at each other, not looking outside either: looking down, into the drinks or into themselves, into that dark secret place the mind goes when paradise is withdrawn from it.

They were wretched creatures. The smell of opium clung to their clothes, but it was not in them. They were, in turn, in shivers and in sweat. Their eyes were haunted.

Opium, Joe thought. Just as it could take away all pain, its absence could hurt worse. Here were the unfortunates who could not cross into the promised land. It lay just beyond the windows, a wonderland of the mind, but they could not cross the desert that was Newport Place. Was it the momentary absence of money? An attempt to rebel against the pull of the drug? Or were they merely waiting, in mute agony, anticipating the rolled balls of sticky resin, the long graceful pipes, the hiss of a flame and the murmur of a girl as she heated the pipe, as the vapours began to roll towards their mouths and send them at last to another, better world?

He watched out the window and saw the shades of Madam Seng's customers as they approached the unmarked doors. He watched them knock, the door half-open – watched the moment of judgement. Those who were chosen disappeared inside. Those rejected carried their rejection with them. Some came into The Edwin Drood and joined the brotherhood of the silent. At least, Joe thought, that explained the clientele.

He watched a solitary figure approach the door and decided to make his move then. He got up and went outside and the cool air was an awakening. He hurried his steps and reached the man in the long black coat just as he was knocking on the door. The man was carrying a round metal canister under his arm.

'Let me help you with that,' Joe said, just as the door opened.

The man turned to him, blinked, said, 'You're the bloke was in the shop the other day –'

'You bring movie?' The man in the doorway, same one as the last time; speaking a moment before he registered Joe, then – 'I told you not to –'

The round metal canister – the man in the coat saying 'Hey, careful with that!' – Joe taking it from his arms and *lifting*, in one smooth motion – 'come here!' from the man in the doorway as the metal lifted, connected with his chin, the sound of the jawbone jarring, perhaps breaking, and Joe kneed him, hard – the man in the coat saying, 'What the hell are you' – the man in the doorway collapsing –

Joe pushed the door open and went inside.

-- London after midnight --

'Is THAT THE film reel for tonight?' a voice said. 'Thank you, I'll take that.' The metal canister was taken from his hands, and Joe stared.

She wore a Japanese kimono, but her face was a Mekong Delta mix, the eyes of a wild mountain creature, hauntingly beautiful, flecked with gold, looking coolly at Joe, studying him. She was not young, but it was impossible to call her old. There was Vietnamese blood in there, and French, and Hmong, and there were laughter lines at the corners of her eyes and Joe thought of the graffiti he had seen that said, *Madam Seng is a Snake Head*. It did not refer to her face.

'Can I help you?' she said. Her English was tinged with Indochina traces. The eyes looking at him, not blinking, studying him, the fallen figure of the doorman behind him. The was no sign of the man from the bookshop. He must have run off, Joe thought. Sensible, in the circumstance. He felt half-inclined to do the same.

'I'm looking for Madam Seng,' he said.

'Why?' she said. And then, 'This place is not for you.'

'Is it the dress code?' Joe said. 'That's it, right? You don't like my shoes?'

'No,' the woman said. 'Though your shoes could do with a polish, if you want to know the truth.'

'Imagine an opium den with a door policy,' Joe said. He felt the urge to bend down and wipe his shoes with his sleeve, but fought it. The eyes regarded him with a trace of amusement. 'Imagine such an establishment without one.'

The doorman groaned behind them. The woman said, 'Get up.' She spoke quietly, but her voice carried. The doorman groaned again, rolled on his side and pushed himself up.

'Sorry about your doorman,' Joe said.

'Not as sorry as he'll be.'

The doorman scowled at Joe, then clutched his jaw. 'Go,' the woman said. The doorman went.

'You are Madam Seng?'

She ignored him. 'This place is not for you,' she said again. This time there was no amusement and the eyes were opaque jade.

Joe shrugged. 'Well,' he said, 'I'm here now.'

'Opium is for people who have already lost something,' the woman said. 'Not for people who are already lost.'

'That's fascinating,' Joe said. She was trying to rattle him. He wouldn't let her. 'Now if you could just answer a few questions...'

The woman smiled. 'Follow me,' she said. She turned her back on him, the canister of film still in her hands.

Joe followed.

The entrance to Madam Seng's was a dark, low-ceilinged corridor. At the end of the corridor was a beaded curtain. Madam Seng did not push it open, but glided through it, the beads parting before her with a light tinkling sound. Beyond...

Beyond was a large room. Two openings, also lightly curtained, led off into other rooms. The air was thick with the smell of opium; the lights were low, paper lanterns the colour of blood glowing faintly, illuminating a scene of drugged languor. There were low sofas, cushioned with embroidered dragons and stars, on which reclined Madam Seng's faithful customers. A three-legged metal brazier was burning charcoal in one corner. Madam Seng's girls moved softly between the lying customers, both women and men, holding fresh pipes for those deep gone into the dream journey, heating the opium in its metal bowls, murmuring softly in languages the customers neither knew nor cared to. Joe felt light-headed, his arms heavy. The woman held his hand. He whispered, 'Madam Seng,' and she nodded. 'You shouldn't be here,' she said, for the third time.

'None of us should,' he said, though he didn't know what he meant by that.

In one corner of the room he saw a projector. The sound of the moving reel was a constant whisper in the room. Against the opposite wall a film was playing, without sound, in black and white. The beam of light travelled from the machine to the wall, catching motes of dust and curls of smoke in its path.

Title: *Weird things have happened there in the last five years.*

Scene: A maid stands at an open door, staring out in horror. She screams without sound.

Joe: 'I am investigating a murder.'

Madam Seng smiled with her mouth. 'Please, sit down,' she said. There was an empty berth beside the projector, facing the far wall. Madam Seng fluffed a pillow and gestured for Joe to sit. He sat down gratefully, his limbs heavy. Madam Seng perched beside him.

Scene: A young woman bursts out crying. A man sits down beside her and looks on in helplessness.

Fade out.

Madam Seng: 'Let the dead bury their dead.'

The opium smell, strong in the room. Joe blinked; it seemed to take forever for his eyes to close and open.

Joe: 'You keep cropping up.'

Madam Seng: 'Like a bad penny?'

Scene: A bat fluttering against a broken window pane. A shutter bangs in the wind.

Joe: 'Like a question mark.'

Madam Seng smiled; this time it reached her eyes. 'I have been taught they should be used sparingly.'

Scene: Two figures coming down a grand staircase. One is a man. He carries a lamp, held high before his face. He wears a black beaver hat and his face is deathly white and grotesque.

There is something unearthly about his appearance. The woman beside him is similarly pale. As they come down the stairs the man in the beaver hat hands the lamp to the woman. At the foot of the stairs they separate.

Joe blinked again; it took his eyes longer to open this time. 'The opium,' he said. Madam Seng nodded beside him. 'It is both a blessing and a curse,' she said. 'Rest.' She put her hand on his brow. Her hand was cool. She smoothed back his hair, gently. 'It is a door one should not open lightly.'

'Are you a Snake Head?' Joe said. Chinese expression: a people-smuggler. Madam Seng shook her head. 'Not in that context,' she said.

What context?

Scene: Two men in a library, talking.

Title: *You mean a ghost?*

'Rest,' Madam Seng said again. 'You should not have come, but now you're here.'

Somehow the words seemed to hold a deeper meaning for Joe. He raised his hand and it was like lifting a tremendously heavy weight from the depths of the sea. When he touched his eyes they were covered in saltwater.

Title: *Not a ghost. Worse –*

Joe's arm dropped back to his side. Dimly, he felt himself sinking, the sea claiming him. Dimly, he heard Madam Seng whispering soothing words in a language he didn't know, nor cared to. She eased him down on the berth, arranged a pillow under his head, lifted up his feet.

Title: *MIDNIGHT.*

Fade in.

Scene: A long-shot of a cemetery, twisted trees bare. Behind, a mausoleum.

Joe's eyes closed, the silent movie receding into nothingness, taking the opium den with it.

Fade out.

-- no place like home --

HE WAS STANDING on Piccadilly Circus and the cars were wrong.
They were like toy cars, like things that ran on batteries. The
statue of Anteros still looked down with his bow and arrow.
There were still tourists in the Circus but they, too, looked
wrong. Strange haircuts. T-shirts advertising brands he'd never
heard of, Gap and FCUK and something called Metallica. A
guy with long hair, faded jeans and wraparound mirrorshades
was strumming a guitar and singing about imagining all the
people living life in peace, his voice reedy in the air.

The pollution was worse.

He looked up and the signs opposite were in neon lights
and the images moved impossibly and the only name he could
recognise was Coca-Cola.

Samsung. Sanyo. Japanese names, but not ones he'd heard
of before.

People had white-coloured wires trailing down from their ears.

He crossed the road, thinking to go to his hotel, but the
Regent's Palace was covered in scaffolding, its windows empty.
He walked down Shaftesbury Avenue and up into Soho and
saw things like the beaks of cranes rotating slowly high above
street level, glass lenses glinting as they caught the light, moving
this way and that as if scanning for prey. On Old Compton
Street there were shops advertising pornographic movies, but
there were no adult cinemas. There were hundreds of titles in
the display windows. Boys on girls, girls on girls, boys on boys.
The girls had breasts that looked like they had come from the
future, they were as large and impossible as spaceships.

A big poster on the corner, an enormous grey eye looking down on the street, a notice: *You are watching Big Brother*.

Shouldn't it have been the other way around?

He walked back down to Shaftesbury Avenue. On the way, he passed a group of silent dancers: they had gathered by the corner of the street and were dancing with no sound, with no order. They all had the same white wires coming down from their ears. A guy in a suit was playing a mute air guitar. When he came to Shaftesbury Avenue he saw a double-decker bus but it too was wrong, with no pole and open platform at the back, the only way in was through the doors in the front and they were closed and the bus wasn't stopping. He crossed the road into Chinatown. No Edwin Drood, no Madam Seng, just a row of Chinese restaurants, red naked ducks hanging from hooks in the windows. He walked down Little Newport into Charing Cross Road. The bookshops were still there. He didn't recognise the names. Up towards Oxford Street, meeting Shaftesbury Avenue for a third time. Large, multi-storey bookshops, but Foyle's was still there; at least that was a name he knew. He went in. There was a counter to his right with the legend: *Information*.

'Do you have any of the Mike Longshott books?'

'Say what?'

'Osama bin Laden?'

The man behind the counter had a something like a television screen in front of him, and a plastic thing with keys. He tapped them, frowning. 'We have a few,' he said. 'Let me print out the list for you.'

He pressed more keys and a small box beside his television screen began to hum and a sheet of paper slid out from inside it and he handed it to Joe. Joe stared at the printed paper. 'What is this?' he said.

The man barely glanced his way. 'What you asked for,' he said.

'But this is all wrong.'

'Complaints department is over there,' the man said. Joe followed his pointing finger. It was showing him the doors.

Joe shrugged, crumpled the paper into a ball, deposited it on the counter, and left.

Up Charing Cross and across St. Giles' Circus and into Tottenham Court Road, which looked like something out of a science fiction paperback. There were rows and rows of stores with gleaming impossible devices on display. One store he passed was full of television screens in its display window, each tuned to a different station, more stations than he thought possible. A man in an office, dancing. Tiny insects, magnified, mating. Two policemen running from an explosion. A schoolgirl in uniform singing silently into a microphone, all the time staring out of her television as if looking out of a prison window. Gigantic spaceships exploding, men with laser guns firing, a monstrous alien blob with a human captive in a block of ice. Joe felt sick. He doubled back, ran down New Oxford, up into Bloomsbury, the air hot in his lungs, traffic lights blinking at him green and red and yellow, glass eyes above moving slowly to focus on him as he passed.

The British Museum. A man selling sausages outside the gate, the smell of frying onions making Joe's stomach knot up. Tourists milling about, cameras flashing. The cameras were odd; too small, he thought. As if they had no film inside.

A man in a robot suit walking down the road, a sign above his head: Half-price tickets. 'There's no place like home!' the man shouted. He stopped by Joe, handed him a leaflet. 'There's no place like home, mate. Get a ticket while they're going.'

Joe blinked, his vision blurred. The tin-man walked away. He'd already forgotten Joe. 'No place –'

'Joe?'

He blinked and opened his eyes. Madam Seng stood above him. 'You had a bad dream,' she said.

-- the man in the beaver hat --

HIS TONGUE WAS thick and unresponsive. He sat up and the room swam. Nothing had changed. The clientele was still arranged artistically on their cushions. The girls administered their medicine. The film continued to play silently on the opposite wall.

Scene: The man in the beaver hat sitting down with another man, who looks dazed.

Title: *Have I been asleep?*

Scene: Close-up on the man in the beaver hat, his grotesque eyes and deathly pallor.

Title: *No, and neither have I.*

'I want to know your role in this.'

'My role in what?' Madam Seng said.

'What was Mo doing here?'

Her eyes, expanding slightly. 'The detective?'

'He had your card.'

She shrugged. 'He came here a couple of times.'

'Why?'

'Why do any of you?'

'No,' Joe said. He shook his head and his vision swam. 'He was investigating something. Some people. He came here... he must have seen them here.' Her eyes regarded him calmly. He described the man in the black shoes.

Madam Seng: 'I don't know why I should even talk to you.'

Joe: 'Why do you?'

Madam Seng: 'You remind me of a boy I used to know.'

Joe: 'What happened to him?'

Madam Seng: 'He...' Slight hesitation. 'Went elsewhere.'

Joe blinked, wanted to sneeze. Held his head in his hands – it felt like a lead weight. 'Do you have coffee?' he said.

'This is an opium house, not a coffee shop,' Madam Seng said, and Joe smiled.

'Please?'

She made a gesture to one of the girls.

'So tell me about these men,' Joe said.

On the opposite wall the film stuttered slowly to a halt.

'I am not a Snake Head,' Madam Seng said.

'But they thought you are.'

'Yes.'

'Where did they want you to take them?'

She shrugged. 'Into fuzzy-wuzzy land.'

'Did they find what they were looking for?'

'No.'

'What *were* they looking for?'

'What are *you* looking for?'

'Lady, I just have a job to do.'

She looked amused. 'That's nice,' she said. 'Lady.'

The girl came back. She carried a silver tray and put it down on the low table beside Joe. Black coffee in a white china cup, a bowl of sugar cubes, a small pouring-jug of cream. She looked up at Joe and smiled. Madam Seng said something Joe didn't catch and the girl left them quickly.

'I'm looking for...' he said, and then fell quiet, and stirred sugar and cream into the coffee, and took a sip; it seemed to set his brain on fire. 'Osama bin Laden,' he said, wonderingly.

Madam Seng slowly nodded.

'I think that's who they were looking for, too,' she said.

-- forget Chinatown --

HE KNEW THE way now. He retraced his steps for the third time, though one had been only in a dream.

'Don't come here again,' Madam Seng had said. On impulse he had leaned towards her, kissed her on the cheek. Her skin felt cold. She pulled back from him and smiled. Her eyes were hidden behind mist. 'Sometimes,' she said, 'you can never go home again.'

He nodded, once. She put her hand on his face, looked at him as if searching for something hidden, the lines of someone else in his face. 'There is no path this way,' she said. 'Forget it, Joe. Forget Chinatown.'

He turned his back on her. As he stepped outside, the air was cooler, waking him. The door closed behind him without noise. The tableau of silent drinkers at The Edwin Drood was undisturbed through the grimy glass. He went down Little Newport and wondered if it had been named for a particularly small and agile chimney sweep. He turned left on Charing Cross Road, crossed Shaftesbury Avenue, saw Foyle's in the distance. On an impulse he went in. Though the hour was late the store was open. There was a girl sitting behind a desk in the front. He approached her.

'Can I help you?'

'Do you have any of the Mike Longshott books?'

'Mike Longshott...' she said. 'Hold on.'

She reached for a thick folder and began leafing through it.

'The Osama bin Laden series,' Joe said. The girl looked up. Closed the folder. A moue of distaste. 'Oh, *those*.'

'Do you have them?'

'We don't stock that sort of stuff here,' she said. 'Try further up the road.'

Joe followed her pointing finger. It was showing him the doors.

With a sense of déjà vu he left the bookstore and continued on his way, walking down London's chartered streets, searching the faces of the night people out at this hour, knowing that he was being watched. He could have gone straight down Shaftesbury Avenue to his destination, but he chose this route, willing an awareness of him. There were no cameras in this London, but still there were secret watchers. He turned on St. Giles, away from gallows that weren't there, walked along High Holborn, feeling in his back the intensity of the hidden watchers increase.

There was no British Museum underground station.

But there had been, once.

Tracked them down to Holborn. Lost again.

Where High Holborn met Bloomsbury Court...

He'd looked it up on his way from the Dog & Bone. A trains and transport bookshop of the kind one can only find in London. A proprietor with hundreds of private notebooks stashed away, recording days spent on foggy platforms, recording times of arrivals and departures. There was no British Museum station there, but there had been, before the war. They said it was haunted, the proprietor said with a whisper, and laughed. They said there was an Egyptian mummy down there. They said there was a tribe of cannibals down there. It was an air shelter during the war. It was a military post. It was home to a group of refugees from a war no one had heard of. It was off High Holborn, but the station building no longer existed. All that remained were the tunnels...

The offices of a Building Society. A shuttered pub. Around the back, a small wooden door, locked and unremarked, grainy wood and peeling green paint. A little way away, a dark-blue police box stood empty, its light dead. Joe approached the door. The handle had been removed. He stared at it. He could feel the silence around him. What lay beyond the door. He could turn back, walk away. Answers were buried underground, in unmarked graves. He breathed in London's night air, then kicked the door. The wood splintered, the door fell back, revealing the darkness beyond. He went towards the darkness.

-- hell is an abandoned station --

WALKING DOWN STONE stairs slippery with moss. His Zippo held up before him, illuminating crumbling brickwork sprayed with ancient graffiti. For a moment he thought of the man in the beaver hat holding a lantern, deathly-pale face coming down the grand staircase. Down and down into the ground. The weight of packed earth above his head. Down to a level surface: a platform. He had Mo's gun, still. He held it in one hand now, the lighter in the other, the flame dancing, his shadow ending at the end of his feet. A voice, as cold as a subterranean spring, spoke through the darkness. 'Mr. Private Investigator,' it said. 'You should not have come here.'

Joe stopped, let the flame die. 'I wish people would stop telling me that,' he said. The unseen speaker laughed. Joe heard a rustling sound, and something brushed against his feet in passing. There were rats down there, he thought.

Some even had four legs.

'Those who go underground,' the voice said, 'sometimes never come back.'

It wasn't the voice of the gentleman in the chequered shirt. Someone else...

Stealthy movement behind him. They must have followed him down the stairs, the ones who were watching above. Joe stepped carefully sideways, felt the wall against his shoulder.

'Nice place you got here,' he said.

Someone spat. 'You're tenacious, Mr. Joe, I'll give you that,' the voice said. 'A useful attribute in your line of work, I would have thought.'

Joe edged forward, the gun raised.

'And obstinate. Which is not so useful. Unable to see what's in front of you...'

Right then he could see nothing. He was going by sound. Two pairs of feet moving behind him, blocking the way out. The voice in front. How many more? He stopped again. Speaking would tell them where he was, but...

He said, 'Osama bin Laden.'

Someone swore behind him in the dark. He didn't understand the words. 'What do you expect to find?' Joe said. The memory of his early morning conversation with one of these men came back to him. 'A face in the clouds?' he said.

'We are trying,' the voice said, and it was no longer cool. It was angry. 'To find paradise.'

'Don't you have to die first to get there?' Joe said.

'Yes,' the voice said. 'That is, precisely, the point.'

'Where is Osama bin Laden?' Joe said.

'Not here,' a new voice said, ahead of him. The man in the black shoes. It was hard to forget his voice. 'I tell you before, you no make trouble.' It sounded genuinely puzzled. 'Why you make trouble? Now kill you.'

'I'll just be waiting ahead for you in paradise, then,' Joe said. A word the girl in Paris used came back to him. '*Nangilima*,' he said. It was the name of a land beyond this land – a word for elsewhere. He knew he wanted a cigarette and fought down the urge. The man in the black shoes said, 'Why he is not here? Why he is not come?'

'Keep quiet,' the first voice said. But the other kept talking. 'You, me, we go. We follow plan. But plan wrong: Where paradise? Why he is not come?'

How many bullets? How many men?

'Maybe hell,' the man in the black shoes said. 'Maybe hell is abandoned station.'

'Keep *quiet*,' the first voice said. And then, 'Perhaps he *is* here.'

Joe said, 'Mike Longshott.'

He inched forward. The voices were closer now. The two at his back hadn't moved.

The first voice said, 'Yes.'

'I could have found him for you.'

'Perhaps,' the voice said. And, 'You shouldn't have come down here.'

'Yet here I am,' Joe said.

'Yes,' the voice said again. 'A pity.'

Joe crouched, gun held in both hands. He heard a scrabbling sound ahead, something heavy being pulled.

'Kill him,' the first voice said.

A click.

Yellow lights came alive, blinding him, and he fired without looking, going by sound.

The sound of gunshots, not his. He rolled, turned, fired again, once, twice. Something hit his arm, throwing him to the ground. Blood pounded in his ears.

Something metallic falling to the ground. Joe opened his eyes, blinked tears against the glare of light. He was lying on the platform and ahead of him one man was slumped against the platform's edge. As Joe watched, the man fell slowly forward, towards the ancient rails. As he hit the track his body seemed to disappear.

Joe blinked, his eyes getting used to the light. His arm hurt; he couldn't move it. He touched it with his other hand and his fingers came back covered in blood. Ahead of him, a man in black shoes, the prone feet vertical. Joe pushed himself up on one arm, stood, retrieved his fallen gun. He walked to the man in the black shoes. There was a hole in the man's chest, pumping out blood. The man was breathing hollowly. Joe crouched down beside him, put his hand on his forehead, smoothed back the sweat-soaked hair. The man's eyes opened, focused on Joe. His mouth moved, shaped itself into a smile. 'I wait ahead for you,' the man in the black shoes whispered, 'in other paradise.'

Then he was gone, and Joe stood up and turned and, for just a moment, before the lights faded and died, saw two more empty pools of blood ahead where the silent watchers had been.

Then, ignoring the pain, he pulled out his cigarettes, shook one out, one-handed, and put it in his mouth, letting the rest of the pack fall to the floor.

In the darkness of a tomb his lighter flicked into being, the tiny flame of light dancing.

He lit the cigarette, blew out smoke. For a long moment he stood there, seeing nothing. Then he began to edge his way forward, towards the stairs and the clean lighted night.

-- the colour of a bruise, blue against black --

STREET LIGHTS, CASTING fates along the dark asphalt. Bloodied entrails, animal bones in curious shapes, rattled and scattered, predicting the future. Clouds above, no stars, the moon invisible. Down these streets a man must go, Joe following a trail of entrails, the scent of old blood, his mouth flavoured rust. Above-ground, breathing clean air. In his head: planes crash into buildings, buses explode, trains scream to a halt, an entire public transport network of death.

His arm felt better up here. He looked at it in the light of a streetlamp and almost laughed – the bullet had merely grazed it. He tore a strip of cloth from his shirt and tied it around the wound. It had seemed worse down below. The pain wasn't bad. What was bad was everything else.

Four men left behind. Need: a drink. Need: sound, music. Need: lives around him. Instead he wandered through a world in black and white. Shadows criss-crossed his face. The stench of blood in his nostrils, clogging.

At St. Giles Circus, almost no traffic – he thought he could see the ancient corpses swinging. Soho Square silent, empty, tall hushed buildings looking down with indifference in their windows.

Joe lit a fresh cigarette, leaned against a dark tree, listened to the silence. Somewhere in the distance, a light, beckoning, the colour of a bruise, blue against black. Four men left behind. Fog: in the street, in his mind. A dank sweet cloying smell. Man in the beaver hat carrying a lantern in the dark illuminating nothing but himself. The blue light beckoned: Joe followed.

Through empty streets. Night is the time of the dead, a graveyard shift. The trains lope home along the tracks, the fog caught in their fur. The lampshades glare. There is respite in quiet night, for restless shades and homeless strays. There is a living coldness in the winds at night, the streetlights mark the passage of the years.

He breathed out a shuddering stream of smoke. Four men left behind. But you are not there. They seek you, seek you everywhere. You are the hand well hidden, and the scalpel that ensures the tumour is removed, the skin is parted so, the ill is healed, the wrong is righted, the world is once more set on course.

Four men left behind. One man ahead, always ahead. The blue light beckoned, not far. Joe thought: God lives in the clouds like smoke, he has a long grey beard.

Not feeling right. Loneliness is magnified at night time. He thought of the long Arctic night, Icelandic suicides, shivered. Pulled out Mo's notebook: last note, page seven, near the top. *Found them*. Joe pulled out a pen, crossed it out.

The light ahead, like a police-box calling out safety. He didn't know where he was, somewhere in the maze of nameless streets. To one side a dirty books store, on the other a bottle store, both shut, *Closed* signs in the windows coated in dust. A closed door, the blue light above it shaped into a musical notation, the name underneath like a period at the end of a long sentence: The Blue Note.

The card in his pocket. The girl – his employer. A matching card in Mo's coat, a scribble in his notebook: Joe knocked on the door.

-- refugees --

A GRILLE IN the door slid back. Eyes regarded him from inside. He could hear the faint notes of a jazz tune. A voice from the darkness: 'What you want?'

Joe: 'A drink.'

'Do I know you?'

'No reason why you should.' He blew out smoke, into the grille. From inside: 'Fuck!' – coughing sounds.

'Are you going to let me in?'

'Members only. Scram.'

Joe – Mo's notebook – recollection: *Met R. At BN*. He said: 'I want to see Rick.'

Silence, a sigh. The voice: 'Everybody comes to Rick.'

Joe – *what-fucking-ever*.

The grill slid shut – the door opened. Joe stepped through.

Beyond the door: tables, a long bar, a small stage. The lights dim. A piano player pounding keys. The tune familiar, but he couldn't put a name to it. Chairs around the tables – occupied. It was hard to make out faces in the gloom.

The voice resolved itself into a shape. 'That wasn't nice, blowing smoke in my face.' Big face. Deep-set eyes. Looking down at Joe, reproachfully. 'I'm asthmatic.'

Joe: 'You're in the wrong line of work.'

The man coughed, put his hand on Joe's shoulder, squeezed. Joe clamped his teeth shut.

'Nobody likes a smartass.'

'I'll try to remember that.'

'Do.' The hand released him, slapped him on the back – the

impact propelled him forward and into the room. 'Rick's in his office, he'll be down soon. Get yourself a drink in the meantime – show's about to start.'

Joe muttered, 'Thanks.' Walked to the bar. Silent figures sitting at the tables: drinks, cigarettes. Waiting.

Passengers in an airport lounge, going nowhere, he thought. There were no clocks in the room. It felt as if time had stopped and been preserved there.

At the bar: a tall thin man. 'Help you?'

'Whisky, double shot. Neat.'

'You look like you need it.'

Joe let it pass. 'And a café Américain.'

Bartender: 'That's just black coffee, isn't it?'

Joe, tired. 'Just do it.' He laid cash on the counter. The bartender made it disappear.

The whisky burned through Joe like lit oil on the surface of a sea. The coffee was black and bitter: oil again, slick and dark, made from the decayed bones of mega-fauna dead long before humanity was born. 'You could power cars with this shit,' Joe said, pointing at the coffee. The bartender, grinning, a slight Russian accent: 'Let's not fight over it.'

Joe shrugged, turned away on his seat, scanned the seated audience.

Impressions: dummies in a store window. No, that wasn't it. But there was something about them that didn't read right. Bars of shadows fell on raised, expectant faces. The sense of a lingering wait, the eyes that stare into a fartherness. Clothes that did not quite fit. The thought of a tree felled, the roots torn out of the ground – helpless in the air. Expectant people – they looked like they did not belong, not here, not anywhere.

He thought – refugees.

The piano-man, singing about love and glory – the singing stopped, piano keys jingled into nothingness. The bartender: 'She's coming on.'

A hush at the Blue Note. Lights dimming further, a single projection – a cone of light catching the stage.

Joe said, 'Keep them coming –' gesturing to the whisky; more money on the counter, but the bartender wasn't listening.

The piano picked up again, stilled.

Joe, waiting.

A single note on a guitar, lingering in the air.

-- over the rainbow --

A FINE HAZE, a mist fell down on the stage. Nozzles in the ceiling, opening like flowers. The falling water – a drizzle, a shower. The light picked out every drop of water, glinting in hundreds of tiny rainbows. He saw her.

She came on the stage, all big eyes and brown hair and pointed pinned-back ears, and there was a silence at the Blue Note like that of an empty and expectant grave. The girl didn't look at the audience. A stool materialised like magic on the stage. Joe watched her through the mist and the beam of concentrated light, and something hurt inside him, and he reached for the shot glass and faltered. The girl sat down. The guitar was a light colour. She plucked some strings. Someone at a nearby table sighed.

The girl sang. Afterwards, Joe found it hard to recall her singing, the words, the music that seemed to wail and gnash its teeth and mourn, in a way that sent tiny men with tiny knives into his guts to work him over. She sang about a place over the rainbow; fingers teasing sadness from the strings though there was no need: it was in the audience that night, touching chill fingers to the napes of émigrés and one lone detective with his hand suspended in its reach for the glass. She sang of a place where the clouds were far, and when she sang she opened her eyes and looked towards the bar, and she saw Joe and he saw her, and the tiny men with tiny knives worked him harder inside, jabbering and mumbling as they cut him up. She sang of a place beyond the rainbow, a place she could not go, or could not come back from. She looked at Joe through the film of water, and her fingers on the strings were an intimate recollection he knew without remembering. She sang of a place over the rainbow, a place far-away and yet so close, so close you could almost touch it. She sang – he thought she sang – for him, asking him to find her.

When it was over the silence draped over the audience like a net rising from the depths of the sea, hauling its catch of mute, silver-scaled fish with it. The girl let her hand fall, and the last notes of the strings hung in the air, unfinished for a long moment. Then she stood and disappeared backstage and the artificial rain ceased falling and the lights came back on and Joe's hand completed its journey to the glass, grasped it, and he downed the shot in one and felt his eyes burning.

A voice behind him said, 'So you are the detective,' and he turned.

'I'm Rick,' the man said. He wore a white evening jacket, was smoking a cigarette.

'I'm drunk,' Joe said, and the man laughed. 'Did you enjoy the show?'

'No.'

Rick nodded. '*Joie de vivre* is something lacking in these parts.'

'Do *you* enjoy living, Mr. Rick?'

'I did.'

The piano player picked up again. Conversation resumed, what there was of it. The bartender brought over a bottle and a glass and placed them beside Rick without comment. Rick refilled Joe's glass, filled his own.

'What do you know about Mo's death, Mr. Rick?'

No reaction from the man – a slight smile, a shake of the head. 'I told him to back off, he wouldn't listen. Dead once, dead twice – who cares.'

'I do.'

'Then you're a fool.'

Joe had no answer, let that one pass. 'What do you know about Snake Heads, Mr. Rick?'

'I know they don't exist.'

'Not even Mike Longshott?'

A hit. Rick's smile fading like Mo's corpse. 'Forget it, detective. Stop chasing rainbows.'

Thinking of the girl, wanting suddenly to see her with a desperation that ached. 'Do you know where I can find him?'

'No.'

'You said that awfully quickly.'

'It happens to be the truth.'

A hunch, Joe playing it. 'But you tried to find out.'

'I stick my neck out for no one, detective.'

'What did you find in the Castle?'

Visible reaction – Rick holding the shot glass too tightly. Ash from his cigarette shuddering down to the floor. 'Nothing.'

'What were you hoping to find?'

'What do you want, detective?'

Joe said: 'Answers.'

Rick raised his glass, regained his smile. 'To answers, then' he said.

'Why?' Joe said, after they'd drunk.

'Why what?'

'Why all this?' Gesturing with his hand, the movement taking in the whole of the Blue Note, the bartender, the piano, the clientele.

Rick shrugged. 'Everybody needs something,' he said. He stood up to go. There were loud bangs on the door, from outside. Rick tensed. 'Excuse me,' he said.

Joe trailed him to the door, felt a hand on his shoulder, stopped.

He could barely see her. An outline, the suggestion of a shape. She said, 'Joe...' and nothing more.

He said, 'I'm trying.'

For a moment she seemed to smile. She leaned towards him. The suggestion of lips touching his – he closed his eyes. When he opened them again, she was gone.

Banging on the doors. People stirring. Rick striding to him. Rick: 'You've got to leave.'

Joe – 'Why' – question uncompleted.

Rick: 'CPD. I don't want them here.'

'What do *they* want?'

But he knew the answer already.

Rick: 'You.'

Another hunch, playing it straight – 'You have an arrangement with them.'

Rick, angry. 'I'm just trying to get by.'

Joe: 'I know. You stick your neck out for no-one.' A slight smile. Rick hit him.

Joe fell back, tasted blood. Rick: 'Get out. There's a back way. Come on. Quickly.'

Joe followed. A small door past the bar. Through that: a narrow corridor, empty. The only light coming through from streetlamps outside, bars on the windows, a criss-cross of shadows falling inside. Another door, a room as empty as the corridor, a back-stage to the bar with no props and no actors. Another door, another corridor – a final door opening on an alleyway outside. Trashcans with no trash, graffiti on the walls – *We'll meet again some sunny day*.

'Go,' Rick said. Joe turned, saw him framed in the doorway. 'They'll be through soon. I can't stop them. Make sure you're a long way away.'

Joe: 'Why are you helping me?'

Rick shook his head. 'I don't want trouble. This way is easiest.'

Joe: 'You're not being sentimental, are you?'

Rick: 'Get out, and don't come back.'

Joe left at a run. The moon cast his shadow on the dirty-grey walls.

-- assault on 22 Frith street --

HE HAD TO know, and he had a plan. It was not a well-formulated plan but, it should work – he'd had some experience already that day. It had the benefit of being simple. He had the benefit of Mo's gun, the muzzle still smelling faintly of gunpowder. He came to Frith Street – eventually, getting lost in the maze of dark streets, but Old Compton Street and Frith Street were still lit and there were people sitting outside drinking beer and coffee and listening to music. There was laughter, which came at Joe like an alien sound. He walked up Frith Street and turned at the door to the Castle and pressed the buzzer and waited, staring at the same blue plaque about the inaugural television broadcast.

'Yes?'

'Mike Longshott,' Joe said.

'Just a moment, sir.'

He waited out the moment. The door opened. The same bruiser as before, in a too-expensive suit, the bulge for a gun under the jacket – 'Thought I made it clear enough last time that you're not to –'

Joe kneed him, once, twice, brought out the derringer, smashed the man's nose in, eased him down to the floor. 'You thought wrong,' he said. He stepped over the man, said, 'Try to breathe.' Walked inside.

Upstairs to the guests' dining-room. Downstairs to the library, smoking lounge, and postal room. A girl behind reception, rising, looking alarmed – 'Don't move.'

She followed the movement of the gun. Joe checked behind

her – an unmarked door made to look like a part of the wooden panelling of the wall – 'What's behind there?'

'Kitchen and service area,' the girl said.

'Open it.'

She went to the door, pushed it open. 'It isn't locked.'

'Get inside.'

He followed her through. A utilitarian corridor, stained walls, smell of garlic wafting through, a bucket of dirty soapy water standing forlorn outside the first door.

'What's in there?'

'Cleaning supplies.'

There was a key in the door. It was dark inside, smelled of cleaning liquids – no windows, a single chair. 'Looks comfortable,' Joe said. He pushed the girl inside, not hard, heard her begin to say, 'Hey, what –' and locked the door behind her. He didn't have long and this was wasting too much time. There was nothing elegant about his plan. Perhaps he could change that.

He found a hidden cupboard behind the desk and dressed himself. A jacket and a tie – dashing. The doorman was coming around. Joe was tired of hitting doormen. Still. He hit him on the back of the head with the butt of the gun, pushed him out with difficulty, closed the door.

He went down the stairs. Down there: wood, plush velvet, soft lighting. A man in uniform, 'Sir, this is a members only –'

'I just joined,' Joe said. He made some cash materialise. The man followed it. 'Always a pleasure to welcome new members, sir,' he said, making the money dematerialise. Joe grinned. 'Where's the post room?' he said. The man pointed. 'Straight and to the left,' he said. 'There's only Millie on duty, sir.'

'Thanks,' Joe said.

He walked down the muted corridor. He was running on nervous energy, a sense of something ending. Sounds of cutlery, clinking, the pop of a bottle, laughter, conversation. He felt like the intruder that he was. At the end of the corridor he turned left – the post room small, a sleepy girl behind the counter, a red Royal Mail post box by the open door.

'Millie,' Joe said, and the girl opened her eyes with a start – 'Sir?'

'The name's Mike,' he said. Smiled friendly. 'Mike Longshott.'

He saw the reaction in her eyes – 'Sir, I –'

'I understand you've been holding some mail for me?'

'Sir? No, sir.'

'What do you mean?'

The girl looked confused – a mirror held up to Joe. 'Your instructions, sir,' she said.

'Of course,' Joe said. 'I might need to change them, though. Now that I'm here.'

Raised voices in the distance. There was a clock above Millie's head – the ticking was driving Joe insane. 'Can we just go over my original instructions?'

More money materialising like magic. 'For your trouble,' he said.

The girl suddenly beamed. 'I have to say I was intrigued,' she said. 'I never thought...'

'You'd see me?'

She nodded. He didn't tell her, the feeling echoing deep inside him. The voices louder – coming closer. 'My instructions – ?' he said, leaving a gap for her to fill.

'All moneys from Mr. Papadopoulos in Paris to go towards maintaining the membership account,' Millie said happily. 'All queries, fan letters, requests and miscellanea to go direct to Mr. Papadopoulos in –'

'Paris?'

'Yes.'

Round and round and round we go, Joe thought. It was a clever setup. Another dead end. Also – Papa D. held out on me.

'Any fan letters?'

'Not really, Mr. Longshott.'

'Anything come in recently?'

'Only this. I haven't forwarded it yet.'

She handed him an envelope. United States stamp, dated two weeks before. Joe put it in his pocket. 'On second thought,' Joe said, 'I think I'll keep the arrangement as it stands. You're doing an excellent job, Millie.'

She blushed. And – 'Could you – ?' A paperback appeared from under the desk; worn, dog-eared. *Assignment: Africa.*

Joe: 'Is there a back door exit from here?'

Millie: 'Yes, right through here.'

Running steps in the corridor outside. Joe closed the door, locked it. 'Problem with the account,' he said, shrugged. Pen on her desk. Opened the book to the title-page, wrote, *To Millie, who looked after me,* and signed it, with a flourish – *Mike Longshott.*

Knocks on the door. 'Follow me,' Millie said. Opened a second door, led him into a narrow service corridor, walked down it, pushed open steel fire doors and let in the night.

'Goodbye, Mr. Longshott,' she said.

'Goodbye, Millie. Thank you.'

There was something wistful in her smile.

Joe walked out and the fire doors closed behind him with a sound like that last thumping of a drum.

-- a sheet of paper, folded accordion-fashion --

HE SAT ON a bench and the night went past him in a blur.

Just sitting there felt good. He had reached the end of the road – there was no trail left to follow, nowhere left to go. Freedom made him light-headed. Opium fumes, alcohol, nicotine and coffee made epic battles in his body. When he closed his eyes he felt like he was falling. There was a gaping darkness underneath. He wanted to let go, fall into it. When he opened his eyes, he saw disconnected images: the girl on the stage, a screen of rainbows hiding her face; another London he had glimpsed and didn't like; Rick, the shadows of the bars falling on his face; the man from the CPD talking about opium, stirring coffee; Madam Seng's hand on his face, her eyes wet; Mo's empty office, the row of books on his shelf slouched like guerrilla soldiers on parade; the woman he met at the airport in Bangkok, searching the board for a flight that would never come.

He couldn't go back to his hotel – the men from the CPD would be there, waiting for him. They had tracked him down to the Blue Note – there had been two warnings, good-cop, bad-cop – he didn't think there would be a third.

He could go back to Vientiane. It seemed very far now, a hot dry place transformed in the rainy season into a lush tropical garden, the dusty streets swept by thick drops of rain, unpaved sidewalks turning to mud, eggplants going out of season, mosquitoes congregating around open drains to pass on gossip and malaria. He still had the black credit card: he could go anywhere.

Anywhere but over the rainbow, he thought. Or perhaps that was wrong. Perhaps the song was upside down. It was returning from the place where the clouds were far behind that was the problem. Sometimes you can never go back, he thought. He wanted more than anything to solve the case: it gave him substance, shape, a backdrop, a script. He could go anywhere and still be nowhere. He could try and find answers at the bottom of a glass, but even those were running out.

He was sorry for beating up on all those doormen, sorry for all the beat-up, worn-out gatekeepers of the world, for all the closed locked doors, for all the dark rooms that would never be lit, for all the hidden secret inscriptions of the mind. He had to admire Longshott, if it really was him, for setting up the mail loop, London-Paris-London, Frith Street to Boulevard Haussmann and back, an endless repetitive loop hiding everything, revealing nothing.

Or maybe not, he thought. Not exactly nothing. He sat up straighter. From his pocket, he brought out the letter he had collected. The Statue of Liberty on the stamp, a postage date of two weeks before. He examined the envelope, determined nothing, tore it open.

A sheet of paper, folded accordion-fashion, slid out and into Joe's hand.

He spread it open on his knees. Began to read. Noted the large, badly-printed typeface, the profusion of exclamation marks – frowned, read on, shook his head – began to laugh, but the laughter cut short.

It was worth a shot.

And he had nothing else.

He read it again, folded it back the way it came, returned it to its envelope. Stood up. The first rays of light were struggling against the grey-black horizon, like prisoners beating against bars. Joe slipped the envelope back into his pocket, patted it. He found a public rubbish bin, wiped Mo's gun clean, slid it into the bin bag.

Walked towards the distant sunrise.

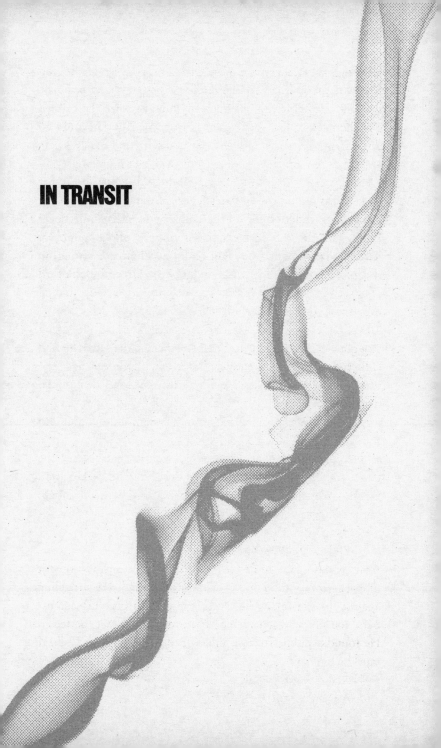

IN TRANSIT

-- the letter from America --

MORNING BREAKING, THE sun a distant lamp carried unsteadily up in the heavens. Rain fell, washing the city, lending the red-grey bricks a sheen of vitality, a coating of moss. Joe had bought coffee at an all-night vendor, Styrofoam cup, the coffee black, two sugars, had it with a cigarette – doctor's orders. His hand holding the cigarette shook.

Early morning, London. He'd gone back to Edgware Road, on foot. Cars roared in rush-hour traffic above his head. He'd gone into a barbershop, a trick shop beside it just opening up. Did all his shopping on the high street – new clothes, new haircut, new hair colour, wore glasses – a suit, a briefcase, a pencil moustache. Oxford pin on his tie. A Rolex watch, fake and heavy on his wrist. He looked at himself in a shop window and nodded to the stranger. 'You'll do just fine,' he told him. The stranger mouthed the words back to him, without sound.

His last call the bank, took out cash on the black card. The letter from America was snug in the breast pocket of his suit. A black cab to the airport, the driver chatty – 'Me, I'm from Baghdad. You ever been?'

Joe saying, 'No.'

'Lovely place,' the driver said, and sighed. 'When I go back, I'll take a black cab with me.'

The drive was slow, the roads busy, the sun still struggled to come out. The rain drizzled down the windows of the cab. The world beyond was smudged.

Red brick houses stoic in the rain. Traffic lights blinked sedately. School kids crossed the road. Joe could smell coffee brewing, bread baking, saw forests of dark umbrellas sprouting in the streets. Postmen marched determined from house to house like soldiers performing a search. Blue-haired ladies were opening doors, turning on the lights in hospice and charity shops. Joe edged the window open, let the smell of rain into the cab, closed his eyes. The cab driver said, 'In my country the rain is different.'

Joe didn't reply.

Outer London spread out from the cab like ripples. Low houses, double-decker buses, somewhere in the distance the bell ring of a school, somewhere in the distance the tolling of church bells, somewhere in the distance, coming closer, the sound of planes, landing and taking-off.

'In my country,' the cab driver said, 'it's very sunny, not like here.'

Joe let it pass. They drove into Heathrow, watched blue-overalled mechanics swarm around a stationary jet, uniformed stewardesses waiting for the shuttle bus, a two-man team clearing out the rubbish.

'Smells like oil,' the cab driver said, and suddenly grinned. 'Just like in my country.'

Joe didn't reply. At the terminal the cab stopped, and Mr. Laszlo stepped out. Rolex, briefcase, tie with tie-pin; glasses, moustache, polished black shoes. He paid for the cab. He went inside the terminal, looked out for men in black. Didn't see them, but knew someone was there.

'Can I help you, sir?'

'I hope you can.' Mr. Laszlo smiled, put his hand on the desk, a heavy gold wedding band on his finger catching the electric light. 'I'd like a ticket to New York.'

The woman checked her folders, went through a list. 'I have a seat available on the next flight. That's in two hours.'

'That,' Mr. Laszlo said, 'would be perfect.'

-- but soon --

THEY WERE LOOKING out for him, but Joe wasn't there, and Richard "Ricky" Laszlo had nothing to do with the CPD, whoever or whatever they were. As he approached the plane, briefcase still in hand (empty but for three shiny-new *Vigilante* paperbacks he had picked up on Edgware Road, to replace the ones he had had to abandon at the hotel; the fourth one, *World Trade Center*, held in his other hand) a light rain was falling and as pale sunlight pierced through the drops he saw her, and stopped.

They stood under the metal plane. She said, 'I thought...' and stopped, and on an impulse he took her hand in his, and it was cold. 'At the Blue Note,' she said. 'You left. I...' Again, a silence punctuating her words. 'When will it end?' she said.

'I need to find him,' Joe said. 'I need to know.'

She said, 'Yes...' He covered her hands in his, trying to warm them. She felt very cold. She looked into his eyes. He wasn't sure because of the rain, but he thought she was crying. 'Stay with me,' she said.

'I...'

She inched her head, regarded him. When she smiled, it reached her eyes. 'I know,' she said. 'I want you to.' She was like a wild bird, there on his hand, ready to take off. 'I want you to know.'

She took her hand away. He let his fall to his sides. Above their heads the engines thrummed. A distant announcer sang the names of far-off cities. 'I have to get on the plane,' he said.

She said, 'Or you'll regret it?' and shook her head, wearing her smile like a veil. 'Maybe not today, but soon?'

All at once she made him uncomfortable. Her eyes were too bright, too knowing. Yet he feared letting her go, sensed how close she was to disappearing. 'I'll find him,' he said.

'And I will find you,' she said. 'I will always find you.' Then she turned away from him. She walked away in the rain, and for a long time he stared after her, long after she had disappeared between the drops.

Then he climbed the stairs onto the plane; it was only when he stepped into the air-controlled environment inside that he realised the once-new paperback in his hand had become damp and soggy from the rain, and as he took his seat he fanned the pages open in his lap, airing them as he stared out of the window onto the tarmac, searching for her, but she wasn't there.

-- a second invasion --

BAGHDAD HAD BURNED before.

On February 13, 1258, the Mongol army of Hulagu Khan swept into the city, looting, burning, and killing. Baghdad's Caliph, Al-Musta'sim Billah, was rolled in a carpet and trampled to death by Mongol troops, ensuring his blood, being royal, did not touch the ground. Palaces, mosques, hospitals and homes burned to the ground. The Grand Library was destroyed, and it was said the river Tigris ran black with spilled ink.

745 years later, it was invaded again.

This time they came with tanks; attack helicopters; fighter jets; smart bombs and guided missiles; a string of communication and surveillance satellites like a pearl necklace strung across the sky, in that thin membrane between Earth and space. They came to wage a war on terror, prompted by an attack thousands of miles away.

That attack had been, like a common modern-day fork, four-tined. Once forks themselves were the subject of a holy war. 'God in his wisdom,' wrote an unnamed member of the Catholic Church, 'has provided man with natural forks - his fingers. Therefore it is an insult to Him to substitute artificial metallic forks for them when eating.' Though this war was not about forks, the attack *was* carried out in the name of God. Four planes had been hijacked and made to crash, two of them into the tallest structures in the city of New York.

Almost 3000 people had died in that attack. The nineteen hijackers had also died.

Two years later, Iraq was invaded (for the second time in a decade) and its caliph, who was now called President, was taken prisoner and, later, executed. He was - terminated - in the appropriately-named Camp Justice in Kadhimiya, a north-eastern suburb of Baghdad. His last meal was chicken and rice, washed down with hot water and honey. He was killed with a rope around his neck at six o'clock in the morning.

The World Health Organization estimated that in the first three years of the invasion of Iraq, 151,000 people of the target population had been killed.

-- closing doors --

HE DIDN'T WANT to think about death. Outside the window, earth had given way to dark sky, sky to an impenetrable layer of cloud and, beyond that, dawn, giving way to empty night strewn with pinpricks of cold shivery star-lights, like holes in the canopy of a world. Going from London to New York was a sort of time travel, racing back into the night. The book was damp in his lap. The paper, already giving off that faint whiff of corruption from its cheap, pulpy pages. The seat was hard against his back. The cabin was in darkness, Joe's seat light the only one still shining. Outside the Earth revolved, slowly, irrevocably, as it hurtled through space at an unimaginable speed. Inside the cabin dinner had been served and cleared, and the smell of heated-up chicken still lingered, mixing, for Joe, with the smell of the book. Like the chicken, the book seemed already dead, its text warmed up unnecessarily. He tried to imagine what lay ahead for him, and found that he couldn't. He tried to picture the city of New York, but it seemed an absence in his mind, a place on the map that had only a hole to mark it. He realised he no longer knew what was true and what wasn't, where fiction began and reality ended. He felt unsettled in his seat, kept turning this way and that, trying to find comfort and failing. He put the book aside and pushed his way through the adjacent seats into the aisle, and made his way to the illuminated sign that meant the bathroom. He felt the floor of the plane through his socks, his toes clutching at the surface as if it were solid, immutable: it was not planes he feared, but the approaching ground.

He closeted himself inside the toilet cubicle, shutting the door behind him. Plastic fixtures, dim yellow lights: his face in the mirror looked like the face of a ghost, staring back at him. He sat down, high above the ocean. When he stared at the wall in front of him he saw that someone had scribbled a note on the light-brown surface, five lines, the handwriting unsteady, the black ink letters spilling up and down from their rows, the thing like an obscene epitaph left by person or persons unknown who would never now, could never now, be known.

As a child I tried to step between the drops
Now I close doors softly

Like a stranger who had wandered in, lost
Into his own home

And does not want to wake its occupier.

PART FIVE:
ESCAPE FROM NEW YORK

-- nothing to declare --

NEW YORK WAS a silent field of lighted butterflies, too numerous to count. Lights rose up into the skies, hovered over the shoreline, swamped out the stars. The captain said, 'Twenty minutes to landing.' Looking out of the window, Joe thought he could see other planes in the skies, circling at a distance from each other as they waited for permission to land.

Inside the immense hall of FDR, Joe lost his bearings for a moment. There was too much of everything there. Too much ceiling, too high above. Too many voices, too many people, bumping into each other like random particles in Brownian motion, thousands of individual stories that intersected for just one brief moment, touched and converged and tapered off in another directions. The floor was cold marble, scuffed by too many shoes. A hidden announcement system seemed never to fall quiet, calling passengers going to or arriving from Paris, Bangkok, Tehran, Moscow, Jerusalem, Peking, Beirut, Nairobi. There was that sense in the arrivals hall of an imperial impatience, tapping its foot, saying: this is the gateway of the world, now get on with it, but in an orderly fashion, please.

'Anything to declare?' The girl was pretty in her uniform. Joe wasn't sure what to say. He wanted to declare he was here to investigate a global conspiracy of mass murder; or say, perhaps, that he was trying to understand a war no one seemed to understand, not even those who were fighting it the hardest; or to explain about the ghosts that kept flickering at the corner of his eyes when they thought he wasn't looking. He said, 'No, nothing,' and gave her an apologetic smile, and she waved him through.

Luggage rolling and turning in an intricate loop... a brown leather bag; a metal carry case, the kind gangsters used to carry money in movies; a beaten-up black-and-brown suitcase with peeling stickers on its wide back that said its owners had visited the Grand Canyon, Yellowstone Park, the Natural History Museum and Graceland. Backpacks with Cyrillic address-tags. Carton boxes with Chinese characters running down the sides. An arrivals board clicking as its slats rotated: Phnom Penh, Damascus, Reykjavik, Baghdad, Kuala Lumpur, Luzon, Cairo, Mexico City, Johannesburg, Rome, Kunming: old cities and new, cities on hills and on planes, on rivers and seas, dots on a wide map each sending out threads of clear light that all came here, all terminated in this terminal, in this city on the edge of a continent, with threads going in all directions until a globe was filled with interlocking bands of light...

Outside the terminal he took a moment to lean against the wall and breathe, though he smelled cars more than anything else. He lit a cigarette. Above his head, planes took off into the skies. The earth seemed to thrum beneath him. FDR was chrome and glass and joyful arrogance.

'Help me,' someone said, and Joe shuddered once and was then very still. He couldn't tell quite when it started. He had the feeling that, even back at the airport in London, he had a sense of them. Shadows at the edge of sight, blurred silent figures, watching him, following him. *Fuzzy-wuzzies*. On the plane, when he came out of the toilet cubicle, in a seat that had been empty before: a young woman, only a girl really, staring up at him with mute enormous eyes – he could see the seat through her. And on the conveyor belt at the airport, amidst the luggage, there were cases and bags that belonged to no one, it seemed, that kept circling indefinitely, like planes overhead which will never now be granted permission to land...

'I can't,' he said. He didn't look, didn't want to see the speaker. He took a drag on the cigarette and went and hailed a taxi and got inside.

'Drive,' he said, and when the driver looked at him with a quizzical expression, Joe said, 'Just drive.'

-- artificial day --

LIGHTS AND PEOPLE and too-tall buildings... it was warm and dark inside the taxi, and smelled inexplicably of aniseed, covering a deeper lingering smell that was familiar. The driver glanced sideways, saw the paperback in Joe's hands and scowled. 'My nephew has that book,' he said. 'Listen to this. A bomb goes off downtown and the police arrest the Easter bunny, Santa Claus, the tooth fairy and Osama bin Laden. They put them in an identity parade and have a witness try to point out the perpetrator. Who does she pick?'

Joe said, 'I don't know.'

'Osama bin Laden,' the taxi driver said. 'Because the other three don't exist.' He scowled harder. 'I don't get it,' he said. Then: 'I told my nephew, I catch him reading this shit again I'll smack him.'

Joe just felt tired. 'Did it work?' he said.

The driver shook his head, slowly and with great deliberation, from side to side. 'No,' he said.

Joe was looking, not at the open book but at the single sheet of paper he had smoothed open between the pages. It was the paper he had found in Mike Longshott's correspondence. Like the taxi driver, he didn't get it either.

The paper read:

Conspiracies and Crime, Murder and Mayhem, Vengeance and **Valor** –
For the **First. Time. Ever!**
Only In **New York City** –

228

A Global **Gathering** of Like Minded **Minds**:

OsamaCon !!!

Where In The World Is Osama bin Laden ??

The shadowy **Vigilante**, the arch-criminal **master**mind, the **enemy** of Western Civilization?

Come and find out – if you **dare**!

Panels, lectures, family entertainment, dealer tables, art expo and costume competition!
An **all-you-can-eat** B.B.Q following the **parade** on Sunday!

Only $55 pre-registration, $65 at the door, The Hotel Kandahar, Lower Manhattan (does not include room price. 10% discount available for members registering early. Kids go half-price). To book dealer tables contact the organisers (*Mike Longshott Appreciation Society, Queens, New York*). Price negotiable.

Be **blown away** – only at the First Annual OsamaCon, coming **soon** –

And then the dates, hotel address and contact numbers, all crowded in at the bottom, as if shying away from the bold, mismatched writing above it.

'What's that?' the taxi driver said.

'This?' Joe said. He shook his head. 'I'm not sure,' he said, folding it closed again. 'Can you take me to the Hotel Kandahar, please?'

'Hotel what?' the driver said.

Joe gave him the address. The driver shrugged. 'You need a girl?' he said.

'No.'

'Everybody needs a girl,' the driver said. Joe said, 'I have one already...' though he wasn't sure he did. An image of the girl rose in his mind again, under the plane, just before it took off. I will find you, she had said. And so far she had...

'Dope?'

'I beg your pardon?'

'You need some dope? I got some Burmese stuff, make you see paradise.'

Under the aniseed, the familiar smell of opium. Joe said, 'Just drive.'

He sat back and closed his eyes against the city they were passing through. The driver drove. Silence like a spider's web shivered behind Joe's eyes.

It was coming up to morning, but New York had an artificial day lit up that was all of her own.

-- towers reaching for the sky --

'I'D LIKE A room.'

A burned-out light bulb in the ceiling fixture meant only a single light shone and the bulb was bare and hanging from its wire. A high-class dump. The man behind the high counter had the eyes of a rabbit – they moved so much it was impossible not to imagine him running from something. He looked as if he'd run for a long time and didn't know how to stop. He shrugged, open palms forward, did a small, strange shudder with his shoulders. 'I'm afraid we're full.'

Joe put down a wad of cash. The black credit card burned a hole in his pocket.

'But we might have something. Let me check.'

Joe put down another, thinner wedge of money. Machine-cut, printed in the US of A. Dead presidents stared up at the man in reception. 'Tenth floor,' the man said. The money disappeared. Perhaps he was an amateur magician.

There was a cut-out of Osama bin Laden, life-sized, at the entrance to the hotel. A wooden table and two folding chairs and a sign that said *Registration*. There was no one sitting there. The man at reception followed Joe's gaze and his eyes opened just a little wider and he said, 'Are you here for the convention?'

'Has it started yet?'

'Pre-registration was today – yesterday, I should say.' Outside, night – like a giant ape – had been defeated by morning's firepower and was toppled. There was no one else in reception, only there was, but Joe wasn't willing to admit it. Not just yet.

231

Only when he moved the shadows in the dusty corners of the room seemed to move with him, and shapes materialised only to resolve themselves into everyday objects when he focused on them. Maybe he was just tired.

He hoped so.

'Your key,' the man behind the reception desk said. Above his head a row of round clocks showed the time in Tokyo, Los Angeles, Kabul and Bombay as well as New York. Only, New York time was frozen at 8:46. 'When do they open?' Joe said, jerking his thumb at the empty desk by the door.

'A couple of hours.'

He didn't *feel* tired. He said, 'Do you have a bar?'

'Through there, but –'

Joe collected his key.

'When do you come off-shift?' he said.

The man shrugged and twitched. His pupils were dilated. 'I don't,' he said.

Joe shrugged and headed for the elevator. 'Go easy on that stuff,' he said. The shadows followed him with dry whispers.

In the room, he prepared a bath. The sound of the running water was soothing. Daylight seeped in through the window-frames. He turned off the water and went and sat down on the bed. He must have fallen asleep, because when he opened his eyes the light was much brighter and when he went to the bath the water was cold and the bubbles had gone, leaving only a film of murky perspiration on the surface of the water. He opened the windows and let in air, and the murmuring voices quieted down. He lit a cigarette and ran a fresh bath.

Outside the window, towers were reaching for the sky like Babylonian minarets. The bed had been made military-fashion; you could bounce a coin off it, if that was your idea of amusement. It wasn't Joe's. The bed looked undisturbed. It always did, even though he must have fallen asleep on it. Sleep, for Joe, was merely an absence.

A khaki-brown blanket was folded neatly and precisely over the bed with its edges tucked into the underside of the mattress. Joe looked out of the window again. He had the feeling that outside the window there should have been hover-cars, men in trilby hats and jet packs, spider-webs of passageways spreading out of the distant tops of the towers. There should have been women in silver suits taking in a show at the tri-vids before indulging in a spot of lunch, the kind that came in three-course pills, great big subservient robots trailing behind them. Instead there was a brown man in overalls collecting rubbish with a long stick outside an adult cinema, and the cars were halted, bumper-to-bumper, beside a traffic light that seemed to be stuck permanently on red. There was a siren in the distance. There was the sound of car horns, a door slamming, someone cursing loudly in American English. Joe shut the window and put out the cigarette and stripped, taking off tie and moustache and Richard "Ricky" Laszlo.

The bath water was warm and soapy. He lay with his head resting on the chipped white coating of the bath. His toes poked out of the water like a jagged reef exposed at low tide. With his ears under the line of the water it was very quiet. He thought – I could lie like this forever. He closed his eyes. No thought, no sound, no sight, no taste, no smell, no touch. For a moment there was no one there, just the empty bath, the water cooling at a rate of zero point one five degrees a minute.

Then flavour came back: ashy taste and airplane food and the phantom-taste of coffee, and Joe blinked and rose from the water, the water sliding off his skin like a benediction.

-- in the pages of a book --

THERE WERE TWO people, a man and a woman, seated behind the registration desk downstairs. The same man was still in reception, tired eyes looking far away. The Osama bin Laden cut-out stared at Joe as he walked past. It could have been looking at the same nothingness the man at reception was. Joe approached the registration desk.

'Here for the convention? Welcome, welcome.' The man had a beard that covered his face like a mile-a-minute vine in a thick and straggly jungle. He wore wire-rimmed glasses, smiled genially, wore a name badge that said, *Hi! My name is Gill.* The woman wore a flowered dress and drop earrings that shook when she moved her head. Her name, according to her badge, was Vivian.

'I would like' – Joe cleared his throat, which felt raw and disused – 'Yes. I would like to register?'

The woman smiled and pushed a sheet of paper towards him. 'Just fill this in, dear.' She had a thin transatlantic accent, a hint of County England diluted with Mid-Western *Américain*. 'Very glad to have you.'

'Am I the first one?' Joe said.

Gill looked shocked. 'Oh, no,' he said. 'There should be a good turnout.'

'People are still arriving, you see,' Vivian said. 'Most people register in advance –'

'The Mike Longshott Appreciation Society,' Gill said, pronouncing the capitals, 'has over thirty members.'

'We just *love* the Vigilante books, don't we, Gill,' Vivian

234

said. It wasn't really a question. Gill nodded. Joe half-expected paratroopers to fall from the quivering brambles of his beard. '*Love* them,' Gill said.

Something made Joe say, 'Why do you think that is?'

Vivian smiled. 'That's a *very* good question,' she said. 'Which, I think, is covered in the first panel tomorrow morning –'

'Eight thirty in the conference room,' Gill said, looking down at what must have been a schedule. 'But, if you ask me,' Vivian said, as if Gill had never spoken, and smiled and shook her head, 'it's escapism.'

'Oh, I don't know,' Gill said, and Vivian said, with a wave of her hand that may have been aimed at Gill, may have been aimed elsewhere, 'Gill takes it all very seriously. He's an amateur historian –'

'It's just, don't you think' – Gill said, then stopped, then smiled and shrugged; Joe decided the two had to be married – 'the question of *what if*. Right? What if the Cairo Conference of 1921 went ahead as planned, with Churchill and T.E. Lawrence and Gertrude Bell dividing up the Middle East for the British? What if they chose a Hashemite king to rule Iraq, and would that have led to a revolution in the nineteen fifties? Or, what if the French war in Indochina somehow led to American involvement in Vietnam? Or if the British held on to their colonies in Africa after the Second World War? You see' – he was in full steam now, his eyes shining like the headlamps of a speeding engine – 'the *Vigilante* series is full of this sort of thing. A series of simple decisions made in hotel rooms and offices that led to a completely different world. And also –'

'And also they're just good *escapist* fun,' Vivian said firmly, and Gill subsided beside her, giving an apologetic smile. 'To read about these horrible things and know they never happened, and when you're finished you can put down the book and take a deep breath and get on with your life. To know it's fiction –'

'Pulp fiction,' Gill said, and the two of them smiled at each other, 'and that's where all these *terrible* things should stay –'

'In the pages of a book.'

'And aren't we lucky that they are? That'll be sixty-five dollars.'

Joe handed over the completed form, fished cash out of his pocket. Vivian said, 'And here's your name tag.' Joe pinned it to his chest. *Hi! I'm Joe.*

'Will Mike Longshott be here?' he said. Vivian sighed and shook her head. 'He is so awfully *reclusive*,' she said, lowering her voice as if revealing a great secret. 'We tried to write to him, didn't we, Gill –'

'We did.'

'But he never answers.'

'Never answers.'

'I see,' Joe said. Behind him, he noticed to his surprise, a small queue had formed. 'Well, thank you again –'

'Thank *you*,' they both said. Their eyes were already on the next registrant. Joe nodded, once, and went in search of coffee.

-- what ifs --

OPERATION NORTHWOODS DID not, officially, exist. The proposal was submitted by L.L. Lemnitzer, then chairman of the United States Joint Chiefs of Staff, to his colleague the Secretary of Defence.

The subject: Justification for US military intervention in Cuba. The date: 13 March, 1962. The objective: Provide a brief but precise description of pretexts for military involvement on the island.

The *Annex to Appendix to Enclosure A* set out the plan in more detail.

///

2. A series of well coordinated incidents will be planned to take place in and around Guantanamo to give genuine appearance of being done by hostile Cuban forces.

  a. Incidents to establish a credible attack.

  1) Start rumours (many). Use clandestine radio.
  2) Land friendly Cubans in uniform "over-the-fence" to stage attack on base.
  3) Capture Cuban (friendly) saboteurs inside the base.

4) Start riots near the base main gate (friendly Cubans).

5) Blow up ammunition inside the base; start fires.

6) Burn aircraft on airbase (sabotage).

7) Lob mortar shells from outside of base into base.

8) Capture assault teams approaching from the sea.

9) Capture militia group which storms the base.

10) Sabotage ship in harbour; large fires - naphthalene.

11) Sink ship in harbour entrance. Conduct funerals for mock-victims.

b. United States would respond by executing offensive operations to secure water and power supplies, destroying artillery and mortar emplacements which threaten the base.

c. Commence large scale United States military operations.

3. A "Remember the Maine" incident could be arranged in several forms:

a. We could blow up a US ship in Guantanamo Bay and blame Cuba.

b. We could blow up a drone (unmanned) vessel anywhere in the Cuban waters... the US could follow up with an air/sea rescue operation covered by US fighters to "evacuate" remaining members of the non-existent crew. Casualty lists in US newspapers would cause a helpful wave of national indignation.

4. We could develop a Communist Cuban terror campaign in the Miami area, in other Florida cities and even in Washington. The terror campaign could be pointed at refugees seeking haven in the United States. We could sink a boatload of Cubans enroute to Florida (real or simulated). We could foster attempts on lives of Cuban refugees in the United States even to the extent of wounding in instances to be widely publicized. Exploding a few plastic bombs in carefully chosen spots, the arrest of Cuban agents and the release of prepared documents substantiating Cuban involvement, also would be helpful.

-- Osamaverse --

JOE DIDN'T KNOW what would be helpful or not. There were other people in the hotel dining room and most of them also had Osama bin Laden paperbacks next to them, and many of them seemed to know each other and were talking, like friends who haven't seen each other in a while and were busy resuming an interrupted conversation. Joe sipped at his coffee, lit a cigarette, people-watched. The room felt more crowded than it was. He tried to ignore that, tried to ignore the suddenly stifling air, the pressure in his chest that made it difficult to breathe. Voices came at him as if through water:

'...represents the renewing vitality of the barbarian horde as it storms the walls of Rome –'

'Sure, it's the reinvigoration of society – destruction before rebirth –'

'A reaction to Anglo-Saxon dominant philosophy – the failure of neo-imperialism –'

'...but is it crime or an act of war?'

'Depends on who's telling the story –' Laughter, a waitress carrying glasses of beer to a table, name tag different from the conventioneers': *Hi, I'm June.*

'Thank you, um, *June*,' two men with beards and hunting vests, clinking glasses – the waitress shrugged, put down their glasses on the table, departed for the bar.

Shadows in the corners of the room, shifting. Voices:

'They say he lives in an airplane hangar and has food delivered to him, the whole place is empty but for a desk and a typewriter right in the middle of all that space –'

'Writes like Hemingway, standing up –'

'I heard from Carl – do you remember Carl? – that he was in Oregon at a bookshop and he found some of the *Vigilante* paperbacks and they were *signed* –'

'*Bullshit.*'

'Signed, and he spoke to the man in the bookshop and he told him, he *told* him there was a man who came in once a month, never bought anything, but after he left all the Osama books were signed. He was dressed like a hunter and drove a pickup truck and he had a cabin in the woods, and –'

'*I* heard' – a new voice, a tall thin man with a stoop leaning into the conversation, mug of coffee unsteady in one hand – 'I heard he was living in the Far East, in Siam somewhere, in an old Buddhist temple in the jungle, all alone but for an old monk who taught him kung-fu, and when he isn't writing he meditates –'

A man at a nearby table, twisting his torso, putting thick arms on the table, saying: 'I heard he lives on a yacht that never comes to land, and he has an army of girls on board who follow his every command –'

'That's ridiculous' – from the thin man stooping –

'One girl follows him around with an ashtray and every time he ashes his cigarette she catches it before it can touch the floor –'

'Did you read what Bolan wrote in the *Osama Gazette* last month?'

The four men laughing. 'A woman!'

'Well, Mike Longshott is obviously a pseudonym –'

'It can't be a *woman*! The writing is clearly masculine –'

A red-faced man at the other end of the room, standing up abruptly. 'Hey! For your information –'

'Oh, hi, Bolan, didn't see you there –'

'I *said* Longshott is a woman, and I stand by that,' the red-faced man said.

'It's a long shot, Bolan...'

More laughter. Joe, thinking: The *Osama Gazette*?

He pushed his chair back, stood up. 'Excuse me,' he said. Four male faces turned towards him – reluctantly, it seemed to Joe. 'What's this *Osama Gazette*?'

The men exchanged glances. Clearly, their looks said, this was a stranger, an outsider in their midst. 'It's a *fanzine*,' one of the men in the hunting vests said.

'A what?'

'It's a small publication dedicated to a scholarly *discourse* of the Osamaverse.'

'The w – ?' he decided not to ask.

The man sighed. 'You can find copies in the dealers' room,' he said. 'It's already open.'

'Where's the dealers' room?'

'Out of here, go down the corridor past the elevator and it's the second door on your left.' He squinted myopically at Joe's name badge. 'Joe. Not seen you around before.'

Joe stared at him, and the bearded man stared back.

'Oh, I'm just a fan,' Joe said.

-- I heart Osama --

HE WALKED DOWN the corridor and the floor echoed underneath his feet. He tried to ignore the silent figures that stood against the walls, watching him with empty eyes. They were just light falling on dust, conjured by tiredness and caffeine, phantoms that should have been laid to rest in the light of day.

A notice on the door said, in large, spiky, hand-written letters, *Dealers' Room*. He opened the door and stepped in.

Tables were arranged with their sides touching each other. There were two rows. The room had the half-festive, half-consecrated feel of a Sunday jumble sale. Joe passed a row of dangling T-shirts. One showed two towers and a flying plane; another had the by-now-familiar face of Osama bin Laden, staring out of 100% cotton. One displayed an "I," followed by a heart, then Osama. I heart Osama. 'They're available in black, blue, red and white,' a woman told him as he passed. 'Medium, large and extra-large.'

Then next table had buttons. They repeated the same motifs. The next one had dolls. Numerous Bin Ladens stared at Joe with black button eyes, their soft plush-toy hands limpid at their sides. The next one, books: Medusa Press titles. He picked up one of Countess Szu Szu's books, leafed through it idly, put it down.

On the next table, Osama pillows. A sign said, *Go to bed with the man from your dreams*. But Joe never dreamed any more.

He found what he was looking for at the end of the row. A solitary man with the same unkempt look as the others he'd seen at the bar was sitting behind a nearly-empty table, making a meal of his nails. He looked up when Joe approached. His name-tag said *Hi! I'm Theo.*

'Hi,' he said. Then he went back to what remained of his nails.

Joe picked up a publication.

The Osama Poems.

By Theodore Moon.

When he leafed to the title page he noticed it was signed, the blue ink smudged across the page. He said, 'You?'

The man nodded without looking up, named a price. Joe looked at the first page.

People fall down like leaves in autumn
The sky is a haze of smoke, burning red.
I see you, on the far shore of sleep
In a place I cannot follow you to
And can never now reach.

He put the book down. There were some cheaply-printed, staple-bound booklets on the table, mimeographed runny blue on dirty white. He picked one up. A sense of futility flooded him. There would be no answers here.

The Osama Gazette, Volume One, Issue 3. A man with a magnifying glass on the cover; through the glass, a miniature city, engulfed in smoke. He looked at the table of contents. *Oil and ideology in the Osamaverse. Fictional Wars #2: Afghanistan. Terrorist, Freedom Fighter or Soldier? Osama bin Laden as a Liminal Figure.* He didn't even know what that meant. *The Twentieth Hijacker Hypothesis.*

Put it down. Yet another publication. *Osamaverse_Stories.* On the cover a man with a portable grenade launcher hiding behind rocks, high in the mountains, a helicopter flying overhead. *The Fifth Plane, by Theodore Moon. Love in the Desert, by Vivian Johnson. A Cause Worth Dying For, by L.L. Norton.*

'You're going to buy, or you're just going to read them here?'

Joe put down the slim book. 'Just browsing,' he said, and wiped his hand, surreptitiously, against his side. He turned to leave. There were no answers there. He opened the door and stepped into the corridor outside, and as he walked down it he could no longer ignore them, could no longer pretend they were not there.

The answers were there, had always been there, only waiting for him to finally face them.

The refugees lined the silent corridor. There were men there, and women, and children, and they were the colours of shadows and dusk. They stared at him and their lips moved, though no sound escaped. He felt his heart shudder like an ill bird, straining against the bars of his body. He walked down the corridor and they parted before him, like leaves in the fall. They were many. Too many. He turned his head, left, right, and they looked back at him with empty faces.

Only one was familiar. He stopped, stared. Black suit, black tie, grey hair – 'Oh, shit.' He turned to run, but there was nowhere left to run. A hand on his shoulder – solid, real. 'Joe.'

He turned. The man with grey hair looked at him, head tilted to one side. 'I told you not to open that door...' he said. He said it softly. He seemed sad. Then he made a minute motion with his head and Joe started to turn, could hear them behind him, knew it was too late even as he –

'Don't knock him out,' the man with grey hair said. Something dark and velvety fell over Joe's head, blocking out the light, muffling sound. He was grabbed from behind, his legs kicked out from under him. He fell, was caught. Was lifted.

He heard someone saying, 'What's going on?' The man with grey hair replying, 'CPD.' Then he was carried, lowered carefully into a small, enclosed space. Something closed shut above him. He thought – the trunk of a car. He heard an engine start off, the vibrations thrumming through the hold. Then the car was moving; it took him with it.

-- dark Arabica --

THE DARKNESS TASTED like dark Arabica. There was a faint whirring sound far away, like a coffee grinder switched on, turning small roasted beans into a soft dark powder like a cloud-wrapped night. There was peace in that darkness. He was tied to a chair. He had been on that chair for some time. His hands and feet were tied to the chair. There was a sack over his head. It was very hot inside the sack. There were small holes cut into the cloth to let in air. The air tasted unused. The rope, where his hands were tied, cut into his skin. He needed, badly, to pee. His bladder was like a nuclear reactor threatening to go off, unstable isotopes excitable, protective shields decaying. But somehow he felt distanced from his body. Somehow none of the reports sluggishly returning to his brain – the pain in the wrists, loss of feeling in left leg, bladder pressure, lungs rattling like an empty can – none of these affected him. There was drool in the corners of his mouth. When he giggled it came out as a tiny warbling sound through the spit, the sound of a drowning bird trying to sing through water. There was a cold numb feeling in his neck where there had been a short, sharp pain earlier.

Sometimes the prisoner tried to sing to himself. The songs had no discernible lyrics, nor, if only the prisoner had given it thought, any tunes. They could more accurately have been described as a humming, a low, long, constant thrum that could have come from hidden pipes behind the walls, from rows of moving cars somewhere beyond the walls, from the electric charge of storm clouds rubbing against each other in the place where sky-scrapers met the sky.

Sometimes the darkness that bound him seemed to expand outwards, into an infinite bubble of space, became a silent prehistoric sea through which he swam, as light as loose leaves, though there was never any shore in sight. Sometimes it constricted about him, and those were the bad times, when the darkness shrunk into a tight, hard ball, like the compacted load of a dung beetle, and he was trapped inside it, unable to breathe, his body defined in sharp lines of bright-light pain, in landing strips marking the drunken flight paths of the fat dung beetles. And sometimes it was as if the darkness was a vast abyss, and he was standing on a precipice of black granite above it, looking down, and a word came and floated up at him from that impenetrable vastness, like the name of a world beyond the world, a reality beyond reality, accessible to him only if he jumped. The word was Nangilima; which seemed a nonsense sound to him, like Heaven. It was a made-up word, or perhaps a name heard once and then forgotten, the memory hiding like a dormouse in the recesses of his mind until now, hinting at a world beyond; if only he could fly.

He couldn't jump. Unseen wires held him suspended above the abyss, and though he pulled at them and thrashed and raged, they wouldn't break. Then there were more and more periods of grey, patches of nothingness eating at his world, growing bigger, lasting longer, times in which he was nowhere and was nothing, but even those went away eventually and the world shrank and there was pain again, a little at first but steadily growing, the world shrinking around him and over his face. It smelled of dark Arabica.

-- clear and present danger --

LIGHT HURT HIS eyes. The room seemed to move around him, wouldn't stand still. He tried to fix his eyes on one spot but as soon as he did the room rotated away in an anti-clockwise direction. His hands felt very light. They were rising up of their own accord. 'Give him a moment,' the man with the grey hair said. Joe tried to focus on him, but the man was spinning away with the room. Maybe they were in one of those rotating restaurants, Joe thought. Only there were no windows here, and no tables, and no diners, and the walls were stained in fantastical shapes the colour of rust. There was a pair of shoes beside him, polished, meeting dark pressed trousers. He leaned towards them.

'Son of a –' He heard someone shout, felt something hard connect with the back of his head. Pain again, but all he could do was open his mouth wider, the blood pounding in his head like a jungle beat, as he spewed out a thin jet of foul water onto the floor. He heard the grey haired man's chuckle, saw one black shoe walking away, leaving footprints of sick behind it. 'You'll feel better in a minute,' the man with the grey hair said. Joe rather doubted it. He dry-retched; there was nothing left to spew.

'There's a basin to your right,' the man said. Joe turned his head, blinked sweat away. His eyes slowly focused. There was a concrete toilet hole and a concrete sink and both were decorated with the same rusty stains. He pushed himself up; staggered; ignored the man's 'Take it easy, now'; and dragged himself to the sink. The water tasted cool. Its touch on his face hurt, but only for a moment. There was no mirror. He was not unhappy about the fact. The pressure on his bladder returned, multiplied. Suddenly it seemed the most important thing in the world. His hands shook as he –

'There's nothing like a good piss, is there,' the man with the grey hair said.

Joe ignored him. He still felt divorced from his body, though the sensation was fading. It was like putting on a suit that had sat in the closet for a while. It took time before you stopped noticing it. When he was done, he washed his face again. There was a metallic taste in his mouth. Leaning on the basin with both hands, he turned his head and looked at the man from the CPD.

Silence stretched between them like the moment between two chess players before a check. Or perhaps it was a checkmate. Joe wasn't entirely sure. He felt pretty beat-up. He didn't think chess players usually kidnapped and drugged each other. When he thought about it, chess seemed like a lousy metaphor. The silence, however, stretched. It hung in the air like a delicate kite, assembled with paper and glue and hope, needing only a tiny breath of air to shatter it and send it tumbling. It seemed a shame to spoil it with words.

'Cigarette?' the man from the CPD said, proffering a pack.

Joe shook his head, though the movement made him nauseous. 'I quit,' he said. The man shrugged and returned the pack to his pocket. Joe stood up, stretched slowly. Aches alternated with numbness, his body a chequered map of opposing states. He patted himself, found a pack of cigarettes, crumpled, and his lighter. Shook one free, put it in his mouth, lit up.

'You said –' the man with the grey hair said.

'I changed my mind.' He blew out smoke. A smile left the man's face. It looked like it had just packed up its bag and moved out for the winter. It didn't look like it was set to return any time soon.

'How do you like it?' the man said. His gesture swept over the room. Besides the basin and the toilet, there was the chair Joe had been tied to and a narrow bed with a grey blanket and a pillow the shape of a brick and the colour of a pumice stone.

'I've seen worse,' Joe said. 'Don't think much of the management, though.'

'Get used to it,' the man said.

Joe shrugged.

'I did warn you,' the man with the grey hair said. There almost seemed to be an apologetic note in his voice; it could have just been an approaching cold.

'Something about not opening doors, right?' Joe said.

It was the man's turn to shrug. 'Too late for that,' he said.

Joe sat down on the edge of the bed. The thin mattress felt like a plank of wood. He dribbled smoke, tapped ashed on to the floor. 'What's the CPD?' he said.

'A committee,' the man said.

'A committee,' Joe said.

'Yes.'

'I see.' He didn't.

'It is a bi-partisan committee on the Present Danger.' The capitals felt as heavy as lead weights. 'It was set up to identify and counter the clear and present danger facing our country's peace.'

'What if there is no clear and present danger?' Joe said. The man with grey hair shook his head. 'There is always a clear and present danger,' he said. 'And right now, it's you.'

'Me? I'm only one man.'

'John Wilkes Booth was only one man,' the man from the CPD said. 'But no, not you specifically. You, plural.'

Joe's cigarette had burned down to a stub. He let it fall to the floor. A look of distaste crossed the man's face. 'Refugees,' he said. 'Fuzzy-wuzzies. Ghosts. Whatever.' He looked at Joe steadily. 'You shouldn't be here,' he said. 'You should not have come.'

The silence was back between them, a flat trampoline, needing only the smallest weight to fall to upset its perfect stillness. The man from the CPD said, 'This is not your place.'

Joe sat back on the bed, his back against the wall. He regarded the man from the CPD through half-closed eyes. The words seemed to come from a long way down, somewhere deep inside him. 'Maybe we had nowhere else to go,' he said.

'I'm sorry,' the man from the CPD said. 'I really am.'

'So am I,' Joe said. It felt as if he spoke into a vast and empty chasm, his words falling like pieces of torn paper down into nothing.

The man from the CPD nodded his head, once. Then he walked out of the cell and closed the door behind him. Joe heard locks slide into place.

Then there was only a solitary silence.

-- cell --

TIME DID NOT exist here. Twice a day a grille would open in the door and a tray would be pushed through. The tray was made of metal, with three cavities forming the shape of a cross. There was food on the tray and water in the basin. The prisoner drank the water and washed himself in it, splashing it onto his armpits, over his face, like a man with a long stop-over at an airport. The food had a chemical aftertaste. When he used the toilet the cell stank. After a while the prisoner stopped noticing the smell.

His thoughts in that time of solitary confinement were not quite thoughts. They were fragments, like a jigsaw puzzle made of torn-up photos all mixed up together. They never seemed to fit. There were memories in there but he could no longer tell which had been real, which hadn't. There was, for instance, a man in a beaver hat, creeping around with a lantern held high in his hand. Bits of dialogue from a silent film's title card, shining-white floating over black screen: *You mean a ghost?*

Not a ghost. Worse...

There was a girl with slightly-slanted eyes and brown hair and pinned-back, pointed ears, but she had no name. There was an airport, fog, a plane waiting to take off. They were not quite dreams, because he never dreamed any more. They were just the fragments of snapshots assembled from somewhere, somewhen else. The plane was going to a land over the rainbow. The girl was getting on the plane. There was an argument. He had on the wide-brimmed hat he'd bought in Paris and lost somewhere on the way.

You must get on that plane, he kept saying. You must get on the plane. She called his name, but it wasn't his name. Maybe not today, he kept saying. Maybe not today.

Sometimes the door would open and they would come in. At first he fought them, but they always overpowered him, easily, and then there would be the quick cold pain in his neck where the carotid artery was and then the numbness. Most of the time he didn't know what they did. Sometimes they stripped him, gloved hands prodded and poked and measured. Sometimes they stripped him and took photos. Sometimes he was back in the chair and there were questions. The man with the grey hair was back, standing with his back to the wall, his face in silhouette. He was asking questions about what the people in the Hotel Kandahar called the Osamaverse. It was like an endless quiz about Mike Longshott's novels. The prisoner said, 'I don't know,' until it became a mantra, releasing him from imprisonment, so that while his body was still there his mind was far away, hovering over the abyss where the next world was, or the next, or the next. 'Why don't you arrest him?' he said once.

'Arrest who?' the man with the grey hair said.

'Longshott.'

The man said something about containable risks, and managing information distribution. The prisoner took it to mean they didn't know where Longshott was. 'We could shut down his publisher,' the man from the CPD pointed out. Sometimes it was as if he were inside the prisoner's head. The prisoner said, 'Why don't you?'

'He's more useful this way,' the man from the CPD said.

Sometimes they stuck needles inside him, drew blood. Sometimes they attached electrodes to his temples, to his chest, took his pulse, measured his heart beat, his brain waves, the phrenological proportions of his skull.

'Tell me the truth, Doc,' the prisoner once said. 'Give it to me straight. Am I going to live?'

The man with the grey hair shook his head with slow, precise movements. 'You're already dead,' he said tiredly. 'You just don't know it yet.'

But the prisoner did. The prisoner drifted in the blackness that wasn't sleep, and as he did, he dreamed of doors in films.

-- doors in films --

ALWAYS, THEY WERE asking him questions. The questions made no sense to the prisoner. The questions were: 'How do cell phones work? What is an iPod? What is in Area 51?' The prisoner didn't know the answers to these questions. They asked him: 'How do you make a computer the size of a briefcase? What is the meaning of flash mobs and how do you control them? What is DRM? What is Asian fusion? Is it nuclear technology?'

There was some confusion as to that last point, but the prisoner couldn't enlighten them.

'What is Star Wars?' They had been very worried about that one.

He understood from them that he was not the first refugee they had interviewed this way. But he had no answers.

Not even for – *especially* not for – himself.

Who was he? Where had he come from? Increasingly, the prisoner felt this world fading away around the corners while he floated in the great peaceful darkness. More and more it seemed to him there were other voices there, the silence broken by half-whispers and mutterings, mumbling, singing, voices etching words into the darkness as if they could leave them there forever.

But they always pulled him back: measuring his sweat secretion, his blood properties, his pupils, his hair, his fingernails, his body temperature inside and out, and they kept asking him questions.

'What is a modem? Who is James Bond? What are smart cars? What is Al-Jazeera?'

They had been very worried about that last one, too.

Sometimes they were gone, just like that, fleeting from the edges of his cell like ghosts, fading away like mist, and he was alone. Twice a day a grille would open in the door and a tray would be pushed through. There was food on the tray and water in the basin. The prisoner drank the water, but he no longer washed. The water tasted like cough medicine. He would ask himself questions. Where do you come from? Where are you going? What is your name? When he pictured the girl he felt better, then worse. She had moved her hand over his, and there was something terribly intimate and familiar about the gesture.

'I will find you,' she had said. 'I will always find you.'

But here there was no motion of light in water. The girl was as barred from the prisoner's cell as the future is inexorably barred from the past. There was only the one door, and it led nowhere. He would study the stains on the walls, searching for patterns in the way they stretched and shrivelled like pulsating, living things. He could see faces in them, clouds, typewriters, mountains. He thought about doors in film.

They were like the *fabriques* in Parc Monceau. Films were constructed landscapes, a fakery made up of the torn pieces of differing locations. A door opened on the outside of a building, in a movie, and it led – more often than not – not into the inside of the building, but somewhere else. There were transitions in film, smoothed over, made seamless, but they were transitions nevertheless, a shortcut through both space and time. Opening a door in film was like prying open a transdimensional gate: it could lead anywhere, everywhere. It was a realisation the prisoner shied from.

More and more the voices crystallized, like a signal strengthening on a wireless radio set. They whispered, shouted, cried, laughed. They jabbered and muttered and mumbled and yelled, their constant babble invading the darkness. He couldn't shut them out.

And more questions. He couldn't shut those out either. 'Describe a stealth bomber. Describe smart bombs. How does a wireless network operate? What do Scud missiles look like? What is Nintendo? What is a Shenzhou-5?'

'Where is Mike Longshott?' the prisoner said. More and more that became his focus, the lode-star to which he could pin the shreds of himself.

'There is no Mike Longshott.'

But he knew they were lying.

Finding Mike Longshott gave him his purpose back. He began to rebuild the detective out of the floating fragments loose in the darkness. He began to map a landscape, a vista of *fabriques*.

'What is your name?' they kept asking him in interrogation. 'What was your name?'

'Joe,' the prisoner whispered. 'Joe.'

'There is no Joe.'

But he knew they were lying.

Then came a time when no one came, and he was left alone in the cell. Though the darkness abated a little, the voices were still there. They sounded louder in the confines of the cell. Mike Longshott, the prisoner thought. And the thought brought with it clarity. He was a detective, and this was his case. He was a detective. In the top drawer of the desk in his office there was an illegal knockoff Smith & Wesson .38, and a bottle of Johnny Walker Red Label: half-empty or half-full, depending.

The voices whispered advice. They were not ready to move on. He thought he recognised familiar voices in the babble, but couldn't be sure. He thought about doors in films. If you opened a door in a fabricated landscape, it could lead you anywhere you wanted to go. But he was afraid of opening the door.

-- yellow-sun brightness --

IN HIS CELL, the prisoner prepared. He was accompanied now
by the voices of the dead, whispering to him, urging him on. He
wished he could shut them within the pages of a book. In the
stains on the walls he now saw faces, nothing but faces staring
back at him. 'Longshott,' he said out loud, tasting the name.
The shadows murmured assent. The prisoner knew what he
was, but didn't know who. He stared at the door, and the door
stared back. He put his hand against its metal surface and it
was warm. There was a long jagged scratch in the grey paint at
the prisoner's waist level. The door had no handle. 'Osama,' he
said, tasting this word, too, like a strange wine, with hints of
acidity and some rust. 'Osama bin Laden.'

The shadows hissed, like puppets in a theatre. I'm ready,
the prisoner thought. He thought of the girl. He pictured
mountains. He undressed slowly: at some point his clothes had
gone, and he was given a prisoner's uniform, blood-orange,
beltless, and he shelled it off with relief and stood there naked,
and with both his hands flat against the surface of the door, he
pushed.

The voices grew in pitch and agitation. Yellow light sipped
under the door, in the process whitening. He thought he could
feel a wind, cold and clean: a mountain wind, flowing and then
surging through the edges of the door. He pushed, and the white
light turned brighter, a yellow-sun brightness, and its warmth
was on his naked skin. He pushed and the door opened, or
perhaps disappeared, and the voices rose into an unbearable
crescendo. For a long moment the prisoner just stood there,

looking out. He thought about freedom. It was what you had when you had nothing left to lose. He stared at the rectangle of bright light and for a moment it was quiet. The voices had fled ahead of him, waited for him on the other side.

The prisoner put his hands against the rectangle of light, testing it. There was no resistance. He could sense the waiting voices. The prisoner shivered, once, and was still.

Joe stepped through the door.

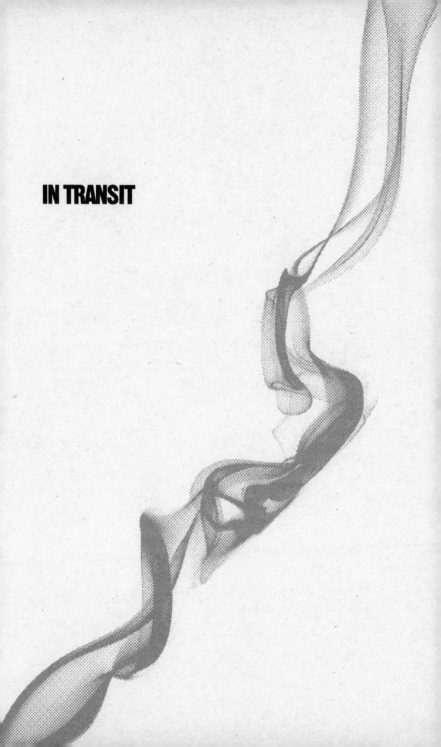

IN TRANSIT

-- ghost stories --

THERE WAS A bluejay outside my window that morning. Its crest was fully raised, suggesting it was excited, or it was being aggressive. They're aggressive birds, the bluejays. They're tough, adaptable, and they've been colonizing new habitats for decades. They like bright shiny objects, like coins, and have a reputation, not entirely deserved, for raiding other birds' nests, and stealing eggs and hatchlings, even the nests themselves. They are very pretty birds, the bluejays. I think this one was a male. I peered at it through the glass and it looked back at me, and the sun streamed in through the window and it looked like it was going to be a beautiful day. I was up early because I had to go to the airport. The colour of a bluejay comes not from pigmentation but from the special structure of its feathers. If you crush the feather, the blue will slowly fade as the structure of the feather is destroyed. I left bed without waking my wife and went downstairs to the kitchen. I put on the coffee and while I waited I looked through my vinyl records and finally put on Duke Ellington's *Mood Indigo*, Duke on piano, Joe Nanton on trombone, Whetsol on the trumpet, Bigard on clarinet, Fred Guy on banjo, Braud on bass and Sonny Greer on drums. I'd bought that album when I was a kid, when they still had vinyl in every shop, and I knew every groove and every scratch on that old record. I poured myself some coffee and listened to Duke Ellington and saw that the bluejay had followed me down to the kitchen and was chattering at me through the window. When I had finished the coffee I went back upstairs, the notes of the piano following me as I climbed, and I got dressed and brushed my teeth and picked up my suitcase, which was already packed. My wife turned over on her back and opened her eyes and gave me a sleepy smile and I bent down and kissed her, and she turned around and went back to sleep. I wish, now, I'd told her I loved her. I went downstairs and put away the record, slipping it into its sleeve carefully and placing it with the others. Before I left, I trailed my hand over the records, absent-mindedly. When I went outside I could no longer see the bluejay. I drove to the airport with my window half-open. I could smell pancakes from a diner further down the street. I got to the airport, left the car in the car-park and went into the terminal building. I had to go to Los Angeles for a meeting, and as I sat on the plane waiting for it to leave I made notes on a notepad, things I was going to say, but mostly just doodling.

THE REASON I was on the bus that day is, there was a lot of confusion around King's Cross, they said there was a power failure, to be honest no one knew what was going on. We were evacuated out from the tube to Euston Bus Station and it was like a sea of nervous, irritable people, too many bodies all together in a crowd, trying to get to work, pushing, and the buses crawling into the station like red-shelled snails sick with a summer cold. I was already late and I had a presentation to give that day and so I pushed my way to the bus and somehow managed to get a seat – I was sitting on the upper deck, by the window, looking out on the station. I noticed one boy detach himself from the crowd, moving away into a relatively quiet area, where he stood and pulled out a packet of cigarettes. He had wavy brown hair and wore earphones and as he smoked he nodded his head in time with the music – I remember wondering what album he was listening too, and also trying to see his eyes. For just a moment, as the bus was pulling out of the station, he looked up, and I think he saw me, we were looking at each other, and he smiled. He had a nice smile. For just a moment I had this crazy notion of getting off the bus, pushing out and through all the waiting people, go up to this guy, say something, I don't know what. Maybe just smile, and bum a cigarette. Maybe ask him what the time was, or if he wanted to go get a coffee. Something. But I never do things like that, and anyway the bus was pulling out of the station, and the guy was looking elsewhere and I sat back and when I looked through the window again, he was gone.

I LIKED TO come to Dahab in April, when Europe was still cold and only beginning to show signs of spring, but the Sinai was hot and dry and beautiful. I liked to sit on the cushions in the beach-front restaurants and smoke a sheesha-pipe and look out on the Red Sea. I loved to sit there at dusk, when there's a kind of hush over everything, and watch the sunset with my shades on. I came to Dahab every year, even after the bombings in Ras-el-Shitan, even after the bombings in Sharm the year after. You can't stop living your life. And it's been quieter there, but you still got the tourists, they came from all over. I've been coming to the Sinai for years. There is no heat like it, not anywhere. The sun is so strong there, and the light suffuses everything with the quality of old, fine clay, making objects seem opaque and fragile. And the hash is good. And I was sitting in the restaurant and thinking about what to order, thinking about a dip of smoky-flavoured roasted aubergines, anticipating the taste of the food on my tongue even before I voiced it, when it happened.

THE BLAST CAME like a thunderstorm in a bay, when the sound rolls and continues to roll, echoing from one shore to the other. I was on a bus from Ugi. It stopped outside the American embassy. I saw a truck stop outside the embassy. I saw a man step out. I saw him swing his arm and heard a popping sound. The last thing I remember seeing is the window crumbling. It moved towards me. It was like being in the sea, the way the current used to wash over me when I was a girl. I must have been thrown back. I put my hand to my mouth and realised I had no teeth. I touched my eyes, but there was nothing there. I didn't feel pain, but I remember worrying about my hair. I tried to touch my hair and couldn't feel it. I was going to get it done that afternoon in a saloon on Ngara Road.

ASSES AND ELBOWS. It was asses and elbows in there. The call came in and we got on the rig, and as we're driving down, the kid in the back – the proby – he said it was an attack. I didn't know what it was, at that time. I don't think anyone really knew. When we got to the building and looked up it was, like, uh – arms and legs, waving – they were jumpers. There was a lot of smoke, a lot of damage in the lobby. The – there were a lot of jumpers. We went into the building, started climbing up the stairs. Single file. After a dozen floors we started taking breaks, every four. Four floors. We made it to the – the thirty-third? Thirty-fourth floor? – people were coming down the stairs, helping each other down, injuries everywhere – I was with my hands on my knees, taking in air, we were talking about hooking up with another company to get up there, all the while there's a throbbing passing through the building, like the sound of a train as it approaches the platform, growing in intensity. Then someone came on the radio, said, 'Drop everything and get out.' He said it a couple of times. We were moving out, when there was a – I don't know how to describe that sound – the ceiling was collapsing, and I remember looking up. That's what I remember. Looking up, and suddenly not seeing anything.

IT WAS THREE days to the elections, it was in the paper that morning, and I stopped on my way to the station for a cup of *cortado*, easy on the milk, leafed through the paper. It looked like it was going to be a nice day. I was thinking – tomorrow's Friday already. I caught the *cercanías* at more or less my usual time. I was going to Atocha, had to change there. It was packed on the train, it always is in rush hour, but I got a seat and was reading the paper, really not paying much attention to anyone around me. I was going to take my wife for dinner that evening, it was our anniversary, and I was looking through the restaurant listings, trying to decide on a good restaurant, what sort of food to order. That was the last thing I remember thinking – what did I want to have for dinner that evening with my wife.

IT PICKED ME up and I went flying through the air. I hit a wall. I remember thinking – this is silly – I remember thinking about red Indians. Like in the Westerns. Red Indians, with war paint over their faces. I... I touched my face, but my jaw was gone. I heard an American woman say, 'Please help, please help my kids,' and I heard another woman shout, 'George, can you help me?' I didn't know who George was. There was a... there was a hand lying on the floor. Just a hand. It had a ring on its wedding finger. I tried to move then, but realised that I couldn't. Something was holding me down. I could hear people, but it all seemed to come from far away. I... I became very thirsty. I didn't feel the pain at first, I guess I was in shock, but it crept over me, slowly, and then I was screaming too, but I don't know if anyone heard me. I remember crying. It became very dark. I don't know how much time passed. Then there were men calling to me, telling me to hold on, and I could hear them, and I tried to talk back but I don't know that I could speak, by then. I heard them pulling someone out and she was alive. I remember being really happy then. Then there wasn't much pain any more, and the voices all faded away, little by little. Then there was no pain at all. I remember thinking that was lucky.

*   *   *

THE PAIN... THE pain was like a boiling sea across my skin. I never knew I had so much skin. I never knew it could hurt so much. I was screaming, begging them to kill me. There were flames eating my flesh, eating me. I couldn't see. I just kept begging them, begging them to kill me. Then I couldn't even think, not in words, all there was was pain, a kind of torture I couldn't stop, I couldn't make it stop, there was fire, fire everywhere. Then there was a sting, something bit me, and the pain began to go away – I don't know how to describe it. The pain went away and I heard someone say, 'The morphine should do it,' and the world constricted, from hell into a hospital bed, and I wasn't in pain any more. It was the best feeling in the world, that lack of pain. I just lay there, and I was so relieved. Then I fell asleep. At least, I think I did.

THERE WAS A heart-shaped stain on the back of the seat in front of me. It was hard to breathe. There was a heavy sick smell where people had been puking. I had a window seat. I looked out of the window. I had my fist in my mouth and was biting on it, so hard I drew blood. I heard someone talking on the phone, talking softly. 'It's getting bad, dad,' he said. There was a child, a girl, and she was crying. I tried not to think about the dead stewardess. They'd stabbed her. I looked out of the window. The sky was so blue. New York was beautiful below. I had always liked flying, before. I tried to shut out the screams. I could feel us descending, and without thinking I popped my ears, like I always do. I popped my ears. I don't know why I did that. I could see the towers out of the window. My left hand was resting on the windowsill. My right was still in my mouth. One of the towers was burning. Someone said, 'Oh, my God, oh, my God,' over and over. The towers came closer, very quickly. Then there was a noise, like a thousand bones, breaking.

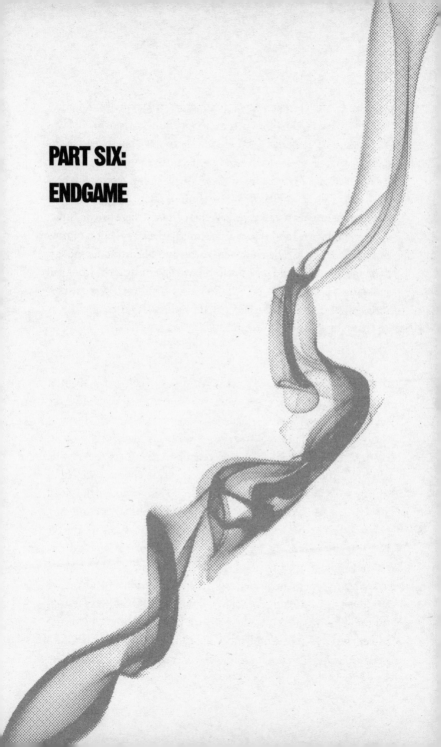

PART SIX:
ENDGAME

-- postcards --

HE CAME TO in a quiet street and was violently sick on his shoes. Only when it was done did he straighten up. There was a queasy feeling in his stomach, a turbulence, a rough sea heaving this way and that in a storm. He puked again, almost daintily, missing the tips of his shoes, a puddle of stomach fluid that was almost clear water seeping into the hard, dry ground below. When he straightened up for the second time he wiped his mouth with the back of his hand, feeling his throat burn with the ejected acid. He took off his hat and patted it, raising a tiny storm of dust.

Joe, the dusty street, the puddle of steaming sick at his feet. There were low-lying houses on either side, small gardens, a few old-fashioned boxed cars parked haphazardly on the side of the road. Joe examined himself. The shoes were leather, soft and worn and brown, and were very comfortable, as if they had been worn by him for a long time. Trousers, a light shirt already beginning to stain with sweat from the heat. He turned the hat over in his hands. It was the wide-brimmed hat he'd bought in Paris, and which he had thought gone. When he looked up, over the roofs of the houses, he could see the mountains rising in the distance, shrouded in clouds. A whole world seemed to be hidden beyond them, just out of reach. He looked down the dusty road and his hands fell to his sides, and for one moment he expected to find two pistols there, strapped to his belt, but there was nothing there and he felt a disappointment he couldn't, had he been asked to put it into words, been able to explain.

The voices had quieted around him. The sun was high in the sky, and there were few shadows. He walked down the road and his feet raised tiny dust-devils with each step. The ground was a desert brown and so were the houses.

The mountains dominated his view. He felt both attracted and repelled by them, as if they hid within their enormous quietude a multitude of secrets, that he would have liked to know and would have been afraid of had they been revealed. He came to a main road. There was a mosque in the distance, minarets rising into the impossibly-bright sky. He passed by a school where children in white shirts played in a yard, pushing and shouting and laughing. Across the road from the school was a shop; he went inside and silently purchased a packet of cigarettes, discovering money in his pocket. The money was inscribed in a cursive script he didn't recognise. So were the cigarettes. 'What is it?' he asked, in English, pointing at the writing, and the seller gave him a bemused look, reserved for tourists everywhere, and said, 'Pashto.'

He stepped out into the glare of the sunlight and lit a cigarette.

All at once the enormity of what had happened hit him, and he sagged against the dusty brown wall, his hand resting against the warm material, finding purchase and solidity in its existence. He wasn't sure what had happened. It all seemed like a bad dream. There was a book he had liked, once, about a girl falling through a hole into a subterranean world that slowly grew more and more into a nightmare. But when the girl could not take it any more, just as she was being attacked by a pack of sentient playing cards, she faced the unreality of her situation and woke up. It had all been just a dream.

Joe wished it had all been just a dream. To think of planes crashing into impossibly-tall towers, of bombs taking out eyes and teeth and fingers, of a silent, secret war he didn't understand, was to think of fiction, a cheap paperback thriller with a lurid cover. There was – there could be – nothing real about such things.

Cars passed on the road as he stood there. He saw compact Skodas and Ladas and a couple of shining black German Mercedes and a Volvo with diplomatic license plates. There were also large Chevies, Pontiacs, Chevrolets and Cadillacs; a United Nations of cars. Across the road, the children were playing at the school. A sign above the building said, in English, Cyrillic script and in the same romantic, cursive script on the cigarettes, that this was the Mohammed Zahir Shah Primary School, and was opened by Ahmad Shah Khan in the year of his inauguration, nineteen eighty two.

It was hot. A plane passed slowly overhead, jet plumes streaking across the sky, descended gradually over the rooftops. The city had a dry, not unpleasant smell. Joe ground the remains of the cigarette and walked on. He could sense the end of his journey, somewhere nearby. He was following instincts, the way a migratory bird might follow magnetic north, the world a map below with borders unmarked. He came to a market, by the river. There were heavy, beautifully-wrought rags on display. A wooden shelf held small glass cups, and next to it was a battered samovar, and Joe could smell the tea as it boiled inside. He could glimpse a couple of old men through a doorless entrance, sipping cups of tea, at the same time sucking on hard candy. He could smell cigarettes, and pipes, and as he walked through the stalls, seeing eggplants and tomatoes, grapes and chickpeas, raisins and nuts and bags of white rice, he could also smell the heavy, sweet scent of the opium that lay, here and there, on low tables, in dark pellets and in bars that were stamped, in English and Pashto: *Product of the Kingdom of Afghanistan*.

Further down there were tables covered in books. He stopped and let his fingers run along the covers; they felt like skin, were warm to the touch. The book titles were in a *mélange* of languages and alphabets, French and English, Arabic and Dutch, Urdu and German and Pashto and Chinese. He picked one up, leafed through it. *A Tourist Guide to the Tora Bora Caves*. Books, he thought, were a sort of migratory bird. Here they rested a while, weary of their travels, before taking flight again, before moving, settling in another nest for a time. They seemed to him like a flock that had descended on these tables, pages fluttering like wings, and here they rested in the shade, enjoying the lull, knowing it would soon be time to go on their way again. Near the books was a revolving stand with postcards stacked on it. A couple of tourists, their pale skins in sharp relief to the muted earth colours of the buildings and the people, were browsing the postcards. The man had a camera around his neck. The girl was pretty in a summer dress. He looked at them and felt a sudden, overwhelming stab of jealousy inside him. It seemed to him he had once been like that, too, somehow completed, and he watched them as they chose and paid for three postcards and walked away, hand in hand: as if they were a postcard themselves.

-- fading --

THERE WERE HOUSES on the hill above the river, and he made for
them. The sun was very strong. Dust devils chased each other
around his feet. In the distance the mountains looked bare and
forbidding, with no sign of vegetation. When he was high up
on the hill he turned, and looked down on the town below.

Kabul looked sleepy in the sunlight. A haze covered the
dust-coloured buildings and reflected off the sluggish moving
cars. Far in the distance, he could hear snatches of music,
conversations, children at play. Another plane came over
the mountains, heard before it was seen, a great metal bird
changing course, descending slowly, casting sunlight off its
wings. There was a lake down below, the snaking river, wide
tree-lined avenues and narrow, serpentine alleyways, an old city
overlaid with the new. It seemed to have sat there for countless
years, basking in the sunlight, patiently waiting in an endless
afternoon.

He watched the plane descend. As it did, the sound of it grew
larger, and in the noise of the engines were voices, calling out.
Joe shook his head, no, no, but the voices continued, growing
louder in the thrumming of the plane.

He watched, as the voices grew into a frenzy around him,
and the city below began to change.

It was a fading. As he watched, parts of the city disappeared,
were blacked out, others shifted, buildings growing larger,
smaller, the city filling with holes that hadn't been there before.

To the drone of the plane joined others: a storm of engines
growing over the city. Their shadows fell on the dry ground

below, and from their glistening bellies fell their eggs, dark metal, matt, whistling through the air.

As they hit the buildings they were born: a multitude of chrysalides emerging from their cocoons. They spread wings of bright flames over the city, gorging themselves on brick and flesh and metal. He watched cars being blown apart, doors and seats and passengers torn and thrown up in the air. He saw roofless houses and doorless homes, a headless child with a football still held under one lifeless arm. The planes were dark clouds in the skies above Kabul. They were migratory birds flying in formation, dropping their charges almost haughtily, as if the city below, this insignificant emptying place that lay huddled in on itself below the mountains, was barely worthy of their notice.

He watched the city as a chequered board of light and dark, illumination sweeping over black squares, shifting, changing, leaving behind the burned-out shell of a car, a crater where a house had been, a fallen doll, somewhere in a street a window, standing upright in the dust, its wooden shutters clanging.

He heard gunshots. Rockets whistled as they flew up into the sky. He watched the lighted lines of tracer bullets racing each other, saw a second sun erupt over Kabul as a desert-coloured helicopter erupted into bright and unexpectedly beautiful flame. He heard screaming, and cursing, and a baby wailing endlessly until it was suddenly silenced, as if the needle of a turntable had been abruptly jerked away. He smelled smoke and urine and roasting flesh and acrid chemical smells he couldn't put a name to. Down below, the city faded and re-emerged, engulfed in smoke that cleared, every now and then, to give him glimpses of another world beyond it. He didn't know how long he stood there, high above the city of Kabul, looking down.

-- strands --

HE SHOOK HIS head, trying to clear it. The drone of the lone plane was long gone, and it was quiet. The city below slept in the sun. There was no sound. Woodsmoke rose from chimneys, and a single bird swooped overhead, once, and dove for shelter in the shade. Joe turned away.

The path led him through the low-lying houses. The sky was a bright cloudless expanse, its colour the startling blue of a far-away ocean. As he walked he peeled away the layers of himself, like a man worrying at a loose tooth. He felt very alone there on the mountain-side. What held him together was little more than a name, an occupation. There was a man named Joe and he was a detective. What led him on, what kept him bound into the strands of that identity, was a question. Up there, he'd felt the closest to the skies he had ever been. Up there, the spirits of the dead wafted in the clean and hallowed air. Up there was heaven.

The house lay at the end of a road. The mud-coloured bricks had been given a lick of white paint that was already peeling in places. A low wall surrounded the courtyard of the house, and a wrought-iron gate was set into the wall like a dash. No smoke rose from the chimney. A lone bird twittered somewhere nearby, out of sight. Joe tried the gate and it was unlocked. It creaked when he pushed it open.

There was grass growing around the house in clumps, separated by patches of dry ground. A tap on the left dripped water, very slowly, two turrets of untidy mint plants growing underneath. A bicycle was leaning against one wall, its tires empty.

Sleep lay over that house like an enchantment.

There was a veranda, empty. Past the veranda was a door. The door was made of wood, unvarnished. Joe walked towards the house and, with each step, the land seemed to expand and contrast simultaneously around him, as if he had encountered a strange region of space and time, a naked singularity. There was a pain behind his eyes that wasn't physical. It was as if all the things that made him up, the threads of his being, were coming unravelled.

The question, for the moment, held him bound. When he reached the veranda, he stood very still, listening. There was no sound. Even the lone bird had stopped singing. The house was hushed, its silence not echoing but mute, the silence of forgotten things, the quiet of abandoned lives. A teddy-bear with missing eyes was slumped with its back to the wall, its fur a patchwork of dye and mould. Joe knocked on the door. There was no answer.

He pushed the door, and it opened.

-- time --

LIGHT FELL SOFTLY through the window on the worn Afghan rug. The room was cooler than the outside. A whisper of wind breezed through the air. There was a ceiling fan overhead, unmoving. There was a familiar smell in the room, though it didn't immediately register. There were two large, comfortable-looking armchairs with the stuffing poking out through holes in the fabric. There was a low coffee table, the wood lacquered, holding an ashtray with three cigarette stubs, and intersecting dark rings where hot glasses had been placed and removed. At the far end, a doorway led into a kitchen. The left wall was covered in a tall bookcase. A large desk sat against the right wall, opposite the window. There were books strewn on the desk, half-opened. Also on the desk were envelopes, papers, pens, coins, seashells, elastic bands, a broken stapler, small round stones, two feathers, a pencil sharpener, a closed bottle of ink: a fantastical treasure map with mountains and valleys, chasms and springs. In the middle of the desk, rising like a mountain, was a typewriter. There was a sheet of paper inserted into the machine. The chair had been pushed back from the desk, as if its inhabitant had momentarily departed and would soon return to occupy it.

Joe stood in the middle of the room and took a deep breath. The smell, lingering, sweet, cloying, familiar. He began to touch things. The armchairs, the coffee table, the bookcase, the walls. They felt solid and real, strangely reassuring. He ran his finger against one level of the bookcase and returned with dust. The books looked like they had been sitting there for an age, unmoving. They were lined up in no particular order he could discern. Letters of the alphabet crowded next to each other in a festive jumble. Tall books sat next to short ones. Fat books squatted next to slim, elegant volumes. Where there was not enough room, books had been piled on top of other books or shoved sideways into available gaps.

Joe let his hands fall to his sides. He turned, half a circle, fingers outstretched. He tried to find a sense of the inhabitant of that room, that house. Was anyone still living there? In one corner of the room, he noticed, a long-necked flower vase stood on a platform, but there were no flowers in it. He turned again, completing a circle, and something caught his eye. On the wall beside the bookcase was what appeared to be a framed photograph. He approached it slowly. On the top, just below the frame, it said *TIME* and, at the bottom end: *MAN OF THE YEAR*. He approached it, cautious for reasons he couldn't articulate. A face slowly resolved itself inside the frame and he took a deep shuddery breath and looked...

The face that stared back at him, framed within, was his own.

-- afternoon dreams --

AFTER A MOMENT he laughed, though without much humour. It was not a photograph at all. It was a mirror, the text painted on to the reflecting surface. What did he expect to see there? Longshott, he thought. Or a man with a long beard and clear, penetrating eyes, the hero of pulp thrillers and suicide killers. Instead all he got was himself. He stared at his own face staring back at him. Did he even know that face? There was a name that went with it, an occupation, but were they themselves real, or were they, too, mere *fabriques*, as fake as a passport could be faked? He shook his head, and the face in the mirror mimicked the movement.

He turned away. Went to the desk. Again, he felt the urge to touch, to feel. He picked up each object in turn, examined it, replaced it on the desk. Pens, blue and black and red. A child's pencil sharpener. He lifted it to his nose and smelled it, but there was no sign of recent wood shavings, no sign of recent use. Stones, pebbles made smooth by water. Seashells that must have come from somewhere else, from a far and distant sea. Their colours were the hues of sunset. He smoothed a feather with his finger. He weighed coins in his hand. Faces etched into the metal regarded him back with haughty expressions, kings and queens and emperors and presidents. He pulled open the drawers, one by one. They were mostly empty. In the second of three drawers he found a single item: a thin, unadorned gold ring, a woman's size. It felt heavy in his hand and he put it back, carefully, and closed the drawer. As he did so, a sheet of paper fluttered down to the ground. He picked it up. A few lines, scribbled – hastily, it seemed – in blue ink that had somewhat smudged on the page. The handwriting was untidy. It took him a while to untangle it. It said:

> we had ankle-length boots
> that let us wade in shallow pools
>
> like resolute explorers
> impervious to rainwater, mud or frogspawn
>
> or those tired warnings, seldom heeded,
> not to go into the puddles on purpose.
>
> that winter I could read the map
> the water charted
>
> and knew the purpose in a snail's
> slow, slimy track as it slid along a window pane.
>
> then the sun came and brought with it
> the end of winter
>
> and meaning dried away
> and was gone with the last of the rains.

The poem vaguely disturbed him. He didn't know why. He put the sheet back on the desk, face down. Next, he looked through the books on the desk. To the left of the typewriter were the four *Vigilante* books. He picked up the uppermost one, the earliest in the series, *Assignment: Africa*. The binding was worn, the spine cracked in places. He leafed through it and saw that it was annotated, in a mix of pencil and red ink, words crossed out and others written in, punctuation examined and found lacking, typos circled in patient, careful loops and rings.

He put it down, and as he did he upset some invisible balance, some delicate equilibrium that had been suddenly disturbed. There was a cascade of papers, pebbles, pens, seashells and coins and the sudden unexpected noise made Joe's palms wet with sweat, made his heart beat faster. He stepped back, tried to calm his breathing. Debris settled on the floor. Silence returned. The air itself was still; the tiny breeze he'd felt before had already departed. The air was thick with afternoon heat, afternoon dreams.

Joe examined the fallout. On the desk, a seismic shift had taken place, a clash of tectonic plates creating a new pattern across the surface. Underneath what had been a miniature mountain of books, a sheaf of pages was revealed.

They were stacked neatly one on top of the other. White pages, edges aligned, the typewritten lines running left to right in single-space. On the first page, centred, surrounded by blank space, a title: *The Last Stand*. Below it, a familiar sub-title: *An Osama bin Laden: Vigilante Novel*.

Below, still: *By Mike Longshott*.

Adjacent to the manuscript was a book open face-down on the desk. The title was familiar, but it took Joe a moment to realise it was the same title he had picked up, briefly, at the market in town.

A Tourist Guide to the Tora Bora Caves. He picked it up, leafed through it. Pictures of mountains, pine trees, cave openings in the bedrock. The place looked quiet and peaceful, the pictures exuding a faint air of disuse.

He moved his gaze to the typewriter. A new sheet of paper was inserted into the machine. It was partially typed. Joe reached for it, pulled it out, gently, his fingers leaving damp prints on the paper.

in the White Mountains. In Pashto its name meant ~~The Black Cellar~~ Black Dust. An extensive network of natural caves, they had been greatly extended in the 1980s with the assistance of the ~~American Central Intelligence Agency the Agency~~ the CIA. Twenty years later they were to become the ~~subterranean~~ grounds for the Battle of Tora Bora between Osama bin Laden's men and coalition troops from the United States and the United Kingdom.

Kabul had fallen. As the tanks rolled into the city, Osama bin Laden's fighters had already left. They went into the mountains, amassing at last in the caves of the ~~Safed Koh~~, the White Mountains, fifty kilometres away from the Khyber Pass.

It should have been the last stand of Osama bin Laden. In the event, it was nothing more than one more battle in an ~~extensive~~ ongoing, prolonged war.

US Air Force B-52H Stratofortress strategic bombers were deployed, fresh from the battle of Kabul. They dropped a steady barrage of ~~bombs~~ ordnance over the mountains, chief amongst them the 500-pound Mark 82 bombs and the 15,000-pound BLU-82 bombs, known as Daisy Cutters. US Special Forces were inserted into the battle zone by helicopters, and British SAS commandos attempted to penetrate the caves, leading to intense close-combat fire-fights. Outside, ~~bomb~~ craters were filled with rubble, and uprooted trees lay on their side.

As the fighting ended, and the caves had been swept clean, no trace could be found of Osama bin Laden, nor of the bulk of his fighters. The Emir had disappeared into the snowy mountain paths, to regroup and continue the fi

-- Longshott --

JOE JUMPED. THE sound was unexpected, loud in the silence. He had been staring at the page for some time. The rest of it was blank. It had been left off in mid-sentence. Joe looked around wildly, but could see no source for the sound, which was, unarguably, a cough. He put the page down on the desk, his heart beating sickeningly fast. He heard a sort of rustling sound, coming from the direction of what he had assumed was the kitchen, the cough again, and light footsteps. Outside a bird, perhaps similarly disturbed, was chattering manically in a rapid percussion. Joe took a step back from the desk.

The shadow came first. It fell down from the open doorway onto the dusty floor, a thin emaciated blade of darkness. Then it stretched, shrank, and a man came through into the room with a gun in his hand.

The man first: tall, thin, with shoulders that stooped a little, as if used to carrying a burden that could not, momentarily, be seen. The clothes hung from his frame as if he had been better fed once, and had since lost his appetite for nourishment. His face, too, was long and thin. He was unshaven. His hair was brown and, like the rest of the man, thinning.

The gun was a single-action revolver: an antique. In his other hand, the man held a polishing rag. The butt of the gun was worn a smooth silver. When he saw Joe, the man stopped still. His eyes were brown and large in his face.

Joe, too, was still. His eyes were on the gun. The man said, 'What are you doing here?'

'Are you – ?' Joe said, and somehow all the questions he

286

wanted to ask were crowding and thronging each other in his head and what came out was, 'Are you going to shoot me?'

'What?' The man looked down at the gun in his hand as if noticing it for the first time. He put it away on the bookcase. 'Don't be ridiculous. I don't even know you.'

'I'm Joe.'

The man stared at him. 'Right,' he said. 'Joe.'

Outside, the lone bird was still chattering away. Inside, the heat felt oppressive. 'Well, Joe,' the man said, moving closer, 'What do you want?'

'I –' As the man's proximity increased, Joe noticed a familiar, cloyingly sweet smell. It seemed to cling to the man, or perhaps to his clothes, like to a suit that had been entombed in mothballs for too long. He said, 'You're Mike Longshott.'

The man stopped beside the desk. His hand rested on its surface. 'Yes...' he said. There was a wondering note in his voice.

'How – ?' Joe said. 'How do you *know*?' He gestured wildly in the air, taking in, in one encompassing sweep, the bookshelves, the *Vigilante* paperbacks, the uncompleted manuscript on the desk.

Longshott slowly nodded. Joe noticed he had a prominent Adam's apple; it bobbed up and down as he swallowed. 'Please,' Longshott said. 'Sit down.' He gestured, in his turn, at the two worn armchairs. 'You are a refugee?'

The question floated between them, lighter than air, unanswered. Then Longshott nodded again, equally slowly, and said, 'Let me make some coffee.'

-- the luxury of waiting --

THEY SAT FACING each other on the armchairs. The coffee was hot and sweet and burned Joe's tongue. It had been flavoured with cinnamon. 'My name,' Longshott said, 'isn't really Mike Longshott. As you no doubt figured.' He shrugged. 'My name is really of very little significance,' he said. 'I picked Longshott because it had a nice ring to it. It sounded like the sort of name you'd find on a paperback.'

Joe nodded, decided the coffee was too sweet for his taste, and took a sip of cool water from the glass resting on the table. 'Do you mind if I smoke?' he said.

'Not at all,' Longshott said. 'My own' – he hesitated – 'pipe is in the other room.'

Joe nodded at that too, as if he had been waiting for just such a confirmation. He extracted and lit a cigarette. The smoke curled lazily in the air. Joe didn't speak. He had, he'd decided, the luxury of waiting.

Longshott was folded into the armchair opposite Joe. He looked lost inside that space, limbs jutting awkwardly like a doll's when its strings had been loosened. He said, 'There was a woman.'

Joe listened to the silence.

-- waxing moon --

THE WAS – THERE had been – a woman. He was working as a journalist, Mike – 'My name really is Mike, you know' – told him. He had developed a habit, gradually – 'I was doing a series of articles on the opium trade, you see' – and had taken to spending some of his leisure time in the smoking rooms where gentlemen – 'Both foreign and local' – of such habits congregated.

'I first saw her on the first night of the full moon,' Mike Longshott said. 'You know, the moon becomes so much more important in places like this. On moonless nights it is so dark, but the stars are beautiful. Beautiful and cold... You can see so many stars out in the desert. But then the moon begins to rise, a little bigger every night – do you know how much light it gives out, how much you can see in the light of the moon?'

Joe nodded. He did know. There was a kind of desperation on moonless nights, when the stars, those alien beings an unimaginable distance away from the Earth, looked down on the world, in a kind of cold strange beauty that gave out no light. The moon was different, and when it came, the darkness was lifted, the light of the sun reflecting off of the moon's surface and illuminating the dark world, giving it a soft silvery shape. The moon rose early when it waxed, like a pregnant woman, her belly growing until at last it was full. The fullness lasted for two days. Then the moon would wane, rising late like a surly teenager, growing smaller again until it disappeared and the darkness returned, and with her the stars.

'Tell me about her,' he said.

Mike Longshott nodded. 'I saw her as I came out of the – the place,' he said. 'She was standing on the street, not doing anything. She was hugging herself, rocking on the soles of her feet. She looked very lost, and vulnerable. I saw her quite clearly in the light of the moon. When I came her way, she turned. Her eyes were warm, I remember that. I remember thinking, they were not like stars. They were like sunlight reflected off the moon. She said, "Do you know where they are?"

'I said, "Who?"

'"I can't find them," she said. I didn't know if she was speaking to me, or to herself. "They were there, but now they're not. Or maybe they are there, but I am not." She shivered, though it was a warm night, and she hugged herself closer. "Do you know where they are?" she said.

'I said, as gently as I could, "No."

'She turned fully to me then. Her arms dropped to her sides. She looked at me, at my face, for a long moment, as if searching for some familiar traces in them, for lines or curves I did not possess.

'Though maybe I did. For, after that long moment had passed, she took a deep breath, and some of the anxiety seemed to go out of her, and she said, "Will you help me?"'

He took a sip of water then, and sat in silence for a while, staring into the air. It was then that Joe realised that the voices who had accompanied him, for a while, from his cell and up the hill, were silent now, and had been for a while. Absent or silent, he didn't know, but he didn't think they had gone. Like himself, they were waiting, listening to a story being told. He said, 'Was she – ?' and Longshott said, 'Yes. She was.'

-- waning --

'YOU MIGHT NOT credit it,' Longshott said, 'but I never learned her story. Oh, I had glimpses of it, from time to time. She spoke in her sleep, sometimes, crying out names – one name in particular. It wasn't Mike.' He shook his head. 'I had the impression she had once had a son,' he said. He was silent then, staring at his hands, lying loosely in his lap. He looked up and his eyes met Joe's and the lines around his eyes were pronounced. 'She... she waxed and waned with the moon,' he said. 'I don't know if it is the same for others. To me, it seemed like enchantment for a time – still does, when it comes to that. I only saw her when the moon was in the skies. I know she craved the daylight. She wanted to see the sun. It hurt her not to be able to. I once asked her where she went, when she wasn't... wasn't there. She didn't know, or was unwilling to tell me. The times of no moon were the worse, for me. She would be gone, an absence, an emptiness no stars could dispel, and every time I worried she will not appear again. My... my habit increased. I smoked more pipes, but they didn't bring me relief. Instead, I began to imagine the world she must have come from. Details of it would come, unbidden, into my mind when I was in stupor. They came to me haltingly, at first. Dates, numbers. Headlines.' He laughed. There was no humour in it. He said, 'Do you know what a journalist is? Someone who hasn't written a novel yet. I couldn't write it in a newspaper. For a time, I didn't need to write at all. Then...'

She had begun to appear less frequently. She was fading, it had seemed to him. Each night she was less substantial, less

there. Only at the full moon did she still seem solid, present –
'She was a present,' he said. 'My present. I didn't think in terms
of past or future. There was only the moment, when she was
there, in my arms, when I could hold her and comfort her and
stroke her hair in the light of the moon...'

It had seemed to him more opium would help, but it didn't.
Instead, that other, imaginary world encroached more and
more on his own, until he could no longer tell them apart.
When walking the streets, sometimes, he thought he saw others
who were like her, shades on the street corners, refugees from
another place and time, but he never tried to talk to them. She
was all he had.

'And then she was gone. She was gone with the full moon as
it set on the horizon. Her hair was spun silver. I held her hand
in mine and it was translucent, I could see the blood vessels
inside, bones like pale crystals. "I think I see them," she said.
That was the last thing she said to me. The next night she didn't
appear, or the next, or the one after that.' He looked up at Joe,
but his eyes weren't seeing. 'I was alone.'

He waited the dark time for the new moon to be reborn. Yet
when it was, she was absent from the night, and he knew she
was not coming back. 'That night I wrote the first chapter. I
hardly sleep any more. When I close my eyes I see him, but
always in the distance, like a cowled figure with clear cold eyes
that are indifferent to me.'

Joe said – whispered – 'Osama.' The name shivered in the
still air, seemed momentarily to assume a shape, a figure, then
was gone.

'Yes,' Mike Longshott said. He shivered too, despite the heat.
'My hero.' He gave a laugh that was more of a cough. His
hands shook. 'Could you – ?' he said. Joe understood him. Far
away, he seemed to hear faint voices, whispering. He rose from
the armchair and walked over to Mike Longshott, helping
him to stand up. 'It's in the other room,' the writer said. There

was sweat on his face. Gently, Joe took his arm. They walked together slowly, the writer half-leaning on Joe's shoulder, and when they arrived in the other room, Joe helped Longshott lie down on the cot the man had prepared for himself long ago, and watched him settle, and something seemed to break inside him, like weak glass. 'Could you – ?' Mike Longshott said and Joe, biting his lips to stop the mist that seemed to have descended on his eyes, nodded wordlessly and helped him prepare the pipe, rolling the ball of resin in his fingers though the smell made him dizzy. He placed the mouthpiece of the pipe in the writer's mouth and lit the flame to heat the resin, watching as Longshott's features slowly relaxed and slackened as he inhaled the fumes travelling down the pipe.

Stupor, Longshott had called it. Joe stayed until the pipe was done, and Longshott's eyes, though opened, no longer saw him. Then, rising, he softly left the room.

HE KNEW SHE would be there, even before she appeared. In a way, he thought, she had always been there, waiting for him on the edge of vision, where light met water and allowed her to form. There was a film of tears on his eyes and he let it stay there. We are all shades, he thought – ghosts, the unexplained. We are bad omens that only appear under certain conditions. He thought of the beds he slept in. They were never disturbed when he woke up. He could never remember sleeping. He was just... he just wasn't there. The realisation did not come as a relief. It was merely there, like the voices of the others, whispering far away. Through blurred vision, he watched the distant mountains where nothing grew. A haze shimmered over red-brown dust, and through the haze she appeared, a small, vulnerable figure, all alone on that swathe of road, empty-blue skies behind her, and the mountains like signifiers of a burial.

'I found him,' he said. His voice sounded hollow, a lost small thing floundering in the open space on that hill above the quiet town. He fumbled in his pockets then and found the black card she had given him back in his office, in Vientiane, which now seemed little more than a dream. He made an attempt to give it back to her, but she ignored the gesture and after a moment's hesitation he let it drop to the ground, where it seemed to disappear in amidst the dust. It was no more real, he realised, then anything else – a prop, a *fabrique*, a folly. He said, 'I found him,' again, and hated the sound of his own voice, but she smiled. She said, 'I knew you would.'

They stood facing each other across the chasm of the hills.

In the background, Mike Longshott's house, a ruined castle, stood in a silence of its own. The heat was heavy on the land, as thick and syrupy as a dream. She said, 'I missed you.'

'No, no,' he said. 'You found me.'

She smiled at that, then frowned. A lock of hair fell over her face and she left it there. Joe had the urge to reach out and move it, held himself still. 'Do you remember?' she said. It was said, he thought, with some urgency. He said, 'I remember you coming to my office. You hired me to find him –' He gestured at the house. He knew that wasn't what she was asking, but he was afraid of the other answer. Suddenly, he was deathly afraid.

The girl glared at him. 'God *damn* it!' she said. Her voice was like an explosion and it startled him. He took a step back and she advanced on him. '*Me*, you bastard! Do you remember *me*? Do you –' She took a deep breath as if trying to steady herself. She looked very angry. He sensed then, or knew from somewhere deep inside him, that she had the kind of anger that could shake the earth and make mountains. And also, something inside him added, a voice he tried desperately to silence, she had that kind of love.

-- Joe --

'YOU LOVE BLACK and white movies and detective novels,' she said. It all came out in a rush. The sun was falling smoothly down the sky. 'You love rum and raisins ice-cream, sourdough bread, butter and not margarine, salads but not with onion.' Her hands were bunched into fists. She said, 'You hate beetroot and avocado, you're indifferent to politics, you like to sleep on the right side of the bed as long as it's facing the wall. You like to turn the pillow over at night so you get the cool side. You hate people who walk slower than you. You can iron but very slowly, have no idea how a washing machine operates, and like to leave your clothes on the floor so you can pick them up again first thing in the morning. You change your underwear every day but will keep wearing the same pair of jeans until they start smelling. You cried when your grandfather died, you like romantic comedies but you won't admit it unless you're drunk, you only drink socially and you smoke too much. Your name is –'

'Joe,' he said. 'My name is Joe.' There was an abyss around him, and the voices of the others chattered like birds far away. He had a sudden, desperate craving for a cigarette. 'My name is Joe,' he said again, holding on to the name as if it were a single tree-branch above rapid waters.

She said another name. The words had no meaning to him. 'You like cowboy hats but won't ever wear one outside,' she said. 'You think of yourself as a cowboy, but you're not –'

He said, 'Hey!' and she almost smiled, but didn't.

'– and you'd argue about if challenged. You like Humphrey Bogart, you re-read Sherlock Holmes stories, you hate it when people sit next to you in the cinema, you like eating chicken and chips and you don't like exercise, you prefer a shower to a bath and you sing when you're in a good mood. You don't like the cold and you don't like humidity. You drink too much coffee.'

'I like coffee.'

'– and you love talking about it,' she said. 'I know.'

'I like –' he began to say, but she stopped him.

'You like to sit in the front on a bus but you like trains, not buses. You hate flying and always order the kosher meal so you get served first and you always ask for a window seat. You try not to drink on flights so you don't have to go to the toilets and you always get dehydrated when you fly. You don't like taking pictures, think ordering take-away on the phone is an extravagance, you like wine but prefer beer, you don't like shopping for clothes –'

'Who does...'

She didn't smile. 'You like to stand in your underwear in the lounge with your hands on your hips and survey your domain. You get very possessive about your personal space. You don't like phones. You gave your penis a nickname when you were thirteen –'

Shocked: 'I never –'

'And you called it Hermann after the commander of the Luftwaffe, which only you think is funny –'

'Well, that's –'

'You like eating standing up by the sink. You like eating chillies even though you always suffer the next day. You dance in front of the mirror when you think no one's looking. You like to bring your upper lip up against your nostrils and smell it. When people ask you where you're from you like to say you come from Japan. Also when they ask where you go. A horse walks into a bar and the bartender says, "Why the long face?" is your favourite joke. You like soup only when you're sick. You smoke too much –'

'Yes, you did say. I –'

'And you know it's bad for you but you still won't stop.'

The sudden silence between them was like a toppled glass: he was afraid of it breaking, knew that when it would, the exploding fragments would hurt. In the still air, there was the ghostly echo of battle helicopters, passing. The loose lock of hair was still across her face. He reached out and his fingers touched her skin and he pushed the lock away. Her skin was warm. He could smell the faintest trace of patchouli. He couldn't read the look in her eyes.

'I remember the explosion,' she said, in a small voice. 'At least, I think I do. Or maybe it's just that, knowing there *was* an explosion, my mind reconstructed it, a memory that isn't real – but how do you know?' she said, almost pleading, it seemed to him. 'How do you know what's real? All of us, imagining lives like something out of a screen.'

'You were a club singer,' he said, remembering the Blue Note, the stage, her singing. She shook her head – tired? angry? – said, 'I worked in a cinema.' A laugh died, still-born. 'And you –'

'I'm a detective,' he said.

She hit him.

He almost fell back. He had not expected her to do it. Her fists were on his chest, pounding him. She was almost a head shorter than him. 'You're – !' She said the name again, the name that meant nothing to him, not unless he let it. She said it again and again, her small fists beating a tattoo across his chest.

He reached out. His arms engulfed her, pushed her close to him, and she slowly subsided against him, warm and real in his arms. He buried his face in the crook of her neck and felt the blood coursing through her.

'Why Vientiane?' he said then, thinking of the life he had been dreaming, and she said, 'Do you remember? We always wanted to go there, and never did... somewhere so remote and secluded, where nothing ever happened and it was always warm...'

'I promised you you'll never be cold again,' he said, and she shivered in his arms. 'I am always cold,' she said.

He held her. He wished he could keep holding her forever.

'You have to choose,' she said softly. Her breath tingled on his skin. 'You have to choose what to be. When you've been stripped of everything: a name, a face, a love – you could be anything. You could even choose to be yourself.'

He held her close to him, there on the hills above the city, as the sun slowly drifted downwards across the sky. Soon it would be dark, the last traces of sunlight fading in a multitude of colours on the horizon.

'I know,' Joe said.

EPILOGUE

-- puddles of rain --

IN THE RAINY season, the unpaved side-streets of Vientiane turn to mud, and water stands still in flowerpots and discarded car tyres. The whole city seems to reach upwards, then, green shoots rising up from the ground, spreading branches and leaves, like open palms waiting to cup rainwater between their fingers. When it rains, it feels as if a sea had been upturned over the city, and the rain falls and falls in a never-ending cascade. In the crowded markets, the ground is paved with packed newspapers and feet squelch as they pass under the market's awnings. Frogs look hopefully out of their deep cages, and the fish swim in the concrete pools with a new purpose, as if sensing an escape. Along the Mekong, sandbags line the bank, piled high on top of each other, a makeshift barrier against flood.

When it rains it drowns sound. There is a silence in the rain, a sort of white noise. It can be very soothing. Before it rains, the wind picks up, dragging the clouds with it, like an angry mother pulling reluctant children by the hand. The sky darkens quickly. In the nights, the lightning is as bright as hope. On such nights, lying awake in his apartment on Sokpalunag, he liked to count the seconds between thunder and lightning, measuring the distance of the storm.

The mornings were warm and bright and as he walked down the road he could see his face reflected back at him from the many puddles. He took to wearing a raincoat and a wide-brimmed hat he'd picked up somewhere, and he cut down on his smoking. His face looked to him as it always did. The air was fresh and clean, pregnant with rain.

In the mornings he liked to walk the half-hour distance from his apartment to the morning market, turning right on Kouvieng, past early-morning monks collecting alms and the women who fed them, past the dogs that sometimes barked at him, past naked chickens rotating slowly on a stick, past the bus station and the vegetable market and the traffic lights and into the small coffee-shop on the corner.

He would sit there, drinking the bitter mountain coffee, and look out of the glass windows at the people coming and going from the market, lives flickering like the light of distant stars as it passes through the atmosphere.

Later, rising, he would walk the short distance to his office by the black stupa, climb the short flight of steps and sit at his desk. There was a fifth of whisky in a drawer but he seldom touched it anymore. There were never any clients, which suited him fine. He would sit in his office and stare out of the window, waiting for it to rain. Sometimes, when it rained, the clouds parted, for just a moment, and sunlight shone through, and at those times he thought he saw a girl standing there, in the place where sunlight pierces rain, looking up at his window, but then the clouds would close again high above and she would be gone.

THE END